Slean roared, more in ang   un
around. She attempted to reac   ws.
But as she twisted, she lost her momentum and dropped out
of the air like a very large, very green rock. When she hit the
ground, the earth shuddered from the impact. Nearra felt the
vibrations even through the thick soles of her new boots.

Catriona cheered. "Well shot, Davyn!" she called back over
her shoulder as she ran toward Slean. Sindri just laughed, as
if he'd found himself in the middle of the greatest game he
could ever imagine: Battle the Dragon. Hands tingling almost
to the point of pain, Nearra feared for both of them. She knew
Davyn's arrow, while proving an effective distraction, had done
no serious harm to Slean. And Slean hadn't fallen all *that* far. In
a moment the dragon would forget all about the irritating pain
in her rump and return to seeking their destruction.

No, Nearra thought. *My destruction.*

THE NEW ADVENTURES

THE NEW ADVENTURES

VOLUME
1

TEMPLE
OF THE
DRAGONSLAYER

TIM WAGGONER

COVER & INTERIOR ART
Vinod Rams

MIRROR
STONE

©2004 Wizards of the Coast, Inc.

All characters in this book are fictitious. Any resemblance to actual persons, living or dead, is purely coincidental.

This book is protected under the copyright laws of the United States of America. Any reproduction or unauthorized use of the material or artwork contained herein is prohibited without the express written permission of Wizards of the Coast, Inc.

Distributed in the United States by Holtzbrinck Publishing. Distributed in Canada by Fenn Ltd.

Distributed to the hobby, toy, and comic trade in the United States and Canada by regional distributors.

Distributed worldwide by Wizards of the Coast, Inc. and regional distributors.

DRAGONLANCE, MIRRORSTONE, WIZARDS OF THE COAST, and their respective logos are trademarks of Wizards of the Coast, Inc., in the U.S.A. and other countries.

All Wizards of the Coast characters, character names, and the distinctive likenesses thereof are trademarks of Wizards of the Coast, Inc.

Printed in the U.S.A.

The sale of this book without its cover has not been authorized by the publisher. If you purchased this book without a cover, you should be aware that neither the author nor the publisher has received payment for this "stripped book."

Cover and interior art by Vinod Rams
First Printing: July 2004
Library of Congress Catalog Card Number: 2003116395

9 8 7 6 5 4 3 2 1

US ISBN: 0-7869-3321-6
UK ISBN: 0-7869-3322-4
620-96595-001-EN

U.S., CANADA,
ASIA, PACIFIC, & LATIN AMERICA
Wizards of the Coast, Inc.
P.O. Box 707
Renton, WA 98057-0707
+1-800-324-6496

EUROPEAN HEADQUARTERS
Wizards of the Coast, Belgium
T Hofveld 6d
1702 Groot-Bijgaarden
Belgium
+322 457 3350

Visit our website at **www.mirrorstonebooks.com**

To my girls:
Cindy, Devon, and Leigh

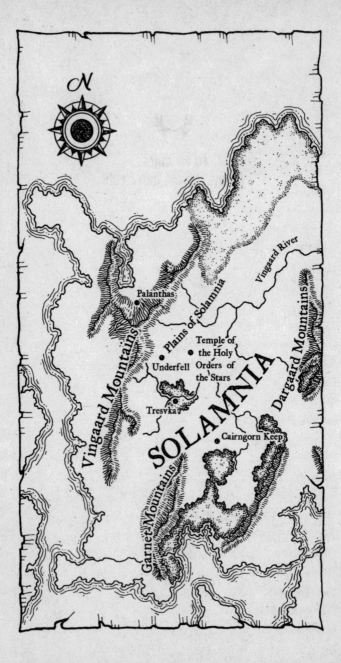

Contents

1   AWAKENING

"Let's rob her!"

"Idiot! Look at her! She's a peasant. Peasants don't have any money!"

"Then let's abduct her! She's young and strong. She'd make a good slave—and good slaves make good money."

The voices—harsh, gravely-gurgly, and not quite human—startled Nearra awake. She didn't know who they were, but it was obvious they weren't friendly. She struggled to open her eyes. As her vision focused, she saw three red-skinned creatures standing around her. Each one wore a grimace, baring sharp teeth that looked capable of tearing through flesh in mere seconds.

A word flashed into Nearra's mind: *goblins*. The thought sent a cold shiver up and down her spine.

"Now look what you've done! You both talked so loudly that you woke her up!" The tall, thin goblin turned away from Nearra to glare at the other two. His red-skinned face had a cruel, almost wolfish aspect.

"What do you mean 'we'?" said the short, pig-faced goblin. He gave the leader a shove. "You're twice as loud as either of us, Drefan!"

The third goblin nodded in agreement, his huge bat-like ears wobbling.

"Don't touch me, you fool!" Drefan drew his dagger from under his belt. He grabbed the pig-faced goblin's black tunic and pressed the blade against his nose. "One more move like that, Fyren, and I'll slice off your nose!"

As the goblins bickered, Nearra sat up and took a quick glance at her surroundings. Trees full of green leaves lined the smooth dirt path where she sat. She had no memory of how she had gotten here. Panic filled her chest. She rose to her feet. She wanted to run but she knew that if she made too much noise, the goblins would realize she was trying to escape. Better to walk for a few yards. Then slip into the woods and lose them among the trees.

"Hey! Where do you think you're going?" Fyren shouted.

Nearra heard the sounds of boots pounding on the dirt path behind her. Too late! The goblins were coming after her! She started running and didn't look back.

She angled to the right and plunged into the forest. Underbrush crashed beneath her feet. She leaped over bushes and fallen tree limbs. Thorns and branches tore her simple turquoise-colored dress and scratched her face, neck, and hands. But she kept running.

Though she had longer legs than the goblins, her dress slowed her down and she had nothing but her body to part the underbrush. Behind her, she could hear the goblins hacking at the vegetation with their daggers.

"There she is! I see her!"

"So do I!"

Running only a few yards ahead of the goblins, Nearra spotted a break in the trees with sunlight and tall grass beyond.

"Stop, girl! Or things will get even worse for you!"

The goblins sounded so close now. A claw scraped the back of Nearra's neck and hooked her collar. She jerked free and kept running.

"I almost got her!"

She put on a burst of speed and ran for the clearing ahead of her. Sweat poured off her forehead and dripped into her eyes. Her breath came in panting gasps, and she knew she wouldn't be able to run much longer.

At the edge of the clearing, she caught sight of a thick branch the right size and length to serve as a club. She bent down, snatched up the branch, and continued until she emerged into open air and sunshine.

In the middle of the clearing, she turned and held the branch before her as if it were a sword. She knew it was foolish to face the goblins armed with only a chunk of wood, but she had no other choice.

The tall one came first.

"Look at what we have here, lads!" Drefan gave a wolfish grin as the other two goblins emerged from the trees. "It seems that the rabbit has decided to stand up to the hounds."

The bat-eared goblin frowned. "Rabbit? But she's a human, isn't she?"

Drefan cuffed his friend none too gently. "You moron, Gifre! I was speaking metaphorically!"

"Meta-what? I'm not familiar with that language, Drefan," Gifre said.

Drefan gritted his yellowed, crooked teeth. "I don't know which of you is the bigger idiot."

Fyren looked at Gifre. "At least we can tell the difference between a rabbit and a human girl."

Gifre nodded. "That's right, Drefan. So don't go getting all high and mighty on us—even if you do speak met-a-for!"

Just then, a dark shadow fell upon the clearing and a sudden wind kicked up. The goblins looked skyward and shrieked. Then they whirled about and dashed back into the trees, running as if their lives depended on it.

Nearra didn't have time to feel relieved at the goblins' retreat. The wind grew even stronger, forcing her to her knees. She heard a loud thump behind her and the ground shuddered beneath her. Abruptly, the wind calmed. An acrid smell filled the air.

She sensed there was something behind her—something big. But she couldn't turn around and look. She couldn't scream. She couldn't run. She was completely paralyzed by fear.

"Greetings, little one." The voice thundered like two large slabs of rock smashing together. The harsh smell grew stronger.

"You can turn around. I'm not going to hurt you." The monster chuckled. "Yet."

But Nearra couldn't move.

"Turn around and face me." The voice no longer held any trace of amusement, and Nearra experienced a renewed surge of fear—fear of not obeying the voice's command.

And so, with her breath caught in her throat, she turned around.

The creature was huge, its green body easily taking up half the clearing. Leathery wings were folded against its scaly sides, and a long barbed tail curled around taloned feet. As large as the beast was, though, its face was the most frightening feature. It grinned at her with a mouthful of razor-sharp teeth. Its eyes were even more terrifying. Big as plates, they weren't the eyes of a mindless animal. They were the eyes of a thinking creature, one that was just as intelligent as any human, if not more so.

"What is your name, child?"

Nearra didn't answer right away. Not because she was afraid—though she was, quite a bit—but because she'd realized for the first time since awakening on the forest trail that she didn't know her own name. A new wave of terror washed over her.

"Well? Speak up! It's the least you can do to repay me after I saved you from those goblins."

Nearra found her voice then. "Saved me for what? Mealtime?"

The dragon let forth a laugh. "You're a bold one, girl. I like that. But you still haven't told me your name. Who are you, girl?" The dragon, eyes glittering, extended her head toward Nearra.

"WHO . . . ARE . . . YOU?"

There was something in the way the dragon repeated the question, as if the words held a special significance she wasn't aware of. As she tried to recall her name, she felt a sudden sensation of dizziness and a building pressure inside her head.

"Nearra," she said. "My name is Nearra." The pressure in her head disappeared as quickly as it had come.

The dragon frowned at Nearra's response, but all she said was, "I am called Slean. What causes you to be in these woods alone, with nothing more than a dead branch for protection?"

Nearra glanced at the piece of wood gripped tightly in her hand. She'd forgotten that she was holding it. The branch seemed an even more foolish defense against a dragon than it had against a trio of goblins.

"I do not know," she answered, trying to keep the fear out of her voice.

Slean arched a scaly eyebrow. "You'll forgive me if I say that seems unlikely."

"It's true. I awoke on the forest path while those three goblins debated what to do with me. I have no memories from before that moment."

Slean considered this for a moment. "And yet, when pressed, you remembered your name. If you have no memories, how do you know that Nearra truly is your name? Perhaps it belongs to someone else entirely."

Nearra shook her head. "I . . . I don't know how, but I know it's mine."

Slean smiled. The sight of her lizardish lips drawing back from her sharp teeth created a truly unsettling effect. "Well then, Nearra, if you don't know how you got here and don't remember anything about yourself, then you have no idea what to do next or where to go, do you?"

With a hollow, sinking feeling, Nearra realized Slean was right. Tears welled in her eyes, but she fought them back. She wasn't going to let the dragon see her cry.

"It would be cruel of me to leave you here, all alone, vulnerable to the many dangers the wood holds," Slean said. "So I'll take you with me."

Nearra felt a flicker of hope. Slean was going to help her!

"In my belly." The dragon opened her mouth wide and lunged forward. Nearra screamed and threw her hands over her head. Her fingers tingled and a voice whispered in her mind.

Yes! Do it! Now! The voice was feminine, sly, and coolly calculating.

The tingling in her hands increased, becoming so painful that it felt as if a thousand needles pierced her flesh from the inside out.

Nearra had no idea whether she imagined that voice or not, but she had the strong feeling that it was very important for her not to do it, whatever it was. Even if that meant getting eaten by Slean.

The tingling in her hands ceased as quickly as it had started. Nearra squeezed her eyes shut more tightly and braced her body to feel the dragon's teeth bite into her flesh.

But they didn't.

Seconds passed. When still nothing happened, Nearra ventured to open a single eye.

Slean was still crouched before her, but now the green dragon's head swayed from side to side, and her eyelids drooped. And then, unable to resist any longer, the dragon fell over onto her side. The ground shook as the monster let out a deep rumbling sound. Somehow, impossibly, Slean had fallen asleep.

"Don't move!" a voice shouted from across the clearing.

Startled, Nearra whirled around, brandishing her makeshift club to defend herself against this new threat, whatever it might be.

2 WIZARD AND RANGER

"A re you unharmed?" a boy of about fifteen shouted as he walked toward Nearra from the edge of the clearing. He wore a traveler's pack and held a bow, arrow nocked and ready. More arrows rode in a quiver slung over his right shoulder and a hunting knife hung from his belt. His sandy brown hair poked out at all angles from beneath his cap, and his deep brown eyes glanced around nervously. Beside him walked a tall, older man garbed in white wizard's robes and also carrying a traveler's pack.

When Nearra didn't respond, the boy asked, "What's wrong with her, Maddoc? Can't she speak?"

"It's the dragonfear," the wizard said. "Whenever a being finds him or herself in the presence of a dragon, they experience a powerful surge of fear. If they become overwhelmed by this fear, they may well panic and lose control. Some attempt to flee in terror, or some become paralyzed with fear. Either way, they are easy prey. She's doubtless still frightened." The wizard glanced at Davyn. "And it doesn't help that you're pointing an arrow at her."

Davyn blushed and lowered his bow, though he did not remove the arrow.

"I'm sorry. My arrow was intended for the dragon, should she suddenly awake."

Maddoc chuckled. "As if a mere arrow could slay such a beast, even one as young as that."

"Young?" Nearra said in surprise. She glanced at the sleeping dragon. "She certainly looks full grown to me!"

"From what I have read about dragons, I believe her to be a juvenile." Maddoc rubbed his close-cropped beard. "But not even an infant fresh out of its egg could be killed by an ordinary arrow."

Davyn blushed more deeply this time.

Nearra felt a sudden need to come to his defense. "That's quite all right. I think it's most brave of you to be willing to face a dragon, armed with nothing more than a bow and arrow."

The boy returned her smile but there was a troubled look in his eyes that hadn't been there a moment ago, as if her compliment had made him uncomfortable.

Maddoc motioned for Nearra to join him and Davyn. "Come, child. We must leave this place. The enchantment I laid upon the dragon won't last forever. Dragons are magical creatures themselves, and there's no telling how a given spell will affect them or how long it will last."

Nearra hesitated, unsure what to do. Could she trust Maddoc and Davyn? The wizard wore the white robes of a mage aligned with good. And he and Davyn had come to her rescue. But so much had happened so fast. Waking up in the forest with no memory, being attacked first by goblins, then a dragon, and finally being rescued by a wizard and a ranger. It was all so strange, like something out of a nightmare.

"If we wished you harm, child," Maddoc said, "we could have simply let the dragon do as she wished with you."

Slean snorted and turned over in her sleep, and Nearra decided that whatever she did, she couldn't stay here. She hurried over to the wizard and the boy, and they led her back into the trees.

In the forest just beyond the clearing, a wizened dwarf wrapped in a gray cloak crouched behind an oak tree. He wore his hood up to protect the pale yellow-white skin of his face from the light, even though the thick canopy of leaves above filtered the sun. Behind him crouched the three goblin bandits: Drefan, Fyren, and Gifre.

"Are they gone yet?" Drefan asked the dwarf.

"I believe so," Oddvar said in a whisper. He rarely spoke louder because he was a Theiwar, a dark dwarf. Dark dwarves lived underground and didn't need to speak loudly because sound carried so well in the caverns. "It's difficult to tell with that dragon still in the way."

"So what did you think of our performance?" Drefan asked.

"I'm not a drama critic," Oddvar said. In truth, he'd thought the goblins' acting job had been less than convincing. If Nearra hadn't been so obviously confused upon awakening, he doubted she'd have been fooled.

He stood. "Let's go," he said to the goblins. "And try to keep quiet for a change. We don't want the girl to know we're following."

"Quiet?" Drefan scowled. "What are you saying?"

Oddvar replied in a low, dangerous whisper. "I'm saying that if you three can't keep your mouths shut, I'll feed you all to Slean."

Drefan's red-skinned face paled almost to pink, but he said, "Bah! What makes you think we're afraid of that overgrown lizard?" The goblin leader puffed out his chest.

Oddvar narrowed his gaze and gave a sly half-smile. "Slean hasn't left yet. If you'd like, I can relay your message to her." The Theiwar turned and started toward the clearing—and the green dragon.

Drefan grabbed Oddvar by the elbow and stopped him. "That's all right, Oddvar," Drefan said in a nervous voice.

Oddvar smirked. He pulled free of Drefan's grip and walked off in the direction he'd originally been heading. He didn't look to see if the goblins followed.

Nearra and her rescuers reached the town of Tresvka just after noon. The summer sun was high overhead, and all three were hot and sweaty as they entered the town.

No one seemed to pay attention to the threesome walking down the middle of what Nearra assumed was the main thoroughfare. Small tents and market stalls lined the dirt road. Men unloaded carts full of coarsely woven rugs and simple wooden furniture. Women haggled in front of stands overflowing with green produce. Horses and oxen clopped down the street, and more than a few stray dogs and cats ran free.

Maddoc had said that the town lay at the intersection of several trade routes, so its citizens were used to seeing travelers come and go. Most of the people Nearra saw were human, of hardy Solamnic stock: pale skin, hard features, and jet-black hair. Maddoc pointed to others who bore the telltale signs of having come from other lands, either by their features or the way they dressed. There were traders and travelers from Hylo, Ergoth, Kharolis, and more. Among the crowd, Nearra could see a scattering of folk belonging to other races, dwarves and elves predominantly.

"Does anything look familiar?" Davyn asked.

Nearra surveyed the simple wooden buildings and the dusty road. Maddoc had said that Tresvka was the human settlement closest to where she had awakened, and so it made sense that the town could be her home. She tried to imagine herself walking through the doorway of the butcher's on the corner or fetching water from the well at the end of the road. But nothing felt familiar. She felt a wave of disappointment.

She shook her head. "No."

"Try to be of good cheer, child," Maddoc said, and set a

comforting hand on her shoulder. "The fact that you haven't lost your entire memory is a hopeful sign."

It was true. As they'd walked through the forest, the wizard had quizzed her on the names of trees, plants, flowers, and animals they saw along the way. She'd been able to name every one. She also knew the name of the country they were in was Solamnia.

Nearra was glad to remember so many things, but none of these details provided so much as a hint to who she was and how she had lost her memory.

"What manner of enchantment erases some memories while leaving others intact?" Nearra asked.

Maddoc smiled. "Magic is capable of almost anything." The wizard looked thoughtful for a moment before continuing. "But I sense no magic associated with your condition. It is my belief the malady that has befallen you is natural in origin, the result of some injury or trauma. Perhaps a blow to the head, for instance."

Nearra reached up and felt around her scalp. "I feel no bumps or cuts, and nothing hurts when I touch it. But something strange did happen when Slean confronted me. I felt a tingling in my hands, and I heard a voice, a woman's voice."

Maddoc and Davyn exchanged a look, and then the wizard said, "I am not a healer, and my expertise in medical matters is limited at best. But perhaps the injury is an old one that for some reason has only now affected your memory. As for the tingling and the voice, they were likely tricks of the mind brought on by the stress of facing a dragon. I'd think no more about them."

Though Maddoc was a wizard, and thus a man of great learning, his words didn't reassure Nearra. It was bad enough that she had lost her memory. Had she lost her mind as well?

They turned the corner and stopped at a ramshackle building. A weathered wooden sign in the shape of a crescent moon hung above the door.

The wizard sighed. "I am afraid this is where we must part company. I have an urgent appointment with the wizard who resides here." Maddoc glanced skyward, judging the time by the position of the sun. "I fear that I'm already very late."

"My apologies, Master Wizard," Nearra said. "If you hadn't come to my rescue, perhaps you wouldn't be late now."

Maddoc gave her a reassuring smile. "Nonsense, child. The reason I'm late—as I'm sure young Davyn can testify—is that I became excited upon seeing the green dragon fly overhead. The great beasts have only recently returned to Krynn, and like any wizard, I'm fascinated by them and wish to learn all I can."

It was Davyn's turn to smile. "At Maddoc's insistence, we tracked the beast for nearly an hour before it alighted in the clearing where we found you."

"Then it is your curiosity that I have to thank for saving me, Master Wizard," Nearra said. "If you hadn't reached the clearing when you did . . ." She thought of Slean's words: *So I'll take you with me—in my belly*. Despite the day's warmth, she couldn't help shuddering at the memory.

Maddoc must have noticed, for he said, "Don't worry. That's all in the past now. As long as you stay out of the forest, I doubt you'll encounter Slean again. Despite being powerful creatures, dragons tend to avoid civilization. At least, so the legends say. Now I'm afraid I really must be going."

"I understand, Master Wizard." Nearra fought to keep the worry and disappointment she felt out of her voice. "I appreciate all you and Davyn have done for me." She turned to Davyn and gave him a grateful smile and then began to walk away.

"Wait a moment, Nearra," Maddoc said. "Where are you going?"

Nearra stopped and turned back to face the wizard. "You and Davyn have an appointment to keep, and I do not desire to make you any later than you already are."

Maddoc looked puzzled for a moment, and then he laughed. "Forgive me, child. I failed to explain my relationship with

TIM WAGGONER

young Davyn. He is not my personal servant. I hired him
guide me to Tresvka. Now that I have reached my destination,
our time together has come to an end. But I do have one more
task for him—that is, if you will accept it, Davyn."

"You have but to name it," Davyn replied.

Maddoc reached into the folds of his white robe and withdrew
a brown leather purse. He handed it to Davyn.

"I cannot delay my appointment for reasons I am not at
liberty to discuss." He smiled apologetically. "But I would not
abandon you, Nearra. Davyn, please see to it that she visits a
healer. There's a good one reputed to do business on Bramble
Street, I believe. I don't recall her name offhand, but if you ask
around, I'm sure you'll have no trouble locating her. Use the steel
in that purse to pay the healer for her services and keep the rest
for yourself. The amount should be more than sufficient."

Nearra felt relieved that she wasn't going to be left on her
own, but she also felt guilty accepting Maddoc's money. "I promise to repay my debt to you, Master Wizard. Somehow."

Maddoc smiled, and a strange, cold look came into his eyes.

"I'm sure you will, child. I'm sure you will."

CHAPTER
3 KENDER TROUBLE

Now that Nearra was alone with Davyn, she felt suddenly uncomfortable. It wasn't that she didn't trust the boy, and it wasn't that he was unpleasant company. But he hadn't said much during their trip through the forest. Maddoc had done almost all the talking. Now that it was just the two of them, Nearra didn't know what to say. Evidently, neither did Davyn, for he remained silent and kept his gaze focused straight ahead. Nearra glanced around, trying to think of something to say when she spotted the smooth silver ring on the boy's hand.

"That's a beautiful ring."

He turned to look at her, a startled expression on his face. "What?"

"Your ring. It's lovely. The way it catches the sunlight . . ." She trailed off, feeling foolish. She wished she hadn't said anything.

Davyn glanced down at his hand as if he'd forgotten he was wearing the silver ring. "This old thing?" He lifted his hand to show her the ring. "It's not even silver all the way through. Underneath the silver plating is iron. I'm sorry, but there's no interesting history behind it. No perilous quests to obtain it, no mysterious enchantments upon it. It's just a plain, ordinary

15

ring. It's been in my family for generations."

"At least you have *something* to remind you of your family." Nearra looked down at her plain dress. "I wish I had more than these clothes to remind me of where I came from. Do you think my parents are looking for me?"

"How would I know?" Davyn said.

"I can't even remember what my parents look like or what it feels like to have a family."

"You're not missing much. Most of the time, parents are more trouble than they're worth."

"But isn't it nice sometimes to, I don't know, have someone looking out for you?"

"I—I only count on one person to look out for me, and that's me."

"Oh." Nearra thought for a moment. "Well, now you can count on me, too." She smiled.

Davyn looked at her in surprise, but before he could say another word, angry shouting erupted from a nearby alley, and a small man wearing a purple cape dashed out into the street.

No, not a man, Nearra realized. A kender.

The kender was on a collision course with Nearra, and as fast as he was moving, Nearra would not be able to get out of his way in time.

Davyn jumped in front of Nearra and shielded her with his own body. He braced himself for impact, but even so, the breath whooshed out of him as the kender crashed into his legs. Fortunately, Davyn was strong and the kender was small enough that the boy wasn't knocked off his feet.

The kender pulled away from Davyn, and Nearra knew that in the next second, he would once again bolt off running like a rabbit fleeing a hungry fox. She grabbed the kender's shoulder to stop him.

"What's wrong, little one?" Nearra asked. "Perhaps we can—" She'd been about to say *help*, but before she could, a huge figure burst out of the alley.

The being, who without doubt was the kender's pursuer, stood seven feet tall, and its body was covered with short, glossy black hair and rippling muscle. But the most striking feature the being possessed was the head of a horned and extremely angry bull.

It's a minotaur, Nearra thought, too surprised by the creature's appearance to realize she'd remembered what it was called.

From the scratches on the minotaur's sides, it was obvious the creature had experienced difficulty squeezing its bulk through the narrow alleyway. In its thick fingers, the beast gripped a large, double-bladed battle-axe.

"Kender!" the minotaur bellowed in a deep, booming voice. "Where are you?"

Nearra expected the kender to shriek in terror at the minotaur's approach. But instead he grinned with delight, as if he were merely playing a game of chase. Another fragment of memory drifted back to her then: kender were rarely afraid of anything, even when—or especially when—they should be.

"Over here!" the kender shouted.

The man-bull turned to look in their direction and he scowled. "There you are!" The minotaur came charging toward them, moving swiftly for a creature of its size and mass.

Davyn shoved the kender aside and drew a dagger from a sheath on his belt. Without taking his eyes off the rapidly approaching man-bull, he shouted, "Run, Nearra!"

Although she was afraid, Nearra had no intention of fleeing. She didn't know what she could do to help Davyn, but she wouldn't abandon him—not after all he'd done for her in so short a time. And she wasn't about to leave the poor kender to the less-than-tender mercies of the beast.

But before Nearra could think of a plan, a young woman came running out of the alley, sword in hand, fiery red hair spilling from beneath her metal helmet.

"Turn and face me, minotaur!" she challenged. "Or is it your people's custom to fight only those who are a quarter of your size?" Her words were brave, but her voice quavered as she spoke.

"Hey!" the kender said in a wounded tone. "I'm three-and-a-half feet tall! That makes me *half* his size!"

Considering how much muscle the minotaur had, Nearra thought the redheaded warrior's comparison to be the more accurate one.

The warrior and the minotaur both ignored the kender's protest. The man-bull's nostrils flared in what Nearra presumed to be anger, and he gave a loud animalistic snort as he turned around slowly to face the red-haired warrior. She stood her ground, and though she trembled, she didn't lower her sword.

"I do not wish to battle the kender," the minotaur said. The man-bull glanced over his shoulder at the kender and snorted in derision. "I would not grant such an honor to one so insignificant." The minotaur's arrogant tone clashed with his bestial appearance.

"Why not?" the kender said, starting to march toward the man-bull. "I think you're just afraid because—*urk!*"

The kender's words were cut off as Davyn grabbed him by his purple cape and yanked him backward.

"Do you want to get killed?" Davyn hissed in one of the kender's pointed ears.

"No," he said. "I suppose not."

"Then be quiet and let your friend handle this!" Davyn sounded confident, but as he glanced at the minotaur, Nearra saw the worry in his eyes.

"Why do you pursue the kender, if not to fight him?" the red-haired warrior asked. "And don't tell me you only want to talk to him—unless minotaurs always hold conversations while swinging a weapon."

"The kender stole something from me," the minotaur said. "I merely wish to retrieve my property."

The kender pulled away from Davyn's grip with an ease that surprised Nearra, and he walked toward the angry minotaur.

"Now I really must protest. I am not a thief! I am Sindri Suncatcher, wizard extraordinaire!"

The warrior groaned.

The kender didn't look much like a wizard to Nearra, but then Maddoc was the only one she'd ever met—as far as she could remember.

"Stay out of this, Sindri!" the girl warrior snapped. "Unless you want this minotaur to use his axe to turn you into two halves of a kender."

"Two halves?" Sindri Suncatcher looked thoughtful. "I wonder what that would be like?"

The minotaur turned to glare at the kender, his grip tightening around the handle of his axe until it looked as if his bulging knuckles would break through skin and fur. "If you do not cease your foolish chatter, you will find out soon enough!"

Nearra almost jumped when Davyn pulled her aside. "Perhaps it would be best if we were on our way," he said softly, presumably so the others wouldn't overhear.

Nearra looked at Davyn, unable to believe her ears. "You showed no hesitation in facing Slean armed with only a bow and arrow. Why are you afraid now?"

"It is my responsibility to escort you to the healer and keep you safe until you have regained your memory," Davyn said. "Getting involved in a dispute between a kender and a minotaur won't accomplish either of these goals."

"We can't leave," Nearra said. "The kender and his warrior friend might need help."

The minotaur took a step toward Sindri and stuck out his free hand, palm up.

"I understand that it is a kender's nature to handle whatever catches his eye. Return what you have taken, and I shall go in peace."

"I don't mean to keep arguing with you," Sindri said in the tone of someone who most certainly *did* mean to, "but I don't know where you get your information about kender. We do no such thing. Oh, every now and then we stumble across objects people have lost, though why they insist on blaming us for their carelessness, I'll never know. But as I said, I am a wizard. I have no need to take objects from anyone, for I possess the magical ability to conjure any item I wish."

Davyn rolled his eyes. "He must be joking."

The red-haired warrior must have overheard, for she said, "Unfortunately, he's not."

Sindri gave his companion a quick scowl. He whispered a few words, then reached into his cape. "Behold!" he shouted, and withdrew his hand with a flourish. He now held a bulging leather pouch.

"My steel!" the minotaur bellowed. "I knew you took it, you little thief! Return it to me at once!"

"You are mistaken," Sindri said. "This purse may look similar to the one you lost—perhaps even identical to it. But this purse magically appeared within one of the hidden pockets of my cape."

"He can't possibly be serious!" Davyn said.

"Maybe he is," Nearra replied. "What thief would ever invent such an outrageous story and expect it to be believed?"

"Even if Sindri is telling the truth, I doubt it will make much difference to the minotaur," Davyn said.

Someone needed to do something or else Sindri Suncatcher was sure to get injured—or worse. Nearra clenched her hands in frustration and a tingling warmth spread through her fingers. It was the same sensation she'd experienced in the clearing when she'd been about to be devoured by Slean. She sensed that whatever this feeling might be, it could allow her to help Sindri somehow. And if that was the case, perhaps she shouldn't fight it.

Sindri made a quick motion with his hand and the minotaur's steel vanished back into his cape. His nimble kender fingers moved with a speed and grace that a human could never copy.

Sindri struck a pose, feet planted well apart, hands lifted into the air.

"I wish I didn't have to do this," Sindri said to the minotaur, "but you leave me no choice. I'm going to have to cast a spell on you."

The red-haired warrior sighed. "Please don't do this, Sindri."

"Hush, Catriona. I need complete silence so I can concentrate."

The tingling in Nearra's hands increased until the sensation was almost painful. She shouldn't have let this, this . . . whatever it was go this far. She felt pressure building inside her skull, as if a crushing headache was coming on. She thought she might faint.

Davyn looked at her with concern and grabbed her hand. Nearra squinted as an intense ray of sunlight reflected off his silver ring. The tingling ceased.

Sindri muttered a few words and threw his hands out in a flourish. The minotaur grunted in surprise as his axe pulled free of his hand and hovered in the air in front of him. As surprised as the man-bull looked, Catriona seemed absolutely shocked. Sindri himself stared at the floating axe as if he couldn't quite believe what he was seeing.

The battle-axe hung motionless in the air for another moment. Then the weapon turned upside down so that the bottom of the handle was pointed directly at the spot between the minotaur's widened eyes.

The axe shot forward and the handle slammed against the minotaur's head. A soft moan escaped his lips, along with a thin line of drool. His eyes rolled back in his head and his body went slack. The minotaur collapsed to the ground, unconscious.

A moment later, the axe fell to the dirt a foot away from the minotaur's head, the blade sinking into the ground with a soft *chuk!*

Nearra, Davyn, Sindri, and Catriona stood in silence for a long moment as they tried to understand the event that had just taken place. At last, Sindri gave out a whoop and jumped into the air, on his face an expression of pure delight.

"Did you see that, Catriona? I told you I was a great wizard, didn't I?"

Catriona gaped in astonishment. Nearra turned to Davyn. His brow was covered with sweat, and his lips formed a small, almost unnoticeable smile.

4 A MATTER OF HONOR

It shouldn't be much longer now," Sindri said. "Bramble Street is just around the corner."

"That's what you said about the last corner we came to," Catriona said.

The kender was unruffled by the warrior's comment. "Well, this time it is."

Catriona shook her head. "I should have known better than to take my eyes off you for so much as an instant. If I'd been watching you more closely, you wouldn't have gotten mixed up with that minotaur."

"It was just a simple misunderstanding," Sindri said. "Luckily, my magic was able to get us out of trouble."

Nearra was glad that Sindri and Catriona had decided to come along with them to make sure they reached the healer safely. Walking with the two of them—and with Davyn—felt right somehow, as if the four were meant to be together.

Davyn had persuaded Sindri to leave the minotaur's money pouch behind when they'd left the unconscious creature. Well, *left* was too mild a word. *Fled* before the man-bull could wake up and come after them was more accurate.

Now Sindri was leading them to the healer, and though Nearra knew she shouldn't get her hopes up, she couldn't help

23

herself. If the healer could restore her memories, then she'd know more than just her name. She'd know where she came from, if she had a mother or father, brothers or sisters. And maybe she'd even learn how she'd come to be in the middle of the forest with no traveling gear, no food, and no water, not to mention how she'd lost her memories in the first place.

But what if she didn't like who she really was? What if there was a reason—a good reason—why she'd lost her memories?

Sindri suddenly came to a halt, and since he was leading the way, the rest of them nearly collided with the kender before they could stop.

"That's odd," Sindri said as he stared at a small shop. The shutters were open and candles hung by their wicks over a wooden rod, on display for potential buyers. "I don't recall this candle maker's shop being here." He frowned. "Why do you suppose they moved it?"

Davyn made a sound in his throat as if he were choking. "I'll go inside and ask for directions." Without waiting for anyone to reply, he walked into the candle shop.

"Asking directions is nothing but a waste of time, since I already know where we're going," Sindri said. "But if it will make Davyn feel better, I have no objection. Besides," he added, almost to himself, "it'll give me a chance to try and remember exactly how I managed to levitate that minotaur's axe."

The minotaur in question, whose name was Jax, was at that very moment returning to consciousness. The first thing he became aware of was a terrible pounding in his head; it was especially bad between his eyes. The second thing he became aware of was that he was looking at an expanse of blue sky dotted with clouds. Strange, but the sky seemed to be directly in front of him, when it should have been—

And then he remembered: the kender. Jax sat up and immediately regretted it as the throbbing in his head increased and a wave of nausea rolled through his gut. He did his best to ignore the pain in his head and the roiling in his stomach. He was a minotaur—a warrior born and bred—and he would not let such minor discomforts get the better of him.

Jax looked around but saw no sign of the kender and his allies. A handful of onlookers stood off at a distance, talking among themselves. One man was laughing, no doubt at Jax's foolishness for allowing himself to be brought down by a kender—a kender wielding magic, but a kender nonetheless. As soon as the people saw the minotaur was awake and looking back at them, they turned and ran.

If Jax's head hadn't been pounding so, he might have gone after them, but he told himself that the rabble wasn't worth the effort.

He looked around for his axe and was glad to see it lying on the ground, along with his pouch of steel coins. Minotaurs usually didn't have to worry about someone trying to rob them. What pickpocket in his right mind would risk coming close enough to a minotaur to do so? But kender weren't exactly in their right minds, were they? Not when it came to "handling" objects that didn't belong to them.

Jax would have loved to have his own hands around the kender's tiny neck right now. If he did . . . The resultant image, gory as it was, made Jax smile.

Still, he had his money back, and more importantly, he had his axe. The weapon had been his father's. He'd given it to Jax on the day Jax had left the island of Kothas to seek fortune and honor in the world. Upon reaching the mainland of Ansalon, Jax began working as a guard for trading caravans. Humans might be intimidated by minotaurs, but that didn't stop them from hiring the man-bulls for their ferocity, strength, and skill with weaponry.

Jax was in something of a dilemma now. Honor was everything to his people, and his honor had been severely insulted by the kender wizard. True, no other minotaur save Jax knew what had happened, and if he never spoke of the incident again, none would. But that didn't matter. Jax knew, and that was enough.

Any other time, he would have immediately set out to find the kender and teach him what it meant to insult a minotaur. But Jax had just signed on to guard a trading caravan leaving Tresvka later that afternoon. If he went in search of the kender, he might miss the caravan's departure. If he weren't there when it left, he would break his word to the caravan-master who'd hired him. Honor would not permit Jax to break his word in such a fashion.

But honor also demanded that he find the kender and teach him an important lesson about showing the proper respect for minotaurs.

The question was, which was more important? Keeping his word or avenging the insult done to him by the kender?

Jax thought about it for a moment longer before deciding there really wasn't any question. He walked off in search of the caravan-master to quit his job. Then he would go after the kender.

5 AN OATH AND NEW HOPE

T he healer lives one street east of here," Davyn said. "She is named Wynda, and we'll know her place because the walls are covered with ivy, and a ginger cat sits on the windowsill when she has her shutters open."

Catriona frowned. "You walked into the candle maker's and came right back out again. How did you have time to learn all that?"

"The man was a fast talker. Let's go."

Davyn started down the street and the rest of them followed. Nearra was worried that something was wrong with Davyn. Ever since they had met Catriona and Sindri, he'd become increasingly irritable, and she wasn't sure why. She wanted to ask him, but she didn't feel she could, not in front of Catriona and Sindri.

Davyn picked up speed, as if he were more eager to get to the healer than she was. Nearra started to increase her pace to keep up with him, but before she could do so, Catriona took her elbow and held her back.

"Tell me, Nearra," Catriona whispered, "how well do you know that boy?"

"I only met him this morning. Remember? I told you about 27

how he and that white wizard rescued me from the dragon. Why do you ask?"

Catriona stared at Davyn's back. Sindri had to run to keep up with the ranger.

"I'm not sure," Catriona said. "There's just something about him that I don't trust."

Though Nearra didn't share Catriona's concern about Davyn, she smiled and said, "Then it's a good thing I have you along to protect me."

Catriona looked at the ground. "I can't protect you. I'm not a real warrior. I'm only a squire."

"You seemed like a real warrior to me when you were fighting with the minotaur," Nearra said.

"What does a girl like you know of battle?" Catriona snapped.

"I'm sorry. I only meant . . . " Nearra couldn't think what more to say.

Catriona saw the hurt in Nearra's face and her voice softened. "Please don't tell anyone. But the truth is . . . I was terrified. I try to hide it, but I'm always scared when I fight."

Nearra thought for a moment. "It seems to me that a true warrior battles on despite her fear. And that's exactly what you did."

Catriona studied Nearra for a moment. "You have no weapons, and you look as weak as a kender. I suppose you do need someone to protect you." She paused and then, as if coming to a decision, continued with firm conviction. "From this moment onward, I vow to serve as your protector, Nearra of the Forest, and I shall continue to do so until such time as you no longer have need of my service. This I do swear."

Nearra was so taken aback by this unexpected declaration that all she could say was "Thank you."

Catriona seemed satisfied with Nearra's response. The warrior nodded once, and then said, "Come, let's catch up with our companions."

Nearra walked faster but the warrior remained at her side, and she didn't let go of Nearra's arm.

They found the healer's place just where Davyn said they would: one street east. Ivy climbed the walls, and a cat lounged on the windowsill.

Sindri grinned upon seeing the small building. "I knew it was here!"

Davyn turned to the kender and Catriona, and he gave them a smile that seemed forced.

"Well, here we are, safe and sound. I'm sure Nearra is as grateful as I am for your help, but there is no need for you to accompany us any further. Come, Nearra. Let's go inside." Davyn stepped up to the wooden door and motioned for Nearra to join him.

Nearra looked to Catriona, unsure what to do.

"I can't think of anything more interesting to do than find out if Nearra recovers her lost memories," Sindri said. "How about you, Catriona?"

Catriona answered the kender, but she kept her gaze focused on Davyn as she spoke. "I have taken a vow to remain at Nearra's side until her mind is whole again. We are coming with you."

Davyn's gaze hardened and when he spoke, his voice was tight with tension. "I appreciate the offer, but we really—"

"You might as well not bother," Sindri interrupted. "Once Catriona makes up her mind, that's it. Several months ago she intervened when I was having a discussion with a deluded alchemist. He refused to believe I'd conjured a vial of water-breathing potion. We were in the middle of a fierce argument when Catriona showed up. Afterward, she decided to travel with me and, as she put it, protect me from myself." The kender leaned toward Davyn and whispered, "I don't really need protecting, of course, but I've found it's best to humor her in these matters."

Davyn's face reddened with anger, then he let out a defeated sigh, the anger draining out of him along with his breath. "All right, you two can come. But only if Nearra approves. After all, we've come to the healer for her sake."

Nearra spoke without hesitation. "I'd like for you to come."

Davyn nodded, gave Nearra a thin smile, then turned and knocked on the healer's door.

Inside the healer's examining room, Nearra sat on a hard wooden table while Catriona stood close by. Catriona had insisted on accompanying her into the examining room, and she'd been equally insistent that Davyn and Sindri—the two males—remain in the outer room while the examination took place.

The examining room was tiny and cramped. Shelves filled with hundreds of jars reached to the ceiling. Nearra read the labels of the jars next to her: Juniper, dried eel skin, goose droppings, sheep fat, wyvern stinger. She nearly gagged thinking of the disgusting potions those ingredients might make. But all the same, she'd be willing to drink anything if it might bring back her memories.

The healer pulled back a panel in the ceiling to allow sunlight into the room so that she might better see her patient. Wynda then walked around the table until she stood behind Nearra. She ran her short stubby fingers gently over Nearra's scalp, pausing now and then to exert pressure on a particular spot as she muttered to herself beneath her breath. She sniffed Nearra's breath, then cut off a lock of her hair and chewed it for several moments before scowling and spitting it onto the floor.

Finally, Wynda spoke. "I cannot tell if you suffer an enchantment, child, but the wizard who aided you said you did not, correct?"

"That's right," Nearra said.

"Then I am at a loss to explain your condition. Your bodily humors are in balance, and you appear strong and healthy."

Wynda made a clucking sound with her tongue as she pondered the problem. "Child, I say this without false pride: I am the best healer in Tresvka, and I have no idea how to help you."

Nearra thought she might cry. "Are you certain? Can't you make some kind of potion to help me?"

"Surely there must be *something* that can be done for her," Catriona said.

Wynda shook her head. "Not by me, I'm afraid, nor by any other ordinary healer. But ... there might be another possibility."

Nearra wondered if she dared to hope again. "What is it?"

"Long years past, there was a temple located deep in a valley somewhere past the northern forest of Tresvka. Many clerics made their home there, sharing their knowledge and working miracles in the names of the divine powers. After the gods turned away from Krynn, the clerics disappeared and the temple fell into ruin. But now that the dragons have returned to Krynn, there are rumors that the gods once more are permitting miracles to be performed in the mortal world. I have recently heard tell that a new group of clerics has returned to the temple and taken up residence there. If I were you, I would journey to the temple to see if the rumors are true and if the clerics might be able to heal you."

Nearra looked to Catriona. "What do you think?"

"I, too, have heard stories of the gods' chosen returning to Krynn after the War of the Lance."

Nearra didn't know—or couldn't remember—what the War of the Lance was. But if Catriona had heard the same rumors as Wynda, then there was at least a possibility of them being true.

"Do you know the way to this temple?" Nearra asked the red-haired warrior, her excitement building.

Catriona shook her head. "Sindri and I have only been in Tresvka for a week or so. We haven't traveled through the land to the north."

"Perhaps Davyn—" But Nearra broke off when Catriona frowned at the mention of the ranger's name.

"If it's a guide you seek, you might find one at the Blind Goose tavern," Wynda said. "It's a favorite gathering place of traders and travelers of all sorts. Odds are that someone there will know the way to the temple."

"Then that's where I shall go!" Nearra said, grinning. Wynda might not have restored Nearra's memory, but the healer had given her renewed hope.

Wynda cleared her throat. "Regarding the matter of my fee . . ."

"Of course," Nearra said, embarrassed that she'd forgotten all about paying the healer. "One of our companions has the money. We shall go fetch him."

Wynda smiled. "Certainly, child. And I hope you find what you're searching for."

Davyn walked into the healer's examining room. Before he closed the door behind him, he listened: Nearra was telling Sindri what the healer had said to her.

Good. That meant no one would hear him speak with Wynda.

The healer held out a hand. "Do you have my payment, young man?"

Davyn removed Maddoc's money pouch from his tunic pocket, then walked over to Wynda. He opened the purse and took out twenty steel coins, but he didn't give them to her right away.

"Did you do as you were told?"

"Yes. I told her that she has no sign of either injury or illness, and that the clerics inhabiting the Temple of the Holy Orders of the Stars might be able to help her."

"And . . .?"

"That she could find a guide to the temple at the Blind Goose tavern."

"Excellent." Davyn dropped the coins into the healer's waiting hand.

Wynda grinned and quickly closed her fingers around the coins, as though she were afraid Davyn might try to snatch them back.

"A pleasure doing business with you," Wynda said.

Davyn nodded. He knew he should have been pleased that meeting Sindri and Catriona hadn't disrupted the plan. But instead he felt unsettled.

He turned away from the healer and headed for the door. They had best get over to the Blind Goose. Oddvar didn't like to be kept waiting.

6 THE BLIND GOOSE

I'm so excited!" Sindri said as he led his three companions down the street toward the tavern. "I've heard of the Temple of the Holy Orders of the Stars, but now I'm actually going to get to see it!" It turned out that Sindri really knew where the Blind Goose was. He'd spent a number of hours there, listening to the stories, the tall tales, and the outright lies the patrons told.

Nearra laughed. "Is there anything you don't get excited about?"

Sindri frowned in puzzlement. "I'm a kender," he said.

"She doesn't have all her memories," Catriona reminded Sindri. "She probably doesn't recall much about kender."

"Lucky her," Davyn muttered. Catriona gave the ranger a dark look, but Sindri ignored him.

"That's right! I forgot!" The kender chuckled. "I accidentally made a joke, didn't I? I didn't remember that Nearra couldn't remember."

"Some joke," Davyn said.

Sindri looked suddenly worried. "I meant no offense, Nearra."

Nearra wanted to say, How would you feel if you didn't know who you were and where you came from? But she knew the little

35

kender wouldn't understand. Instead she smiled. "No offense taken, Sindri."

"Good. Then let me tell you something about kender. We are extremely curious about everything."

"And this curiosity results in kender having an almost total lack of fear," Catriona added. The warrior sounded almost envious.

"You mean a lack of common sense," Davyn said.

Sindri ignored him. "Our curiosity is strongest when we're young. Around the age of twenty or so, we go through a stage of our lives known as wanderlust. It came upon me earlier than it does others." Sindri smiled smugly. "But then I've always been advanced for my age. I suspect that accounts for my skill with magic as well."

Davyn rolled his eyes.

"What do you mean by wanderlust?" Nearra asked.

"Oh! You don't remember much, do you?" Sindri said. "Wanderlust is a time when young kender are compelled to travel throughout the land seeing and doing as many interesting things as we can. These travels might go on for a number of years before we finally return home and settle down."

"It sounds to me as if kender have found a way to get the most out of life," Nearra said. "Travel and adventure when young; home and family when older."

"If they survive long enough to get old," Catriona muttered.

Nearra ignored her. "Have you ever seen a dragon in all your travels, Sindri? Slean is the only one I have seen—as far I can remember."

"I'm sorry to say that I have never come across any of the magnificent beasts," Sindri said. "I'd love to see one!"

"Speak for yourself," Catriona said with a shudder.

"Why do you suppose dragons returned to Krynn after all this time?" Nearra said.

"I have heard stories about the War of the Lance," Catriona said. "Stories of how the Dark Queen Takhisis brought dragonkind back to the world in an attempt to conquer all of Krynn, and how a group of brave heroes armed with the legendary Dragonlance finally defeated her. As to how much of the story is true and how much is exaggeration, I cannot say."

"Well, all I can say is that I hope we can find someone at the Blind Goose who not only knows the route to the Temple of the Holy Orders of the Stars, but who also knows a thing or two about avoiding dragons," Davyn said.

"Do you think they are as fearsome as the tales say?" Sindri said.

"They're worse," Davyn answered, "because they aren't just stories anymore; they're *real*. So you'd best hope we don't see a dragon. That is, if you wish to survive your time of wanderlust."

Sindri sighed. "I see your point."

The kender didn't sound all that convinced to Nearra. But she was more concerned with what Davyn had said: I hope we can find someone at the Blind Goose . . . You'd best hope we don't see a dragon.

She looked at Davyn. "Does that mean you're coming with me to the temple?"

Davyn shrugged. "If you'd like . . ."

Nearra smiled. "I would. Very much."

Davyn looked at her for a moment before returning her smile. "Then I will."

Nearra had been so involved in the conversation that she hadn't noticed the street had grown narrow here, the buildings smaller and crowded together, sometimes leaning against one another for support. The gutter overflowed with fruit rinds, spoiled vegetables, picked-clean animal bones, and other disgusting garbage. The companions had to step around animal manure covered with buzzing black flies. The heat from the afternoon sun warmed the manure and the air was thick with a sickening stench.

Nearra stepped carefully as she walked, and clamped a hand over her mouth and nose to shut out the smell. But Sindri inhaled deeply and grinned.

"What a stink! Every time I come here, it smells worse!"

A pack of grubby dwarves walked by. They huddled close together, not speaking, and they cast furtive glances about as they walked, as if constantly alert to the possibility of attack.

"Is it safe here?" Nearra asked, trying not to sound as worried as she felt.

"It is as long as I am at your side," Catriona said.

"Of course it's safe," Sindri said, sounding surprised anyone could think otherwise. "I've never had any trouble here."

"Just like you didn't have trouble with the minotaur, eh?" Davyn said.

Sindri gave the ranger a dirty look but didn't say anything.

Near the end of the street, they came to an especially rickety-looking building. Nearra saw a sign hanging over the door. On it was a faded, lopsided painting of a bird that might or might not have been a goose. A black blindfold covered the bird's eyes.

Nearra pointed. "Is that it?"

Davyn opened his mouth, but then he quickly closed it.

Sindri said, "Yes, that's the Blind Goose. Let's go!" The kender started running toward the tavern, but Catriona grabbed a handful of his cape and stopped him.

"Let's go slowly," she said. "We don't want to draw any more attention to ourselves than necessary. Especially in a place like that," she added under her breath.

As they approached the tavern entrance, the window shutters burst into splinters and a man came flying out headfirst. He landed in the street muck with a loud gasp as the air was knocked out of his lungs. The man lay still for a moment, then rose shakily to his feet, groaning with the effort. He staggered down the street, seemingly none the worse for wear.

Catriona looked anxiously at Nearra. "Perhaps you should wait out here while Davyn and I go in and look for a guide." From the tone of her voice, it sounded as if she would rather not go in at all. "Sindri will watch over you."

"Do I have to?" the kender whined.

Nearra felt a sudden surge of anger. "What are you saying? That I can't handle myself in a dangerous situation?" Nearra was at a loss to explain her anger. She knew that Catriona was only looking out for her, but for some reason the idea that the warrior thought she was helpless infuriated Nearra.

"Since awakening in the forest, I've encountered goblins, a dragon, and a minotaur, and the day is only half over. If I can deal with all that, surely I can deal with some drunken thugs in a seedy tavern." Nearra was surprised to hear herself say these things. It was almost as if the words weren't hers but someone else's.

"I do not mean to criticize you," Catriona said, "but in each of those situations you had help. And given your condition, in many ways, you are like an infant that has only been born this morning. Perhaps you can handle yourself in a dangerous situation, but do you know for certain if you can? From what you've told us, you had no weapons when you first woke in the forest. Do you remember if you've been trained to use any kind of weapon?"

Nearra thought hard, but she could not recall ever having been trained to do *anything*, let alone fight. She didn't speak. Her silence was enough of an answer.

Catriona nodded. "It's settled, then. Sindri, stay here with Nearra while Davyn and I go into the tavern."

Nearra felt her anger building, rising near the boiling point. She balled her hands into fists and they began to tingle and grow warm.

How dare she speak like that to me! The thought echoed through Nearra's mind, but it felt alien, as though it belonged to someone else. A woman with a cruel edge to her voice . . .

Nearra fixed her gaze on Catriona and began to raise her hands . . .

But then Davyn was standing next to her, gently but firmly pushing her hands back down.

"It's all right, Nearra," he said in a soothing voice. "We won't be long."

He smiled and Nearra felt the tingling—and her anger—subside. "I'll wait," she said.

Davyn nodded, then turned to Catriona. "Let's go." Without waiting for Catriona to respond, he started toward the tavern's entrance.

Catriona scowled. It appeared she didn't like taking orders, at least not from Davyn. But she followed, and the two of them went inside the Blind Goose.

Sindri sniffed the air. "Does that smell like dead cat to you? Let's go see!"

7 WANTED: ONE GUIDE

A

s they stepped into the tavern, Davyn scanned the room, looking for Oddvar. The Theiwar wouldn't be expecting him to be accompanied by anyone except Nearra, and Davyn needed to figure out a way to let Oddvar know that the plan was still on track.

The patrons, mostly male and mostly human, sat at tables and chairs made of stained and scratched wood. The dirt floor was smooth and packed down from all the feet that had trod upon it over the years. The room was dark, the only light coming from the window with the now-broken shutters. But the patrons liked it that way. The Blind Goose wasn't the sort of tavern where people went to be seen—quite the opposite, in fact.

Davyn spotted Oddvar sitting on a stool at the end of the bar. The Theiwar wore the hood of his cloak up, despite the dimness of the room. On the counter before him was a clay mug, most likely filled with the bitter dark ale Oddvar favored. The dwarf sat between two humans—a bald man with a black patch over his left eye, and a slender man with shoulder-length blond hair. A traveler's pack rested on the floor between the blond man's feet.

"Let's go speak with the tavern keeper," Catriona said.

Since that meant they would have to go over to the bar where 41

Oddvar was, Davyn nodded. As they began making their way through the crowd, Davyn noticed that more than a few eyes followed their progress—or more accurately, Catriona's progress. The red-haired warrior was certainly a striking figure—tall, attractive, with an aura of strength and confidence. Davyn wasn't worried about Catriona; he knew she could take care of herself. But he was glad that Nearra had stayed outside. He knew he shouldn't feel such a thing but he did. She was nicer than he'd expected, and braver, too. He was impressed by the way she was handling the loss of her memories. If it had been him, he didn't think he would handle it half as well.

Stop it, he told himself. You're here to do a job, so do it!

The tavern was crowded, and it took some jostling and elbowing before Davyn and Catriona reached the bar. There were no seats open, so Catriona had to lean in between two customers and say, "Barkeep, I have a question for you."

The tavern keeper, who was wiping a mug with a filthy rag, looked up. "What do you want?" he said.

"My companions and I seek a guide to the north. The healer Wynda said we might find such a person in your establishment."

The tavern keeper frowned and glanced toward the end of the bar where Oddvar sat. The Theiwar lifted his index finger off the counter.

The tavern keeper jerked a thumb in Oddvar's direction. "Try the dwarf."

Catriona nodded. "My thanks, good sir."

The tavern keeper burst out laughing. "Good sir, is it? It's been a long time since this pesthole has seen such courtly manners! Do you fancy yourself a knight? You're certainly dressed for the part!" The tavern keeper laughed again, his merriment spreading to the others seated at the bar.

But Catriona was far from amused. Quick as lightning, she drew her short sword and pressed the tip against the roll of flab beneath the tavern keeper's stubbly chin.

"Do not make fun of Knighthood," she said in a low voice. "You are not worthy to so much as speak the word."

She hesitated, then removed her sword point from the tavern keeper's neck.

"For that matter, neither am I." Catriona sheathed her sword in a single smooth motion. The tavern keeper's face was pale, and a tiny trickle of blood ran down his neck where the sword had barely pierced his flesh.

Catriona and Davyn moved down the bar toward the dwarf. But just as Davyn was about to say something to the Theiwar, the man on his right—the one with blond hair—turned around and said, "Did I hear right? Are the two of you seeking a guide?"

The man had a friendly smile, but there was something calculating in his gaze. He brushed his blond hair back over his ears—his pointed ears—and Davyn realized that he wasn't a man at all, but rather an elf.

Before Catriona could answer, Oddvar turned and spoke in his soft, whispery voice. "I believe they intended to speak with me."

The elf turned to look at Oddvar. His smile remained in place, but his voice took on a skeptical tone. "I mean no offense, friend, but you are a Theiwar, are you not? Unless I am mistaken, your people live in underground caverns and rarely venture into the light of day."

"Not all Theiwar are the same," Oddvar said, his voice slightly louder now. "Are all elves?"

The elf's smile didn't falter. "As I said, I meant no offense. But I can see that even in here, where there is little light, you wear your hood up to protect your sensitive eyes."

"So?" Oddvar challenged.

"So these two seek a guide to lead them through the land to the north. There's forest up there and the woods are hardly the sort of place your people frequent. While I, on the other hand, am Kagonesti, and my people have a deep affinity for the forest and the creatures that live there."

Oddvar frowned. "Are not Kagonesti elves generally dark-haired and possessed of brown skin?"

The elf's smile almost fell away, but he managed to maintain his good cheer, if barely.

"I am half Kagonesti and half Silvanesti. It is my Silvanesti heritage that gives me my lighter colored skin and blond hair. But in all the ways that truly matter, in here—" the elf tapped his breastbone—"I am completely Kagonesti."

"So you are a *half-breed*." Oddvar said this last word with a sneer.

That was it for the elf's smile. "Have a care, dwarf. Up to this point I have been civil to you. It would be a shame if our conversation were suddenly to become less than pleasant."

Oddvar's large eyes glittered with anger, and his left hand disappeared beneath the counter, to grab his weapon, no doubt.

"Hold, both of you," Catriona said. "There is no need for this. We shall decide which of you to hire—if either."

The elf turned to face Catriona, his smile restored. "Of course, my lady. My name is Elidor, and I am entirely at your service."

Oddvar snorted but said nothing.

"That matter can be decided quite simply," Catriona said. "Which of you has had more experience traveling through the lands to the north?"

Davyn decided he'd better say something. "More to the point, do either of you know the way to the Temple of the Holy Orders of the Stars?"

Oddvar opened his mouth to answer, but Elidor jumped in before the dwarf could speak.

"I not only know the route to the temple, I have been there," the elf said. He looked at Davyn. "It is a beautiful place—tall glass spires, crystalline domes. The courtyard is paved with multi-colored tiled mosaics and filled with an assortment of amazing foliage. It is a divine place in every sense of the word."

Catriona was nodding to herself, and Davyn knew he had to do something fast before Catriona gave Elidor the job.

But just as Davyn was about to say something, he heard Nearra scream.

Sindri had grown bored with the dead cat—thank the gods—and had turned his attention to a strange-looking mold growing on the side of a building when Nearra saw the minotaur stalking down the street toward them.

She wasn't certain the minotaur had seen them yet, but she was sure that it was the same one they'd encountered earlier—he had a black coat of fur, wore a leather kilt, and carried an axe sheathed on his back. And there was no mistaking that furrowed brow or those angry eyes.

Nearra bent down close to Sindri's ear and whispered, "Don't look, but the minotaur that was chasing you earlier is—" but that was all she got out before Sindri turned and headed straight for the man-bull.

When she first met the kender, Nearra thought his almost total lack of fear was charming. But now she could see that it could quickly become annoying—if not downright deadly.

"Sindri, stop!" she called.

"Why? I took care of him once before, and I can do so again." He frowned. "I'm just not sure how I did it." He shrugged. "Oh, well. I'm bound to remember sooner or later."

For Sindri's sake, Nearra sincerely hoped it would be sooner.

"Halt, minotaur, or I'll be forced to cast another spell on you!" Sindri planted his feet on the street muck and raised his arms in what Nearra assumed was meant to be an intimidating wizardly pose. Unfortunately, the kender looked more like a child stretching to see how high he could reach.

Still, the minotaur stopped. He fixed Sindri with a hate-filled glare, but he did not take another step toward the kender.

"I have been searching all afternoon for you," the minotaur said in a low, rumbling voice. "You have insulted me, and I have come to reclaim my honor."

Sindri blinked several times, clearly puzzled. "I don't understand. You got your money back, didn't you? Or rather, I left you the substitute I conjured. Did the purse contain fewer coins than the original?"

"No money was missing," the minotaur said.

"Well, there you go." The kender lowered his arms. "It's all settled, then."

Now it was the minotaur's turn to look confused. "No, it isn't! There is still the matter of my honor!"

"You keep using that word: honor. What precisely does it mean to you?"

The minotaur stared at Sindri for a long moment before answering. "You mean you truly do not know?"

"I've heard the word before, of course. I've always thought it meant worrying too much about what other people think of you. But I must be wrong. I can't imagine anyone going to all the trouble you have simply to improve another's opinion of one's self. That would be pathetic, don't you think?"

The minotaur had been growing increasingly angry as Sindri spoke. Now the man-bull's face was so contorted by rage that he truly did resemble an inhuman beast. With a roar, the minotaur ran toward Sindri, hands stretched out in front of him. He was so furious that he wasn't going to waste time drawing his axe; he was going to fight the little wizard barehanded. It wouldn't be much of a fight, Nearra thought, given the difference in their sizes.

Nearra wished there was something she could do to help Sindri, and once more the warm tingling erupted in her hands, stronger than before. A picture flashed through Nearra's mind— an image of the minotaur's hooved foot slipping in the street muck, causing the man-bull to lose his balance.

And then it wasn't simply an image anymore. The minotaur's right hoof slid on something wet and disgusting lying in the street. He wobbled, unbalanced, but he was moving far too fast to slow down. He barreled toward Sindri, completely out of control, wildly waving his arms in a vain attempt to regain his balance.

Just as the minotaur was about to slam into the defenseless kender, Sindri nimbly stepped aside, and the man-bull continued slip-sliding forward, straight for the entrance of the Blind Goose Tavern. The minotaur crashed into the tavern door, his speed and bulk reducing it to instant kindling.

The strange tingling sensation in Nearra's hands began to fade and she felt a trifle dizzy.

Nearra looked at Sindri. "Are you all right?"

The kender was grinning. "Did you see the way he hit that door? *Pow!*"

Sindri was obviously unharmed. Nearra hurried toward the tavern—careful to keep from slipping herself—and hesitantly walked through the now-open doorway.

The minotaur lay sprawled on the dirt floor, beneath him the splintered remains of a table, as well as a pair of very unhappy customers. The minotaur groaned and started to rise, but one of the men he'd pinned grabbed a broken table leg and cracked the man-bull over the head with it. The blow didn't seem to injure the minotaur, but it did enrage him further. He roared and reached for the man. The man's friend pulled free from the remnants of the table and grabbed another table leg. He swung wildly, trying to free his friend. But instead of hitting the minotaur, he nearly hit Nearra.

Nearra screamed but dodged the blow just in time. "Davyn! Catriona! Time to go!"

It was dim inside the tavern, but Nearra could just make out the figures of Davyn and Catriona standing near the bar. With them were two men—one tall and one short. Catriona pointed to the tall one, and then the three of them began hurrying toward the entrance, leaving the short one behind.

Looks like we've found our guide, Nearra thought. She then stepped out of the way to let Davyn, Catriona, and a handsome blond elf exit the tavern.

Catriona shot Sindri a look. "I see your horned friend managed to track you down."

"You missed it, Catriona! Just as the big cow was about to get me, he suddenly slipped and went crashing into the tavern! Do you think maybe I cast another spell on him without knowing it?"

Davyn gave Nearra a quick look before turning to Sindri. "We can worry about that later. We need to get out of here before the fighting spills into the street."

The sounds of combat inside the tavern had become louder and more violent. It seemed the brawl had spread to include the rest of the Blind Goose's customers.

"You mean before the minotaur comes outside looking for Sindri again," Catriona said.

Nearra looked at the elf. His right hand twitched near the pack slung over his shoulder and then fell still.

Nearra frowned. She'd had the impression that the elf had been holding something. And had she seen that same hand reach out as the elf had run past the minotaur? It had all happened so fast, she wasn't sure.

He smiled. "My name is Elidor." He reached out to shake Nearra's hand.

"Introductions later," Davyn said, grabbing Nearra's hand and pulling her down the street. "Running now."

Oddvar stood with his back against the bar, warily watching the fighting and doing his best to stay away from it. He could fight well enough when he had to, but he preferred to use stealth and cunning whenever he could.

He still had hold of the poisoned dagger he'd intended to use on the elf. He was now tempted to use it on the idiotic minotaur who'd come crashing into the tavern before Oddvar could prevent the cursed elf from stealing his "job" as Nearra's guide. The Theiwar had no idea who the redheaded girl in chain mail had been, but obviously the boy had experienced some unexpected complications. Whatever had gone wrong, Oddvar knew his master wasn't going to like it, not one bit. He slid the poisoned dagger back into its sheath and skulked off in search of a back door.

8 DINNER AND DISGUISE

Elidor had said they could reach the temple in only a couple of days if they traveled by horseback. But since there wasn't enough of Maddoc's money left to buy horses for them all in addition to the supplies they needed, they would have to walk. That meant the trip would take four days, perhaps five depending on how often and long they needed to rest.

To prepare, they purchased dried beef from the butcher and rye bread from the baker. Then they stopped at a cobbler to get sturdy walking boots for Nearra. At the market, they bought a traveler's pack for Nearra as well as water skins and rain cloaks for the entire group.

"We'll be traveling through the forest north of Tresvka at first," Elidor said. "But when we reach the plains, we'll need to protect ourselves from the sun's rays. We can wear our rain cloaks with the hoods up, and if they get too hot, I can weave us some simple but serviceable hats from rushes, leaves, and twigs."

"You can?" Sindri asked, eyes wide with wonder.

Elidor laughed. "Of course, my small friend. I am Kagonesti."

The companions knew there was an excellent chance the minotaur was still searching for Sindri since the kender had now humiliated him twice. So they'd taken precautions. While

51

the others had been buying supplies, Davyn and Catriona had visited several taverns and spread the word that the kender wizard called Sindri Suncatcher had departed Tresvka on a special mission to the south.

Catriona and Sindri had been staying at a small but respectable inn, and they decided that the others should join them there for the night. The five companions would set off on their journey at dawn.

While the purse of coins that Maddoc had given Davyn was significantly lighter after shopping, there was still enough left for the five of them to eat dinner. Davyn felt it would be safer to leave Sindri behind while the rest of them ate, but Catriona refused to leave Sindri alone. The companions gathered in Sindri's room to decide what to do.

"I need to eat," Catriona said. "Tomorrow we start out on a long journey."

"Of course you need to eat," Davyn said, sounding irritated. "But if we want to keep the minotaur from finding Sindri, we can't have him sitting in the common room with the rest of us. An elf can always brush his hair over his ears, sit in a dark corner, and with luck, pass for human."

"Not that he'd want to," Elidor said, smiling to show that he was only joking.

"But it's not so easy to disguise a kender," Davyn finished.

"If we keep arguing, there won't be any food left downstairs," Catriona said.

"And I haven't had a decent meal in . . ." Nearra paused. "Well, I don't remember when. But I'm starving! Let's just go downstairs and eat. What are the odds that the minotaur will come to this particular inn looking for Sindri?"

"He could always eat here in his room," Davyn said.

"What?" Sindri yelped. "And miss all the fun downstairs? I'd rather have the minotaur catch me! Why don't I go find that beast and settle this once and for all." He grabbed his cape and headed for the door.

"No!" they shouted. Catriona snatched him by the hood and pulled him back.

They all started arguing at once then.

Catriona yelled, "Be silent!" The warrior lifted the hood of Sindri's cape and smiled slowly, a twinkle in her eye. "I think I have a better idea."

It was busy in the common room that night. The thick stone walls made for a welcome respite from the heat outside, and almost every table was full of men and women eating and talking. Many were citizens of Tresvka who'd just come here for a good meal and to be entertained by the bard strumming his lyre in the corner. Servers ran back and forth bringing ale from the bar and steaming mutton stew or venison roast from the kitchen. Overseeing it all from the doorway, the huge innkeeper stood, his arms crossed and his face contorted into a permanent scowl.

Davyn, Nearra, and Elidor took a table in a dark alcove as far from the entrance as they could get. Catriona arrived several moments later carrying a wooden crate.

"Where did you find that?" Davyn asked.

"In the kitchen." Catriona set the crate on the bench and out popped Sindri, wearing Catriona's rain cloak.

"This crate used to hold potatoes," Sindri said. Catriona turned the crate over and gestured for Sindri to climb up.

The kender scampered onto the top of the crate with the ease and agility of a squirrel. He grinned as he looked around. "So this is what the world looks like to you big folk!" He laughed. "Your heads are up so high, I'm surprised you ever notice anything beneath your noses."

"Shh, Sindri!" Catriona said. "Try not to draw attention to yourself!" She adjusted the rain cloak to cover the crate and pulled the hood up, concealing Sindri's pointed ears.

Davyn snorted. "He doesn't look human. His head's still kender-sized."

Catriona frowned. "Maybe so, but he looks good enough to pass for human at a distance."

"A very long distance," Davyn muttered. "Say ten or twenty miles."

When the serving woman brought their food, she gave Sindri a strange look. But she set their dinners onto the table without a word. They had all ordered the same thing: mutton stew with onions, peas, and beans served in trenchers of bowl-shaped dark bread. As they ate, Nearra turned to Elidor.

"I'm afraid I don't recall much about elves," she said. "Perhaps you could refresh my memory?"

The elf laughed. "There's so much to tell, I hardly know where to begin!" He thought for a moment. "Well, for one thing, though I appear to be a teenager, just like the rest of you, I am in fact sixty-three years old. Since my people typically live to be over five hundred, even a Kagonesti isn't considered a full-fledged adult until the age of eighty."

"What does Kagonesti mean?" Nearra said.

Elidor's eyebrows lifted. "You really don't remember much, do you?" He took in a deep breath then continued, "There are several different races of elves. Silvanesti claim to be the first elves of Krynn. The Qualinesti are smaller and darker than their Silvanesti cousins. Dimernesti and Dargonesti are sea elves. The Kagonesti are known as wild elves. I happen to be part Kagonesti and part Silvanesti."

Sindri tore off a hunk of bread from his trencher and spoke as he chewed. "I've heard that Silvanesti elves don't approve of having children with other types of elves. If that's true, how could you be half Silvanesti and half Kagonesti?"

Elidor glared at the kender, and a tense silence fell over the table.

Sindri, who had been in the process of taking a bite of stew, stopped, the spoon halfway to his mouth.

"Did I say something wrong?"

Elidor gave the kender a smile that seemed forced. "The

matter is a sensitive one among elves, and we do not usually discuss it with those of other races."

"Oh," Sindri said. Then he shrugged and returned to eating as if nothing had happened.

Nearra hastened to change the subject. "Elidor, what can you tell me of the Temple of the Holy Orders of the Stars?"

Elidor cleared his throat. "Well—"

"Oh, let me tell the story!" Sindri said. "One of the things I love most—besides magic, of course—is collecting stories, especially stories that deal with magic. That's why I'm so excited about going to the temple. I learned all about it from a wizard named Fizban at the Inn of the Last Home." Elidor nodded and Sindri continued, his voice taking on the tone of a practiced storyteller.

"These events took place before the Cataclysm, so it's difficult to tell how much of the story is fact and how much is legend. But according to the tale, the temple was founded by a cleric named Elethia. It was her dream to create a place where priests and priestesses of all the gods could live and work together. Clerics from all over Ansalon came to be part of Elethia's dream, and her temple grew in size, beauty, and power. But one day a fierce red dragon called Kiernan the Crimson decided to claim the lands surrounding Tresvka as his own."

Nearra couldn't help shuddering as Sindri said the word dragon. Once again she saw Slean's eyes, heard her harsh voice, saw her mouth opening to display twin rows of sharp teeth . . .

Sindri continued. "Kiernan began attacking the trading caravans, demanding they pay him tribute if they wished to live to complete their journeys. The caravan masters had no choice but to give Kiernan whatever valuables he desired for his treasure hoard. The dragon, of course, was too clever to go anywhere near the Temple of the Holy Orders of the Stars, but word of Kiernan's harassment reached the clerics nevertheless. It was Elethia herself who chose to leave the temple and confront Kiernan.

"By this time the red dragon had grown much bolder, and the beast began flying over Tresvka, threatening to burn the town to ashes if the citizens didn't pay him tribute. The people of Tresvka decided to pay. But just as Kiernan was about to fly away with the valuables he had forced the townsfolk to gather for him, Elethia arrived.

"She demanded that Kiernan leave the tribute, depart Tresvka and the surrounding lands, and never return. Kiernan, however, was an evil, proud dragon and refused. He attacked Elethia. Wielding the holy power granted to her by the gods, she fought back. Ultimately, Elethia placed a blessing upon an arrow and fired it at the raging dragon flying high above. The holy arrow flew straight and true and struck the beast in the eye. Kiernan crashed to the ground, dead, a threat no more."

When Sindri's tale ended, everyone was silent for a moment, then the kender grinned sheepishly. "I hope I told the tale well enough. I've only heard it told once, and I'm not sure I did the story justice."

"You did a fine job, Sindri," Catriona said, her tone gentle for a change.

"Indeed," Nearra said. "It seems you are also a wizard with words when you wish to be."

Sindri blushed, then his gaze immediately darted around the room like an impatient hummingbird. He nodded his head in time to the bard's music. Nearra agreed with Davyn. Sindri's disguise wasn't an especially effective one, but it made her smile to see the kender enjoying his masquerade so much.

"'Ere now, wot's yer problem?" Nearra looked up and saw a bald-headed man with a nose ring and a scar running down the middle of his face from crown to chin. The man was glaring straight at Sindri. The kender looked around to see if he was addressing anyone else. Finally, Sindri said, "Do you mean me?"

"Yeah, I mean you! I been wash . . . wash . . . watching you for a while now. And I got a question for you. What in the name of Paladine is wrong with yer head?"

Nearra could tell by the way the man slurred his speech—not to mention his blood-shot eyes—that he'd partaken of too much ale this evening. And he was obviously the type who was made belligerent by drink.

"Why, whatever do you mean, my good man?" Sindri then blinked several times to feign puzzlement.

Nearra had to keep from rolling her eyes. The kender might be a wizard, but he certainly wasn't an actor.

"I mean yer bloody head!" the drunk said in exasperation. "It's too small for yer body! I've heard tell that some savages who inhabit distant lands shrink the heads of their enemies. Is that wot happened to you?"

"So our friend has a small head. What is it to you? Go back to your table and leave us in peace." Davyn's eyes narrowed. "I'm sure there's a mug full of ale somewhere that's calling your name."

The man scowled. "Are you calling me a drunk?"

"No," Davyn said. "I'm saying you are drunk, and I'm asking you to go bother someone else."

The man made a sound low in his throat that was nearly a growl. He reached beneath the belt of his tunic for his iron mace. His fingers fumbled clumsily as he struggled to draw the weapon.

"Take that back, boy, or I'm gonna bath . . . bath . . . bash yer head in!"

Sindri sighed. "This was fun at first, but it's beginning to grow tiresome. If you don't do as my friend asks, I'm afraid I'll be forced to cast a spell on you."

"Not now, Sindri!" Catriona hissed.

"A shh . . . a shh . . . a shpell? Wot, you some kinda wizard?" He laughed. "Well, that would 'splain the size of yer head. You musta shrunk it when one of yer spells went wrong!" He roared with laughter.

Sindri frowned. "Very well. You leave me no choice." He lifted his arm and rolled up the sleeve of Catriona's cloak until his small hand was visible.

"You've got teeny arms, too!" This set the drunk off into fresh peals of laughter.

Sindri concentrated and wiggled his fingers.

At first, nothing happened, which only made the man laugh harder. Nearra feared that whatever magic the kender possessed was going to fail him.

But then the bald man's nose ring began to quiver, and he stopped laughing. His eyes crossed as he tried to look at the ring.

"What the—?"

He started to reach for the ring, but before he could get his hand on it, the ring suddenly flew across the room. Unfortunately, the man remained standing where he was. He screamed and clapped his hands to his face in an attempt to staunch the flow of blood.

While he was howling in pain, Catriona got up, removed the mace from the man's belt, and clonked him over the head with it. The man stopped yelling and fell to the floor.

Catriona looked at Sindri and grinned. "That was a good spell, but sometimes more mundane methods are just as effective."

"Indeed," Elidor said.

Catriona motioned for the innkeeper to come over and remove the unconscious man.

Nearra looked at Davyn. He was simply sitting there with his eyes closed, his hands curled into fists. Nearra was surprised. Was he afraid? Nearra tapped Davyn's arm and he opened his eyes.

"So much for not drawing attention to ourselves," he said.

9   TALES AND SCHEMES

After they finished their meal, the group decided to turn in early and get some rest before setting out in the morning. They headed upstairs, the males to Sindri's room, and the girls to Catriona's. Unfortunately, there was but a single bed in the warrior's small room.

"Take it," Catriona said. "I will sleep on my bedroll."

"I can't do that," Nearra protested. "I've imposed on you and the others too much already!"

"I am used to spending the night on my bedroll. I will be perfectly comfortable." Without waiting for Nearra to respond, Catriona began undoing her bedroll and spreading it out on the floor.

"I . . . very well. Thank you." Nearra climbed onto the mattress, but she did not cover herself with the woolen blanket. Though the air had cooled somewhat with the coming of night, it was still hot out, and even with the shutters open, the room was stuffy.

Catriona didn't even remove her chain mail vest, though she did take off her metal helmet.

"Isn't it uncomfortable to sleep in that vest?" Nearra asked.

Catriona smiled. "One gets used to it. A warrior is always prepared for whatever may come. I'd rather put up with a little 59 discomfort than be without my armor should the need for it suddenly arise in the night."

Nearra wanted to ask what "need" the warrior thought there might be for her armor tonight, but she wasn't sure she really wanted to know.

Catriona lay down on her bedroll and said, "Would you mind blowing out the light, Nearra?"

Nearra sat up, leaned over, and blew out the candle on the nightstand next to the bed. Her eyes began to adjust to the darkness at once, and there was more than enough moonlight filtering through the open window to help the process along. Soon she could see almost as well as when the candle had been burning. She lay back and stared up at the ceiling, waiting for sleep to come and terrified of what might happen when it did. It had been only a mere twelve hours ago that she had woken on the forest path. What if she woke tomorrow morning to find goblins hovering over her once again? How had she gotten on the path in the first place? She strained to find something in her mind that might give her a clue, but all she could think of were the terrifying teeth of those goblins.

The air felt humid, and Nearra's skin was coated with sticky sweat. She tossed and turned, trying to get comfortable, but the mattress was too lumpy, and her mind was swirling.

"Can't sleep?" Catriona asked.

"This is probably going to sound strange, but I'm not sure how to sleep," Nearra said. She was so frustrated and frightened she thought she might cry. "I don't remember ever falling asleep before. I can't even remember where I spent last night."

Nearra rolled over to face Catriona and saw that the warrior was lying on her side, head propped on her hand. "So you truly have no memories at all?"

"I have no personal memories beyond knowing my name. But I have many general ones."

"Like how to speak, how to walk, and how to feed your-self?"

"Yes, things like that, but nothing about my past. It's awful not knowing."

Catriona was silent for a moment. "You might not believe this, Nearra, but in a way, I envy you."

Nearra was shocked by the warrior's words. "You're right—I don't believe it."

"Tell me, Nearra, do you recall anything about the Solamnic Knights?"

"The name sounds somewhat familiar, but—no, I don't."

"They are an ancient and revered order of fighting men and women dedicated to protecting the weak and downtrodden and upholding the highest standards of morality and chivalry. At least, that's what they once were. After the Cataclysm—a time of great destruction throughout Ansalon—the Knights lost the respect of the people for not being able to, or as some said, being unwilling to do anything to prevent the Cataclysm. For centuries after, the Solamnic Knights were reviled by the folk of Ansalon, but then came the War of the Lance, and the Solamnic Knight known as Sturm Brightblade. It is mainly thanks to him that the knighthood regained its honor. Today the Solamnic Knights seek to restore their order to its former glory."

"And . . . you are one of these Knights?" Nearra guessed.

"No!" Catriona practically shouted. Then, in a calmer voice, she said, "But I was in training to become one."

Catriona fell silent, and Nearra thought the girl would say no more, but then Catriona took a deep breath and continued her story.

"I was a squire who served a Solamnic Knight named Leyana. She was also my aunt. One day we were patrolling the plains on horseback, searching for a group of bandits that had been harassing trading caravans. We found the bandits easily enough, or rather, they found us. They attacked, and I became frightened. I tried to flee, but as I started to ride away, the bandit leader caught my horse's bridle and stopped me.

"He pulled me from my horse, disarmed me, and set me on his

mount in front of his saddle. He pulled a dagger, pressed it to my throat, and ordered my aunt to surrender or else he would kill me. I wanted to shout for my aunt to ignore the bandit's command, but I was too terrified to speak. My aunt didn't hesitate; she dropped her sword—" Catriona reached out and patted her sword in its sheath lying beside her. "The same sword I carry today. My aunt then raised her hands and surrendered."

Catriona stopped speaking, and even with the moonlight, it was too dim in the room for Nearra to tell for certain if her friend was crying. Nearra decided to pretend that she wasn't, for the sake of the warrior's dignity.

"What happened then?" Nearra asked in a soft voice.

"Two of the bandits killed my aunt before my eyes while the bandit leader laughed. I feared I was to be slain as well, but the surviving bandits, seeing how grief-stricken I was, thought it more amusing to let me live. The bandit leader threw me to the ground and they rode off laughing.

"I wept and cursed the bandits, though I knew it was my own cowardice that had caused my aunt's death. After a time, I stopped crying. I draped my aunt's body over her horse's saddle, tied her securely so she wouldn't slip off, and began the long ride back home. I told the other Knights what had happened, and after my aunt's funeral service, I took her sword, an old chain mail vest and helmet, and departed in shame and disgrace. That was five months ago."

Nearra felt sorrow for her new friend. "But you were only a squire. Surely the other Knights would have understood what happened."

"Perhaps they would have," Catriona said. "But I cannot forgive myself. I have vowed to travel throughout the land, living without a home and performing chivalrous deeds until such time as I finally redeem myself and regain my honor."

"And when will that be?" Nearra asked.

Catriona didn't answer. She lay down and rolled over, her back to Nearra. Several moments later the warrior's breathing deepened, and Nearra realized that Catriona had fallen asleep. Or at least she wanted Nearra to believe that she had.

Nearra lay back down and looked up at the ceiling once more and waited for sleep to come. She had to wait a long time.

Oddvar sat in an alley with his back against the wall. Now that it was finally dark, he didn't have to wear his cloak, though he could have done without the light from the moons above. Solinari was three-quarters full, while the red moon Lunitari was half full. He could have done without the temperature, too. The caverns where the Theiwar lived were pleasantly cool and damp, not hot and sticky like Solamnia in summertime. But if Oddvar ever wished to return home and get revenge on the cursed dwarf wizard who'd exiled him, he'd have to continue to serve his master and serve him well. As payment, he'd been promised enough magical power to destroy the Theiwar wizard, and since Oddvar desired vengeance more than anything, he intended to be a very good servant, indeed.

After a time, Oddvar heard a soft flapping of wings. The shadow of a dark bird passed over Solinari, and then the bird landed next to the dwarf. The black falcon folded its wings against its sleek body and looked at Oddvar with a piercing gaze.

The Theiwar seemed to listen attentively for several moments, though if anyone else had been in the alley with him, they would have heard nothing.

"Yes, my lord," Oddvar said in the merest of whispers. "I am currently in the alley next to the inn where the children sleep. They plan to leave for the temple at sunrise. But there have been certain . . . complications."

The falcon cocked its head, and its small black eyes gleamed with what Oddvar took to be restrained anger. Oddvar then spoke of how Davyn and Nearra, for reasons unknown to the dwarf, were now accompanied by a redheaded warrior and a kender. He also told the falcon how the elf at the Blind Goose had been hired as their guide instead of him.

The falcon regarded Oddvar for a few moments, then the dwarf nodded. "I will do as you command, my lord."

The falcon bobbed its head, as if nodding, then spread its wings and once more took to the sky.

Oddvar stood, picked up his cloak, and put it back on. Then he silently walked out of the alley. Making sure to keep to the shadows, he made his way toward the northern edge of town. He needed to meet Slean and tell her of the plan for tomorrow.

Oddvar grinned. For the first time in his life, he was actually looking forward to a sunrise.

Maddoc released his hand from the mirror's pulsating surface, severing the psychic link to his falcon. He sat in a high-backed leather chair in front of a huge fireplace. To his left stood the large upright mirror that allowed him to contact Shaera, his beloved familiar. His white robe was gone, exchanged for one that was a far more appropriate shade of black. Though there was room for much more wood in the fireplace, only a few logs burned. Since Maddoc was the only one in the room—not counting his faithful pet, of course—he saw no need for a large blaze. The wizard was a practical man and despised waste.

"That boy is more of a disappointment than ever," muttered Maddoc. Lying next to Maddoc's chair, the Beast growled softly and lifted its horned head. Its eyes, red slits deeply set beneath a furry red brow, glared at Maddoc. The creature's enormous back, covered in long, sharp bony ridges, nearly came to the edge of the armrest.

"I was sure my plan would succeed after the goblins led the girl to that clearing. Slean confronted her, just as instructed, and I sensed the power rising in the girl. But she fought it down before the Emergence could take place, forcing Davyn and me to intervene. I gave the boy simple instructions. He knew what he was supposed to do. Is he too stupid to follow orders?"

After Maddoc had left Davyn and the girl in Tresvka at the building with the sign of the crescent moon—an empty building, which in fact Maddoc owned—he'd hurried back home to Cairngorn Keep. He intended to oversee the rest of this game from his keep, leaving Davyn and Oddvar—as well as those three goblins—to serve as his agents in the field. Maddoc hadn't expected his plan to be this difficult to execute, but the black-robed wizard wasn't prepared to give up just yet. No, not at all.

There was one thing he hadn't planned for, though: the traveling companions the girl had accumulated. Davyn knew he was supposed to prevent others from joining him and Nearra.

"Davyn is not performing well, my friend." The Beast growled again, louder this time. Maddoc reached over with his left hand and scratched the monstrous creature on its head between its four horns. The Beast rumbled its satisfaction and settled down. "Still, it is too late to relieve him of his duties. I'll just have to let events proceed from this point on and do my best to control how they play out. One way or another, I will succeed."

Maddoc folded his hands over his stomach and gazed up at the tapestry hanging over the fireplace. It was an ancient, elaborately detailed piece of craftsmanship ten feet tall and four feet wide. The weaving remained tight and the colors vibrant, as if the tapestry had been finished yesterday instead of centuries ago.

The tapestry portrayed a woman with a narrow face and long, raven-black hair. She wore a dark green dress trimmed with red fur. Her complexion was ivory-white, though Maddoc didn't know if that was an accurate representation or merely artistic license on the part of the weaver. Her eyes were a striking shade of violet. They reminded Maddoc of the way a predator's eyes gleamed just before sinking teeth into its prey.

The woman in the tapestry wore a sun-shaped medallion around her neck, and lying on the ground in front of her feet sat a silver sword with a jewel-encrusted hilt. Maddoc had researched the woman in the tapestry for many years, trying to discover what had become of the two artifacts, but in all his studies, he had never found so much as a single reference to the location of either one.

Asvoria—or rather, her image—stood before a wall of gray stone covered with strands of climbing ivy. Maddoc had once believed the wall she stood in front of was the outer wall of this very keep. After all, hundreds of years ago, this keep had once been Asvoria's home. But after living here himself for nearly two decades and finding no sign of either the medallion or the sword, he was no longer so sure of that. Still, it was early in the game, and Maddoc had every confidence he would ultimately triumph.

He smiled at the image of Asvoria. He was looking forward to finally meeting her.

10 ON THE NORTHERN ROAD

Nearra was lost in a world of endless darkness . . . a world where there was no form, no substance. She had no body in this placeless place. She was a being of pure thought, a wandering spirit trapped in eternal nothingness . . .

And she wanted out.

Nearra opened her eyes and sat up. Sunlight came through the open window, its illumination a welcome sight after the endless nothingness in her dream. Just a dream, she thought. But such a strange one . . .

Then the events of the day before came flooding back to her. Her heart pounded as she glanced quickly around the room. She let out a deep breath. No goblins, no dragon.

Catriona was already up and dressed, her bedroll put away in her pack. She stood before the open window. The sunlight made her red hair seem to blaze with its own internal flame. The warrior's eyes were closed, and her lips moved as she whispered some sort of morning devotion. Nearra wondered if this could be a ritual of the Solamnic Knights, but given how sensitive Catriona was about her past, Nearra knew better than to ask. 67

After a moment, Catriona opened her eyes and turned around to face Nearra.

"Did you sleep well?" the warrior asked.

Nearra thought about the world of darkness in her dream. "More or less," she answered. "But I will say this: waking up in a bed at an inn definitely beats waking up surrounded by goblins."

Catriona laughed.

The five companions walked down the long path toward the northern edge of town. Each carried a traveler's pack filled with food, water, and other supplies.

Sindri looked up at the sun, which had only just started to clear the rooftops of Tresvka's buildings. "Isn't it beautiful?"

"You may not find it so after you've marched beneath its warming rays for a few hours," Elidor said.

The kender ignored the elf. "The sun is very important to my family, you know. It's the reason for our surname: Suncatcher. Human mages draw their power from the three moons: white-robed wizards from Solinari, red robes from Lunitari, and black robes from Nuitari. But we kender know that the strongest magic lies with the power of the sun. Long ago, it was prophesied that a member of my family would one day become a great wizard and be the first to tap the sun's magic. My family has been known as the Suncatchers ever since."

Catriona seemed to be paying no attention to the kender's story. Probably because she's heard it before, Nearra thought. Given how much Sindri loved to talk, Catriona had doubtless heard the tale numerous times.

"And I suppose you think you'll be the one to fulfill the grand prophecy," Davyn said with a hint of mockery in his voice.

Nearra frowned. She liked Davyn, but she didn't always like the way he treated Sindri. But if the kender noticed Davyn's tone, he didn't react to it.

"Maybe. After all, someone in my family has to be the one. Why not me?"

Elidor smiled, amused. "Why not indeed?"

"You know, there's something I never understood about that story," Catriona said, surprising Nearra. So the warrior had been listening after all. "You mention a third moon, the one where evil mages get their power. But there are only two moons in the night sky."

Sindri opened his mouth to explain, but before he could speak, Nearra said, "That's because Nuitari is visible only to the eyes of those who wear the black robe." She frowned, then looked at the others. "How did I know that?"

They all looked at Nearra, then at each other, clearly at a loss. Finally, Davyn shrugged. "I suppose it's just one more of your memories returning." He paused, then quickly added, "Assuming it's true, of course."

"Oh, it is," Sindri said. "I try to learn as much about magic as I can at every opportunity, so that I will be ready when it's my time to take the Test of High Sorcery at the Tower of Wayreth."

"While I am no mage, I too have learned something about magic in my travels," Elidor said. "From what I understand, those who wish to join one of the orders of wizardry begin studying with an archmage during childhood. When they are ready to take the Test of High Sorcery, they must first declare allegiance to a particular order." The elf smiled. "I do not believe the mages have an Order of the Sun."

Sindri scowled. "Then perhaps it's high time somebody started one!"

Elidor explained the route he had planned as they walked.

"Tresvka is more of a way station along the trading routes than anything else," the elf said. "The main routes go east and west across the plains, and these are the ways most traders travel. But there are always folk who for one reason or another need to travel through the forests. There is a main path—not really wide enough to be called a road—that runs the length of the southern forest."

"That's where I woke up," Nearra said.

Elidor nodded. "There is a similar path through the northern forest and out into the plains, but unfortunately, it begins to curve eastward long before reaching the temple you seek. So while we shall be able to make use of this path for part of the journey, eventually we shall be forced to leave the path and forge our own trail."

Nearra wasn't worried about traveling through the known sections of the northern forest, not with her new friends accompanying her. But the idea of leaving the path and traveling through wild territory did frighten her. Yesterday in the southern forest, she had encountered goblin raiders and a green dragon. What new dangers might await her?

Their footsteps thumped as they crossed the wooden bridge over the Vingaard River. Though it was early, the bridge was already busy with travelers entering the town. A woodcutter pushed a wheelbarrow full of firewood in from the woods. Behind him, a farmer drove a wagon filled with vegetables headed for the market at the center of town. Neither one gave the travelers a second glance as they passed.

On the other side of the bridge, the road cut through a field of tall grass. In the distance, Nearra could just make out a stand of trees: the northern forest.

Bees buzzed lazily above the tall grass on either side of the road and birds flew about, singing to one another. Blue sky, fluffy white clouds—a perfect day for traveling.

But as they walked along, Nearra became increasingly uncomfortable. The straps of her pack dug into her shoulders, and her new boots were stiff and beginning to make her feet ache. And to top it all off, though it wasn't even midmorning yet, it was warming up quickly. It appeared the day was going to be a hot one.

Nearra wiped sweat from her forehead with the back of her

hand. "Somehow I didn't expect adventuring to start out so uncomfortably."

Elidor laughed. "I'm not sure I'd call a simple trip like this an adventure, but even so, you know the old saying about adventures, don't you?"

"She doesn't know much of anything," Sindri said. "She's lost her memory."

Nearra knew the kender was only trying to be helpful, but she wished he'd chosen his words more carefully.

Elidor acknowledged the kender's statement with a nod, then turned once more to Nearra. "The saying goes like this: an adventure is someone else having a very difficult time a thousand miles away."

Nearra frowned. "I'm not sure I understand."

"What he means," Catriona said, "is that often the idea of adventuring is much more fun than the reality."

There was a hard edge to Catriona's voice, and Nearra knew her friend spoke from bitter experience.

"Especially when the reality includes something like that!" Elidor pointed skyward, and they all looked up to see a large, winged reptilian form circling high above.

It was Slean.

Sindri clapped his hands in glee. "A dragon! I've finally seen a dragon! Do you think she'll come closer? I hope she does. Maybe I should yell for her to come down." Before Sindri could do so, Catriona clamped her hand tight over the kender's mouth and spoke softly in his ear.

"I know this will be hard to get into that one-track kender mind of yours, but just because the dragon is interesting to look at doesn't mean she won't kill us if she gets the chance." Catriona slowly removed her hand.

"So I shouldn't say anything?" Sindri asked, clearly confused.

Before Catriona could reply, Elidor said, "We're too easy to spot here on the road—get in the grass and stay down as low as you can!" Without waiting to see if the others would follow, Elidor ran off the road and dove into the tall grass.

Catriona grabbed Sindri's hand and hauled him off the road while the kender stared up at Slean with a grin of delight. Davyn took Nearra's upper arm and the two of them followed after the others. The grass was two feet tall at the most, and they quickly discovered it provided minimal cover.

"Everyone curl up into a ball," Davyn said, "and make yourselves as small as you can. With any luck, the color of our clothes and packs will help camouflage us."

Most of the party was dressed in browns and greens, but Sindri wore his purple mage's cape, and Nearra had on her bright turquoise dress. Catriona had tried to talk her into putting on a tunic and leggings before they left town, but Nearra declined. The dress was the only link she had to whatever life she'd lived before losing her memory. To her, that was reason enough to keep it. Now, however, she wished she had listened to Catriona: the color of her dress stood out too much against the green of the grass.

Even though all Nearra could see was grass and soil, she closed her eyes tight. She could sense Davyn curled up beside her, and she was grateful for his presence. She felt an urge to reach over and take his hand for further comfort, but she was not only afraid of how Davyn might react to this, she didn't want to move and risk attracting Slean's attention.

Go away, she thought. Please go away and leave us alone!

Several moments passed, and Nearra began to hope that Slean hadn't spotted them and had flown away. But then Nearra was gripped by a sudden intense fear. It was all she could do to keep from leaping up, screaming in terror, and running back toward town. She understood what was happening to her. After all, she had experienced the same feeling yesterday.

Nearra knew that the fear she was feeling meant that Slean was coming closer, perhaps even preparing to attack, but she also knew that if they had any hope of surviving, they would have to resist the dragonfear. Although all she wanted to do was lie curled up in a ball and shiver, Nearra forced herself to open her eyes and turn her head to look at Davyn. His jaw was clenched tight, and there was a determined look on his face as he struggled to fight the dragonfear, too.

"We need to do something," Nearra whispered.

"I know," Davyn replied through gritted teeth. "But what can we do against a dragon? If only Maddoc were here—"

It was Slean herself who offered a suggestion.

"Give me the girl and the rest of you can go free!"

CHAPTER

11 DRAGON'S PREY

Davyn was the first to stand. "You can't have Nearra!" he yelled. The sound of his words seemed to blunt the dragonfear—or perhaps it distracted Slean so that she wasn't able to generate as much fear in them. Whichever the case, Nearra was able to move again, and she stood, as did the others.

Catriona drew her short sword and looked up at Slean's scaled underbelly, searching for a vulnerable place to attack. Unfortunately, it didn't look to Nearra as if the dragon had one. Maddoc had said that Slean was a young dragon, but even so, she looked more than capable of killing them all.

Davyn dropped his pack and began to string his bow. Neither Catriona's sword nor Davyn's arrows would be much use against a creature as powerful as Slean.

Then Nearra remembered her dagger. Catriona had insisted she visit a weaponsmith and buy a dagger just like the one the warrior carried in her own traveling pack. At the time, Nearra had felt it would be useless to her, since she could not recall ever having learned how to use a dagger.

A dagger would be even less effective against a dragon than a sword or a bow, but it was Nearra's only weapon, so she slid off her pack and quickly removed it. It was foolish, but she felt 75 safer with the knife in her hand.

Nearra had no idea why Slean wanted her specifically—if only she could remember! She knew that she should step forward so the others would be safe. She shouldn't let her friends risk their lives for her. But Catriona was right. She knew nothing of battle. And what could Nearra do against a fearsome dragon? The dagger in Nearra's hand shook and Nearra realized she was trembling.

She turned to Elidor in the hope that he had drawn a weapon to protect her—but when she looked, she could find no sign of him. It was as if the elf had vanished.

Perhaps he's planning some sort of sneak attack, she thought. Or perhaps he's run off and abandoned us. If so, she supposed she couldn't blame him. They'd hired Elidor to guide them to the Temple of the Holy Orders of the Stars—not to fight dragons for them. Still, she couldn't help feeling disappointed. She'd almost begun to think of the elf as another friend.

Sindri raised his hands above his head and curled his fingers into mystic gestures. "Beware, dragon! I am the wizard Sindri Suncatcher, and if you do not depart at once, I shall visit a powerful enchantment upon you!"

Slean stopped circling and hovered twenty feet above them, flapping her wings to remain in place. The wind generated by her wings was strong enough to nearly knock the companions off their feet. The dragon fixed her reptilian gaze on Sindri. For an instant Nearra feared Slean intended to snap up the kender in her jaws and make a snack out of him. But then the great beast burst out laughing, filling the air with the acrid scent of her breath.

Nearra remembered something Maddoc had told her yesterday.

A green dragon such as Slean doesn't breathe fire. Instead, she spews a cloud of deadly gas called chlorine.

The smell burned Nearra's nasal passages and her throat. She coughed and tried not to gag. This was only the merest residue of gas, breathed out when Slean was laughing. Nearra didn't want to even imagine what a blast of full-strength chlorine gas would be like.

Slean looked down at Sindri, her mouth stretching into a hideous grin.

"A wizard, eh? You're the smallest mage I've ever seen, wee one. Tell me, what sort of spells do kender cast? A curse of annoyance? A glamour of ridiculousness?" Slean laughed again, and wisps of yellow-green gas curled upward from the slits of her nostrils.

The usually good-natured kender scowled, but as he opened his mouth to reply, he was cut off by the sound of a battle cry echoing across the grassy field.

Nearra and her friends all looked westward in surprise. A minotaur came running toward them, battle-axe held high. It was Jax.

"What in the name of all the gods is he doing here?" Davyn said.

"What does it matter?" Catriona answered. She pointed her short sword at Slean. "We've got a bigger problem to worry about!"

Slean looked at the charging minotaur, then turned back toward Nearra. She narrowed her reptilian eyes. "You surprise me, girl. Not only have you managed to find yourself protectors, but one of them is a minotaur as well."

Nearra wasn't certain, but Slean seemed to turn her gaze to Davyn for a moment before rising higher into the air and flying off to meet the minotaur's attack.

Nearra didn't know whether the minotaur had originally intended to engage Slean in battle, but now the man-bull had no choice. Slean flew lower until she was skimming just above the grass. The minotaur didn't slow his charge. If anything, he picked up speed.

Though Nearra had lost her memories, she doubted she'd ever witnessed such bravery before.

Then, just as Slean and the minotaur were about to collide, the dragon gave a powerful beat of her wings and arced skyward. The minotaur swung his axe in an attempt to strike a blow. But the dragon was too fast, and the man-bull's swing missed as she flew out of reach.

Slean laughed as she ascended. Nearra realized the dragon was toying with them. Slean could destroy them all whenever she wished, but like a cat playing with a mouse, she wanted to have fun with her prey before killing them.

The minotaur bellowed in frustration, but he wasn't about to give up. He drew back his axe, aimed, then hurled the weapon skyward. The battle-axe tumbled end over end through the air, flying faster and farther than any human could have thrown it.

Slean was still flying straight up. She didn't see the axe coming. But she sure felt it when the sharp edge nicked her right wing. The tear was slight, but it was enough to make Slean let out of grunt of pain and dip to the side, her balance thrown. In seconds the dragon managed to right herself. She curved around and glared at the minotaur.

The battle-axe fell to the ground, slicing into the earth with a soft *chuk!* at least a dozen yards from where the minotaur stood. The man-bull began running toward his axe. He moved far more swiftly than Nearra expected for a creature of his size. But no matter how fast he ran, Nearra doubted the minotaur could retrieve his weapon before Slean reached him.

Nearra felt the first hints of tingling in her hands, but the sensation was muted, distant. Whatever strange power she possessed, she knew she would not be able to summon it before Slean killed the minotaur.

"Someone do something!" she shouted in frustration.

Catriona looked to Davyn. Davyn looked back, both unsure exactly what they could do to help.

"I know!" Sindri said. "I'll levitate the axe into the minotaur's hands!" The kender frowned in concentration and pointed toward the axe and began wiggling his fingers. At first nothing happened, and Nearra feared that Sindri's magic was going to fail him. But then the battle-axe pulled itself out of the ground and shot toward the minotaur. Jax caught it deftly in his out-stretched hand.

Nearra clapped Sindri on the back. "You did it!"

The kender grinned so wide it seemed his face might split in two. "Nothing to it."

Axe in hand once more, the minotaur was ready to meet Slean's attack.

"We can't let him face the dragon alone," Catriona said, and sprinted through the grass toward the man-bull and Slean.

"Wait for me!" Sindri shouted, and took off running after Catriona.

"Idiots," Davyn muttered as he wiped the sweat off his brow. He lifted his bow once more, drew an arrow from his quiver, and nocked it. He pulled back the string and squinted one eye shut as he aimed. He waited for a shot and released the string with a *twang!* The arrow flew straight and true. It struck Slean on her right hindquarter, lodging between two scales.

Slean roared, more in anger than pain. The dragon spun around. She attempted to reach the arrow with her front claws. But as she twisted, she lost her momentum and dropped out of the air like a very large, very green rock. When she hit the ground, the earth shuddered from the impact. Nearra felt the vibrations even through the thick soles of her new boots.

Catriona cheered. "Well shot, Davyn!" she called back over her shoulder as she ran toward Slean. Sindri just laughed, as if he'd found himself in the middle of the greatest game he could ever imagine: Battle the Dragon. Hands tingling almost to the point of pain, Nearra feared for both of them. She knew Davyn's arrow, while proving an effective distraction, had done no serious harm to Slean. And Slean hadn't fallen all that far. In a moment the dragon would forget all about the irritating pain in her rump and return to seeking their destruction.

No, Nearra thought. *My* destruction.

12 HIDDEN MAGIC

Davyn's skull throbbed as if an ogre were pounding on his head with a heavy rock. Davyn hoped Sindri wouldn't attempt to cast any more "spells." He didn't know if he could take using his ring again so soon. If he used it more than three times in a single day, he got a skull-splitting headache. Sometimes he even passed out.

The ring allowed its wearer to move objects solely with the power of thought. Davyn had used it to fend off the minotaur yesterday, as well as the drunk in the tavern last night, allowing the others to believe that Sindri had saved them with his "magic." He didn't want to have to answer their questions about why a simple ranger should possess a magical ring.

But now that Sindri had a taste for telekinesis, there seemed no stopping his urge to cast "spells." Davyn shouldn't have continued to fuel Sindri's delusion by levitating the minotaur's axe. But he was beginning to feel caught in his own deception.

Using the ring a second time to guide his arrow toward Slean was foolish, he knew. He was a skilled archer, but he wasn't capable of shooting an arrow that far, and he'd wanted to make the shot look good. After all, he was supposed to be trying to stop Slean. He'd been more surprised than anyone when the arrow not only hit the dragon, but actually penetrated her flesh. 81

The arrow wouldn't really hurt her—for a creature her size, it would be like getting a splinter under the skin for a human. But Slean was a green dragon, and they were known for their vicious tempers. If she became too angry, she might well forget that she was supposed to be holding back—and if she began fighting in earnest, Davyn doubted any of them would survive.

Slean was on the ground now, using her teeth to try to pull out the arrow without snapping the shaft in two and leaving the arrowhead lodged in her rump. While the dragon was absorbed in this delicate task, the minotaur ran to attack her. Nearra stood far behind him, a dagger clutched in her hand. Davyn didn't know if the man-bull was capable of hurting Slean. Minotaurs were rumored to be very strong. The battle-axe looked heavy and its blades looked sharp. But he knew Nearra had no chance of defending herself. Davyn had to do something.

Despite the pounding in his head, Davyn nocked an arrow, took aim—making sure that he wouldn't hit Catriona, Sindri, or Nearra—and fired.

The arrow flew past Slean's face, missing her by mere inches, exactly as Davyn had intended. Davyn knew green dragons preferred to avoid physical combat whenever possible. They were far too vain to want to risk getting injured. It was Davyn's hope that Slean would take to the sky to avoid the minotaur's blow, thus saving the man-bull's life, as well as the lives of his foolish comrades.

The arrow's movement caught the dragon's attention. She ceased tugging on the shaft stuck in her hindquarter and looked up. The minotaur was only a few yards away and closing fast. She spread her wings—just as Davyn hoped—and prepared to launch herself skyward.

But before Slean could lift off the ground, Elidor stood up. He'd been hidden in the tall grass less than fifteen feet from Slean. The elf held a knife in each hand, and with swift, graceful motions, he hurled first the right knife, then the left.

The first blade struck Slean on the bony ridge of brow over

her left eye and bounced off without doing any harm. But the second knife hit the corner of her eye, where the tear duct would be on a human, and sank to the hilt.

Slean froze for an instant. Then blood gushed from her wounded eye and she roared in pain and fury.

"Uh-oh," Davyn whispered.

Catriona and Sindri wisely stopped running toward Slean when she roared. But they stood their ground, waiting to see what the dragon would do next.

Slean turned toward Davyn and gave him an accusing look. She then returned to face the minotaur and opened her mouth wide. The dragon made a coughing-chuffing sound, and a cloud of yellow-green gas shot out of her mouth toward the minotaur.

With lightning-quick reflexes, the man-bull threw himself face-first onto the ground to prevent the deadly gas from getting into his eyes and lungs.

Slean then whirled toward Elidor, but the elf was no longer there. It was as if he had vanished. Slean wasn't about to give up, though. She sprayed chlorine gas across the field where the elf had last stood, moving her head back and forth to cover as much ground as she could.

There was a breeze coming from the northwest, directly behind Slean, and the wind wafted the cloud of yellow-green gas toward Catriona, Sindri, and Nearra.

This is it! Davyn thought. If Nearra and the others inhaled the gas, then surely Nearra would—Nearra!

He glanced down at the silver ring on his right hand.

Davyn dropped his bow, clenched his ring hand into a fist, and struggled to concentrate past the throbbing pain in his head.

The cloud of chlorine gas came toward them. Maddoc had said the gas was deadly, and as fast as it was coming, there was no way they could escape.

The tingling in Nearra's hands had increased to the point where it felt as if they were on fire.

But just before whatever was about to happen to Nearra could happen, Catriona's sword flew out of her hand and floated in mid-air for a split second before beginning to spin, slowly at first, but then faster and faster until the sword became a steely-gray blur.

The tingling in her hands began to diminish, and the presence inside her—whatever it was—disappeared.

Nearra looked to Sindri. "Are you doing this?"

The kender frowned in puzzlement. "I'm . . . not sure."

The sword continued spinning, creating a loud whirring sound. The blade whipped up a fierce wind that blew the chlorine gas away from the three companions and back toward Slean. The gas engulfed the dragon.

Slean roared, "Enough!" She began flapping her wings—further dissipating the chlorine gas—then leaped into flight, an arrow protruding from her backside and a dagger sticking out of her eye. She rose into the air, gaining altitude quickly, then circled once before heading northward. Within moments she was lost to view.

Catriona's sword stopped spinning and dropped to the ground. Nearra looked to her two companions. Neither Sindri nor Catriona appeared to have been harmed. The spinning sword had successfully protected them all from the deadly gas.

The minotaur stood up, as did Elidor. Both the man-bull and the elf also escaped the chlorine's ill effects.

Grinning in happy disbelief, Nearra turned to look back at Davyn and saw the ranger lying in the grass, unconscious.

High above the field, a black falcon paused for a moment before turning and flying off after the wounded dragon.

13 HONOR RESTORED

It took every ounce of will Slean had not to turn around and slay every one of the annoying little pests.

She wasn't all that upset about the wounds she had suffered. The arrow in her rump was embarrassing, but not serious. And though the dagger wound hurt like blazes, the eye itself didn't seem to be damaged. She could still see out of it. No, what made her insanely furious was the humiliation of it all. She could have easily destroyed those brats, but Maddoc's oh-so-precious plan wouldn't allow it.

Slean spotted a clearing on the banks of a small stream. Good. She could use the water to clean her wounds. She stopped flapping her wings and began to descend, gliding gracefully toward the ground.

She decided to go to work on the arrow first, since removing it would be less painful than extracting the dagger. She curved her long serpentine neck around and gripped the feathered shaft in her teeth.

Once she had finished tending to her injuries, perhaps she could forget about Maddoc and his idiotic plan. He was a powerful wizard, but not so powerful that he could compel her to obey him. Still, he had promised her payment for her services—a very special payment which, if Maddoc could truly deliver it, would be worth any amount of pain and humiliation.

Slean managed to ease the arrow out and spat it onto the ground. Fresh blood welled forth from the wound, and she began to lick it clean.

Slean cherished freedom, as all dragons did, but unlike some others, she was obsessed with keeping hers. She was young as dragonkind reckoned age, and she had a long life ahead of her. She intended to remain free and enjoy it. When Maddoc had first approached her, the wizard told her that he knew of a way to ensure that she would never be forced to leave Krynn again, and he would tell her how she could accomplish this feat—*if* she served him well.

But if she were forced to endure much more humiliation at the hands of those brats, she'd kill them all—the girl included—and Maddoc and his precious plan could go to blazes.

Slean took a deep breath and let it out in a sigh accompanied by faint wisps of chlorine. She couldn't put it off any longer. Time to get to work on the dagger.

This was going to hurt.

Slean reached her foreleg toward her wounded eye and clasped the dagger's hilt between two claws. She gritted her teeth and then pulled.

The dragon's roar of pain echoed through the forest, sending terrified birds and animals fleeing in all directions.

Nearra and her companions continued following the road north, with the minotaur behind them all the way. Since telling them his name was Jax, he'd not said another word, and they all walked along in silence. By noon, they decided to rest. They sat beneath large elm trees near a brook where they ate rations of dried beef and drank from their water skins.

Jax sat apart from the others, glaring at Sindri from time to time. The companions watched him nervously. Finally, Elidor broke the silence.

"I'm sure everyone is wondering the same thing as I," the elf said. "Why did you help us against the dragon?"

"Not that we're ungrateful," Nearra hurried to say.

"Just confused," Catriona added.

Jax didn't say anything for a moment. Then he took a deep breath and began talking slowly. "After the humiliation I suffered at the tavern, I spent the rest of the day and evening searching for the kender throughout Tresvka. I questioned several tavern keepers and merchants who told me they had heard rumors that the kender wizard planned to travel south at the first opportunity. But I am a minotaur," he said with pride, "and my people are by no means fools. When I asked where they'd heard the rumors from, the tavern keepers and merchants described two young humans—descriptions I recognized as two of the kender's companions. The conclusion was obvious: the rumors had been planted to trick me.

"I decided to play a hunch. If the kender and his friends wanted me to believe he was heading south in the morning, then I would hide in the grass near the northern road and wait to see if they went that way instead. When I first spotted all of you, I was pleased that my hunch had proven correct. I had been about to stand up and go running toward the kender when the green dragon appeared in the sky. I experienced a touch of dragonfear, but I guess I was too far away to get a full dose of it. Besides, I am a minotaur warrior. We are trained to resist fear.

"I wasn't certain what I should do next. I watched as the dragon glided downward, sunlight sparkling off its green scales as if they were highly polished emeralds. If the dragon attacked, I knew you would all most likely be killed. And while the kender might be a wizard of sorts, I doubted he had the power to stand against a dragon. If he had, he wouldn't be hiding in the grass alongside the rest of you."

Jax paused a moment before going on.

"I didn't want to see the kender dead. I only wanted to restore my honor, and I could not see how lying hidden and letting the dragon slay my enemy would accomplish that. Then when I heard the dragon threaten the girl, I knew what I had to do. Honor would not permit me to hold back and watch while an innocent was threatened and there was a battle to be fought. I stood, drew my battle-axe, and charged toward the hovering dragon. The rest you know. I have to say that you all fought well against the dragon, even the kender. I did not think anyone but a minotaur was capable of such bravery."

"You'd be surprised what 'inferior beings' such as ourselves can do when we have to," Davyn said. He'd regained consciousness not long after Slean had fled, but he'd been in a terrible mood ever since.

"I did not say that you were inferior," Jax said. "But you did pass out during the battle, did you not?"

Davyn got to his feet, wincing and touching his hand to his head. "So?"

Jax stood as well. "So either you were overcome by the dragon's gaseous breath, or you succumbed to the fear she projected. Which was it?"

Davyn hesitated. "I don't know," he said. "Perhaps a little of both."

Jax sniffed. "A true warrior does not know fear."

Now it was Catriona's turn to rise. "We *all* felt the dragonfear." She shuddered at the mention of it. "But we fought on regardless."

"I can't believe I was lucky enough to see a dragon," Sindri said.

"I can't believe we were lucky enough to survive," Catriona said. "I should have run faster. Perhaps I could have reached Slean in time to strike a blow before she released her gas. As it was, we all would have died if it hadn't been for your magic, Sindri."

"Don't be too hard on yourself, Catriona," Sindri said. "After all, it was your sword which blew the gas away."

Catriona was not cheered by the kender's comment.

"We were fortunate to escape with our lives," Elidor said, "and we wouldn't have been able to if it hadn't been for Sindri's magic."

The kender grinned.

Jax snarled. "The same magic he used to steal my money pouch, I'll wager!"

"I don't have to steal!" Sindri protested. "I can conjure whatever I need!"

"Stop it, all of you!" Nearra said. "If we're all going to travel together, we can't keep arguing like this! That is, if Jax intends to continue traveling with us."

Everyone looked at the minotaur and waited for him to answer.

Jax grunted.

"Obviously you want something, or you wouldn't have accompanied us after the fight with Slean," Nearra said. "So what do you want from us?"

"It's not what I want from you," Jax said in his deep, rumbling voice. "It's what I want from him." He pointed at Sindri.

Nearra looked at the kender. Sindri didn't appear frightened, of course, but he did look confused. "I gave you your money," he said to Jax. "What else do you want?"

"My money disappeared once more, after the . . . incident at the tavern."

Sindri sighed. "I suppose you want me to conjure some more for you."

The minotaur shook his head. "I believe my purse was stolen by someone who took advantage of the confusion when I was in the tavern."

"Then what else do you want?" Catriona said.

"My honor restored," Jax said. "Twice now you have humiliated me. Honor means everything to my people, and I cannot allow such insults as what the kender did to me to go unanswered."

"Oh," Sindri said. "Well, I'm not sure what I've done, but I don't want to insult anyone. So if I've done so, I most sincerely apologize."

The minotaur looked at Sindri for a long moment before finally nodding. "I accept your apology."

The companions waited to see if Jax would say anything more, but he remained silent.

"That's it?" Davyn said. "All you wanted was for Sindri to tell you he was sorry?"

"Yes," Jax said.

"No offense, but it seems like an awful lot of trouble to go through just for an apology," Davyn said.

"That's because you are not a minotaur and do not fully understand the importance of honor," Jax said.

Nearra feared that Davyn would take that as an insult, but before he could respond, Catriona stepped in.

"The Knights of Solamnia have an oath they live by," the warrior said. "*Est Sularus oth Mithas*. It means 'My honor is my life.'"

Jax looked at Catriona and inclined his head in acknowledgement of her words.

Davyn opened his mouth as if he intended to reply, but he said nothing. Instead he looked thoughtful, considering what both Jax and Catriona had said.

"So what will you do now that you have what you came for?" Elidor asked.

Jax thought for a moment before answering. "As I said, the five of you demonstrated great bravery against the dragon." He glanced at Sindri. "And the kender used his magic to save us all—myself included—from the beast's poison gas. I would accompany you on your journey and provide assistance should you encounter any more difficulties."

"Don't look at me," Elidor said. "I'm just a guide the others hired. You'll have to ask them."

Catriona and Sindri looked at Nearra.

"We travel for your sake," Catriona said. "The decision should be yours."

Nearra turned to Davyn, but he seemed to purposefully avoid looking at her, as if he didn't want to influence her decision one way or another.

Nearra smiled at Jax. "I would be honored to have you travel with us."

Jax opened his mouth and bared his teeth in what Nearra hoped was a smile. "Then I shall."

No one else said anything, but Nearra sensed the tension among the companions ease a bit, and she knew she'd done the right thing.

"I'm curious, Sindri," Elidor said. "I confess that I know little about wizardry, but I thought that mages carried spellbooks with them and needed to read and memorize their spells anew each time after casting them."

"That's how human wizards do it," Sindri said. "And elf and dwarf mages as well. But I don't have to memorize written spells and gather special ingredients to work my magic. I guess I'm what you'd call a natural wizard. My spells just happen. For quite a while, all I could do was conjure small objects, but then yesterday—when Jax first confronted me, as a matter of fact—I was suddenly able to perform feats of telekinesis. Since then I've been levitating objects all over the place!"

Davyn grimaced as if he'd just bitten into a piece of rotten fruit.

Elidor arched an eyebrow. "Really? And that was the time when you and Catriona first met Davyn and Nearra?"

Sindri nodded.

Elidor's eyes narrowed. "How interesting," the elf said.

"Perhaps you can now satisfy *my* curiosity," Catriona said to Elidor. "The way you sneaked up on Slean was most impressive, as was your skill with throwing daggers. I'm surprised that a simple guide would possess such abilities."

Elidor smiled, but there was no humor in his eyes. "I'm a sort of jack-of-all-trades. Guiding travelers is only one of the things I do to make a living. But as for the skills you ask about, they are common enough for my people. Elves are known for our grace and stealth. In addition, we tend to possess talent for weapons that require aim and accuracy, such as bows and arrows, as well as throwing knives."

Catriona looked skeptical, but she said nothing more.

Elidor rose to his feet, signaling that the conversation—and the rest break—was over.

"Shall we resume our journey?" he said.

14 ATTACK

Oddvar crouched behind a fallen log a few yards off the main trail through the northern woods. Though there was plenty of shade here, he wore his cloak with the hood up. Sundown was still too many hours away to suit him.

The Theiwar had a perfect vantage point from which to observe Davyn and the others as they walked by. He was surprised to see that, in addition to the elf, a minotaur now accompanied them. It seemed that Davyn was more of a threat to Maddoc's plans than Oddvar had thought.

Oddvar hunkered down behind the log and held his breath as the companions passed. The Theiwar was so quiet and still, and his gray cloak so closely matched the color of the log, that even if one of the youths had walked right up to him, they still would have had a difficult time detecting the dwarf's presence.

When the companions had gone by, Oddvar stood up, but he still didn't lower his hood.

Where are those goblins? he wondered. After Slean's performance had failed to cause the Emergence, Maddoc had ordered Oddvar to contact a band of goblin mercenaries that lived underground and arrange for them to ambush Davyn and the others. Oddvar had given the job to Drefan, Fyren, and Gifre since they were goblins themselves. He told them to meet him right here on this log after they had met with the mercenaries. The three goblins should have been back by—

Oddvar's thoughts were interrupted by a rustling in the underbrush on the other side of the trail. An instant later, Drefan, Fyren, and Gifre poked their heads out of the greenery and looked around, frowning in confusion.

Oddvar should have expected this, the three goblins had found the right section of the forest, but they were on the wrong side of the trail.

He hoisted his stumpy legs over the log and walked to the edge of the trail.

Drefan was the first to see the Theiwar, and the goblin leader raised his hand in acknowledgement and opened his mouth to speak.

Oddvar quickly made a slashing gesture across his throat to indicate the goblin should keep quiet.

The crimson skin of Drefan's face turned light pink—the goblin version of going pale. Fyren and Gifre took one look at Oddvar and their faces paled to pink, too.

Oddvar instantly understood what had happened. The stupid goblins thought he meant that he wanted to cut their throats!

He shook his head to let them know they'd misinterpreted, but the goblins paid no attention. They turned and fled in terror, crashing noisily through the forest.

Oddvar sighed. At least they hadn't screamed.

He chanced looking down the trail in the direction Davyn and the others had gone. He was relieved to see that none of them had turned around. Perhaps they hadn't heard the goblins' flight, or if they had, perhaps they'd assumed some forest animal had made the noise. Since none of the youths were looking, Oddvar risked dashing across the trail in pursuit of the three goblins.

And when he finally caught up with the fools, perhaps he really would slit their throats.

"How long does it take for a new pair of boots to become broken in?" Nearra asked no one in particular.

They had entered the forest hours ago. Walking on the uneven path was taking its toll on Nearra's feet.

"It depends on how much you walk in them," Catriona said. "A few days, perhaps longer."

"A few days? By then there won't be anything left of my feet! They'll be worn down to nubs!"

Catriona, Davyn, and Elidor laughed, but Jax remained silent. Nearra wondered if the minotaur had a sense of humor. If so, she'd seen no sign of it so far.

"It's a good thing we're taking you to a temple full of clerics, then," Sindri said. "Maybe they'll be able to heal your feet."

"Clerics?" Jax said.

Nearra realized that no one had informed the minotaur of the purpose for their journey, so she told him all that had happened to her since waking up on the trail of the southern forest yesterday morning.

When she was done speaking, Jax said, "It is a strange story. One that is difficult to believe."

The minotaur walked at the rear of the group, and Catriona—who was up front with Elidor—had to look over her shoulder to address the man-bull.

"Are you saying Nearra is lying?" the warrior said, a challenge in her tone.

"No," the minotaur said evenly. "But humans have a tendency of being . . . over-imaginative."

Before Catriona could get into an argument with Jax, Nearra said, "Nevertheless, it's true. On my honor."

Jax opened his mouth as if he intended to dispute the story further, but then thought better of it. He accepted Nearra's statement with a nod.

The six companions continued walking, and Nearra thought

the matter was settled. At length Jax said, "My people tell stories of a time when priests and priestesses could perform miracles in the name of our god Sargas, the Great Horned One. But these days, very few minotaurs believe the tales were true."

"People used to believe that dragons were only myths," Elidor said, "but the great beasts have returned to the world. Who's to say that miracles haven't returned as well?"

Jax thought on this for a time. Eventually, he said, "I would have to see such a miracle to believe it. Some of my ancestors were priests, but when they could no longer fulfill their promises of healing, my people came to believe the priests had lost the favor of Sargas, and they were disgraced. Since then, no one in my family has entered the priesthood." Jax paused, and when he continued, his voice was uncharacteristically soft. "I would very much like to see a miracle, even a small one. It would restore my ancestors' honor—in my eyes, if in no one else's."

"Not to criticize your abilities as a guide, Elidor," Davyn said. "But shouldn't we have left the trail by now?"

"Wondering why you bothered hiring me in the first place, eh?" Elidor said. "After all, who needs a guide to travel such a simple, well-defined trail as this? Believe me, I understand completely. But I'll start earning my keep soon enough. We should reach the point where we'll need to leave the trail right around nightfall. We should probably start looking for a good campsite now, and then tomorrow—"

Elidor broke off. He stopped walking and cocked his head to one side, as if listening to something.

Everyone gathered around the elf, concerned.

"What is it?" Catriona asked as she drew her sword.

Elidor frowned as he listened, though Nearra couldn't hear anything. Did elves possess better hearing than humans? She didn't know.

"I'm not sure," Elidor said. "It sounds like—"

"I'll tell you what it *smells* like," Jax interrupted, his large nostrils flaring. "It smells like goblin."

As if responding on cue, a dozen short, squat figures stepped out of the forest and onto the trail in front of the companions. A strong, rank odor like rotten fruit filled the air. The goblins wore bits and pieces of rusty, ill-fitting armor—leather vests, chain mail, plate armor, helmets, gauntlets—and the pieces clanked as the goblins moved. Scavengers, Nearra thought. They were like parasites, living off the people they victimized.

The goblins brandished scavenged weapons as well: daggers, short swords, spiked clubs, hand axes, every kind of weapon Nearra could imagine.

Catriona stepped in front of Nearra. "Stay behind me," she said softly, and Nearra felt a stab of fear.

Davyn nocked an arrow and took aim at the goblin in front, but the ranger didn't fire.

Nearra realized that the others had formed a semicircle in front of her to protect her. She felt at once grateful and ashamed.

"Go now and you shall not be harmed." Catriona was trembling, but her voice was strong and steady.

The goblins burst out laughing.

The one in front—who was slightly taller and fatter than the others—spoke.

"You speak bravely for one who is outnumbered."

"There are six of us and twelve of you," Jax said. "And considering that you are *goblins*—" he said the word as if it were something nasty to scrape off the bottom of his hoof—"each of us counts for two, perhaps three of you. Thus I say it is you who are outnumbered."

The goblin grinned, displaying crooked, yellowed teeth. "Look behind you and count again, minotaur."

"Oh, please!" Elidor said. "That's one of the oldest tricks in the Book of Stupid Goblin Ploys."

Jax sniffed the air. "It isn't a trick."

The companions glanced over their shoulders and saw another dozen goblins had stepped onto the trail behind them, making a total of twenty-four.

Without saying anything, the others shifted their positions until their semicircle became a true circle, with Nearra protected in the middle.

This is ridiculous! thought Nearra. I have the power to take care of myself! She had felt that power several times since she had first awakened, whenever she was in danger. She concentrated on trying to make her hands grow warm and begin to tingle, but no matter how hard she tried, she felt nothing. Maybe I'm not in enough danger, she thought. Maybe it would be better if the others weren't protecting me . . .

"So now the odds are even," Catriona said, though she didn't sound as confident as she had a moment ago. "We have little of value. All you'll gain by attacking us is death."

The goblin leader sneered. "Death is what we seek. But not ours—yours." The leader spoke a harsh command in the goblin tongue, and the two bands of red-skinned creatures shouted battle cries as they surged forward.

15 FROM BAD TO WORSE

Davyn grabbed Nearra's hand and tugged her toward the trees. He held his bow in his other hand, though now the arrow pointed toward the ground.

"Come on! The others can handle the goblins!"

Nearra didn't know what to do. She didn't want to abandon her friends, but the tingling sensation hadn't started yet. She was terrified of the goblins, so she allowed Davyn to pull her off the trail and into the trees.

"Don't stop!" Davyn said, not letting go of her hand. "Keep running!"

Hand in hand, they crashed through the underbrush, fleeing as the sounds of battle erupted behind them.

Catriona saw Davyn pull Nearra to safety. Though she didn't completely trust the ranger, she was glad he had done so. Right now, this was a very bad place for someone who didn't know how to fight.

But then the goblins were upon her and Catriona had no more time to think. Though she was only a squire and technically had no right to do so, she let out the Knights' traditional war **99** cry, fought to ignore the fluttery feeling in her stomach, and moved in to attack.

A goblin came at Catriona with a spiked club. The goblin swung wildly, with more enthusiasm than skill. She side-stepped, easily avoiding the blow. She brought her sword around in a backhanded swipe and struck the goblin in the face with the flat of her blade. Her aunt had taught her never to take life—not even the life of a creature as loathsome as a goblin—unless there was no other option.

The goblin shrieked in pain and staggered backward, but he didn't fall. Leathery red lips drew back from sharp, foam-flecked teeth. He snarled and attacked once more.

Catriona felt the cold icy grip of fear squeeze her heart as the goblin ran toward her, waving his spiked club, eyes blazing with lust for her blood. The goblins weren't skilled warriors and they weren't especially strong, but there were so many of them. Even with the aid of Sindri, Elidor, and Jax, how could she hope to stand against them all?

Her fear made her hesitate almost long enough for the goblin's club to connect with her ribcage. But in the end, her training took over. She jumped back to avoid the blow. With the goblin off-balance, she thrust her sword forward. The creature cried out in pain one last time before stiffening and falling to the ground.

She felt a surge of triumph, as well as gratitude to her aunt for teaching her so well. But she had little time to celebrate, for another goblin came at her, this one wielding a rusty hand axe. Catriona felt fear rise again, but she fought it down and ran forward to meet the attack.

Soon she fell into a rhythm, fighting and dispatching one goblin after another. She parried strikes from all sorts of weapons: long knives, spiked clubs, halberds, flails, maces, and more. It seemed almost as if she were fighting the same goblin over and over, only somehow he managed to switch weapons when she wasn't looking.

During those few seconds when she wasn't attacking or defending, Catriona glanced around to see how her companions were faring. Jax was having no problem whatsoever with the goblins. The minotaur cut them down with his axe as if he were a farmer reaping a field of wheat. Elidor held a pair of his throwing knives, but instead of hurling them at the goblins, he gripped them tightly and used them as miniature swords. Moving with inhuman speed and agility, he turned aside blows and lashed out at his attackers with devastating results.

It was Sindri she was most worried about. The kender had virtually no training in the arts of war. Unless he was able to make use of the magic skills he seemed to have recently acquired, she feared the goblins would strike him down.

Sindri jumped aside just as a goblin swung a flail at him.

"You call that an attack?" the kender said. "My great-great grandmother has a steadier hand and surer eye than you! She's easily twice as fast, too!"

The goblin snarled in rage and lunged at Sindri, but the kender stuck out his foot, tripping the goblin. The red-skinned beast staggered forward, unbalanced, only to end up spitted on the sword of another goblin standing nearby.

Catriona smiled grimly. She had forgotten about the kender ability to taunt a foe into a mindless rage. More often than not, it resulted in the foe making a foolish—and in this case, deadly—mistake. Sindri could take care of himself.

"Hey, you!" Sindri called. "The one with the face like red-colored cow manure!"

A dozen goblins turned to look at the kender.

Of course, there was such a thing as being too good at taunting.

The goblins ran toward Sindri, shouting.

"Death to the kender!"

"Slit his gizzard!"

"Save me the wishbone!"

Catriona tried to run to her friend's aid, but just then the large goblin leader—who was large enough to be a hobgoblin—stepped into her path, and grinning with its fang-filled mouth, swung a war hammer at her head. She brought her sword up in time to counter the blow, but it was a close call. As strong as the goblin was, she didn't think she would be able to defeat him in time to go help Sindri.

The goblin swung again with his hammer, this time at her back. As Catriona spun around to block the weapon, she saw Elidor standing still in the middle of the battle. He reached into his tunic and pulled out what looked like a bulging purse. He opened the sack, poured steel coins into his hand, and then hurled them into the air above the onrushing goblins. He then spun around and threw another handful over the heads of the second group of goblins.

Both goblin squads halted instantly, as if they'd had a stasis spell cast over them. But this wasn't a magic spell: it was a monetary one.

"Steel!" one of the goblins shouted.

"Mine!" another yelled.

"Get your hands off my money!" screeched the leader.

Within seconds, the goblins had forgotten about Catriona and the others and were fighting each other for possession of the coins littering the ground.

Catriona looked at Elidor with a mixture of amazement and admiration. The elf threw the empty purse over his shoulder and smiled. "Sometimes it pays to have your enemy do the fighting for you," he said.

Goblins argued, screamed, and shrieked as their battle became increasingly more savage.

Catriona looked at the spot where Davyn and Nearra had fled into the woods. "Come on! Let's go before the goblins remember we are here!"

Jax scowled. "Minotaurs do not run from battle."

"We are not running *from* anything," Catriona said. "We are running to Nearra and Davyn. There may well be other goblins in the forest—or worse threats. They may need our help. I took an oath to protect Nearra, and I will not fail her!"

Still scowling, the minotaur ignored her and turned to Elidor. "That was my money you threw, wasn't it, elf?"

Elidor tried to smile, but Jax was far too intimidating—especially when holding a double-edged battle-axe.

"Let's quibble over such minor details after we've found Davyn and Nearra, shall we?" Elidor didn't pause to listen to the minotaur's response. Instead, the elf turned and dashed past Catriona and Sindri and plunged into the trees.

Without waiting to see how Jax would react, Catriona ran to catch up, Sindri following close behind.

"We should slow down!" Nearra said as she ran. "If we don't, we'll lose the others!"

"We're still too close to the trail," Davyn said. "Just a little farther, and we'll be safe."

They continued running, dodging around trees, ducking beneath branches. Sweat poured off Davyn's body, his heart pounded, and his breath came in ragged gasps.

They ran past a copper boulder. Then the ground sloped downward, and the trees became sparser, their branches broken off and their bark scarred as if someone—or some*thing*—had been hacking away at the trees with a large axe or club.

Davyn knew the reason why the trees looked this way, and a cold fear gripped him. Not fear for himself, though. Fear for Nearra.

They slowed down until they stopped, unable to run any farther. They both gulped air as they struggled to catch their breath.

"What's . . . that . . . smell?" Nearra said between breaths.

The air was thick with a rank odor, slightly different from the smell of goblin. It was earthier, the scent of a large creature that spent all of its time in the wild.

It was an ogre.

The bestial giant came lumbering from behind an ancient oak tree. It fixed its bloodshot eyes on Davyn and Nearra and grinned.

"It's about time you two got here," the ogre rumbled, its words almost unintelligible. "Ugo worked up powerful hunger while waitin'." The ogre began to salivate, and thick drool ran out of one corner of his mouth and dripped in long, sticky strands to the forest floor.

Ugo stomped toward them, dragging a large bleached bone that served as a crude club. He stared at Nearra and licked his lips with a gray-black tongue.

During the flight through the forest, Davyn had kept hold of his bow, though he had dropped the arrow he'd nocked somewhere along the way. But he had more in his quiver. He drew one now, nocked it, and took aim at Ugo's heart.

The ogre stopped his advance and frowned in puzzlement. "You want to hurt Ugo?"

Davyn released his bowstring and sent the arrow flying.

Ugo was too slow to avoid or block Davyn's arrow, and the shaft struck his chest. But though the point stuck, the ogre didn't appear to be in any pain. In fact, he laughed and brushed the arrow away as if it were nothing more than an annoying insect.

"Ugo not hurt by arrow." The ogre pulled down the collar of his animal-hide tunic to reveal a vest made of reptile scale underneath. The ogre grinned as he let his tunic collar slip back into place. "Ugo now have armor made from wyvern scales. Wizard give as payment."

"Then I'll just have to aim a bit higher, won't I?" Davyn started to draw another arrow from his quiver, but before he could nock it, Ugo bellowed and charged. Though the ogre was slow, Davyn didn't want to risk taking the time to try another shot. It was unlikely he'd slay the ogre with a single arrow, but the man-beast could easily kill them with a single blow of his bone club. They needed to keep out of the ogre's reach if they wanted to stay alive.

Davyn let the arrow fall back into the quiver and grabbed Nearra's hand.

"Come on!" he shouted. "We can't outfight him, but we can outrun him!"

Nearra didn't move. Davyn thought she might be frozen with fear. He tugged on her hand, trying to get her moving before the ogre could get close enough to take a swing at them with his club. But no matter how hard he pulled, Nearra didn't budge. It was as if she'd turned to stone.

Davyn glanced toward Ugo and saw that the ogre was almost upon them.

Davyn knew they had only one other chance: his ring. He'd never been able to use it more than three times a day, but he knew it was theoretically possible. It was only a matter of willpower and inner strength.

Davyn concentrated as hard as he could, and imagined all the arrows in his quiver flying out and shooting toward Ugo, piercing his tough hide as if he were an ogre-shaped pincushion.

One arrow trembled, and then another. But before any of them could rise into the air, a white-hot bolt of pain lanced through Davyn's skull. The young ranger cried out as he began to lose consciousness.

Forgive me, Nearra, he thought. The world spun around him and everything began to grow dark. He felt his hand let go of Nearra's, and then he was falling toward the ground.

16 DOORKNOBS AND
SECRET NAMES

Catriona easily found Davyn and Nearra's trail. She could see the broken branches, snapped twigs, and crushed plants that they'd left in their wake, and what's more, she could hear them crashing through the forest somewhere ahead of her.

At first Catriona had been glad that Davyn had taken Nearra off the trail, but now she was beginning to worry. Instinct told her that something wasn't right, that Davyn wasn't simply trying to get Nearra safely away from the goblins. He was taking Nearra too far from the road and moving too fast, as if he were trying to get away from the rest of them as well as the goblins.

The Knights of Solamnia worshiped Paladine, the chief god of Good, and though Catriona wasn't a Knight, she hoped more than anything to redeem herself and prove worthy of becoming one someday. She whispered a prayer for Nearra's safety and hoped Paladine was listening.

She heard a noise and glanced over her shoulder. She saw Sindri struggling to catch up to her. The kender was fit and agile, but his legs were far shorter than Catriona's, and there was no way he could hope to keep pace with her.

She found herself suddenly torn between two oaths: should **107** she continue running as fast as she could to catch up to Nearra and Davyn, or should she slow down so that she didn't outdistance Sindri? She had sworn to protect both of them, but by trying to help only one, she could well be putting the other's life in danger. And there was no way she could possibly protect both. But what if, by choosing one over the other, she caused harm to come to the one she didn't choose? She'd failed her aunt when the bandits had attacked, and Leyana had paid for Catriona's cowardice with her life. Catriona was determined not to fail anyone else again—ever.

She finally decided that Nearra needed her the most. Sindri had more experience at dealing with the hazards of traveling than did Nearra, who in a very real sense had only a day and a half of experience to draw on. Besides, Sindri had his magic to protect him, though exactly how he had suddenly become capable of performing spells of telekinesis, Catriona didn't know.

"I'm going to try to catch up to Davyn and Nearra!" she called back to Sindri.

"Go ahead!" the kender shouted in reply. "I'll find you!"

Sindri sounded excited, as if she'd just proposed they play a game of hide and seek.

Kender, she thought, with a mix of fondness and exasperation. Not for the first time, she envied Sindri's ability to resist fear or indecision. Then she focused her thoughts on running as fast as she could.

She continued following Davyn and Nearra's trail until she came to a copper-colored boulder. She nearly tripped as the ground began to slope downward, but she managed to maintain her footing and kept on running.

Catriona found them in time to see Davyn fall to the ground. Catriona wasn't sure what had happened to the ranger. From what she could see, it didn't look as if the ogre had been close enough to strike him. But whatever had caused Davyn to lose consciousness, she couldn't worry about him now. It was Nearra whom she was sworn to protect.

TIM WAGGONER

108

Nearra stood motionless as the ogre approached her. She's paralyzed with terror, Catriona guessed. Not that she could blame Nearra. The ogre might not have been as fearsome as Slean, but he was formidable enough in his own right.

"In the name of the Knights of Solamnia, I command you to stop!" Catriona shouted, managing to keep the fear she felt out of her voice. Though technically she had no right to say this, she hoped that by evoking the name of the Knights, she might catch the ogre's attention. She had no illusions that the creature would obey her. She merely hoped to distract him long enough so she could reach him before he could harm Nearra.

The ogre turned to look at Catriona and blinked several times.

"Ugo kill you next. You wait turn."

"I would rather go first, if it's all the same to you." Catriona continued to approach the ogre, moving slowly and circling to his right, hoping to lure the beast away from Nearra and Davyn.

The ogre followed Catriona with his gaze, then turned back to look at Nearra. "This one could be trying to fool Ugo. Might run away if I kill you first." The ogre's face then brightened. "Ugo know! Ugo break blond girl's legs so she can't run, then Ugo kill you first!"

Before Catriona could say anything else, Ugo raised his bone club, obviously intending to take a sideways swipe at Nearra and shatter her legs.

Catriona knew there was no more time for talk. She shouted a battle cry and charged, short sword in hand, hoping she could reach the ogre before it could harm Nearra.

Sindri was breathing hard when he finally caught up to Catriona. The chase had been great fun, even if he had snagged his cape on a branch and torn it. But when he saw the scene that awaited him, Sindri knew this was no longer a game.

A huge ogre stood in front of a motionless Nearra, while Davyn lay on the ground, not moving. Catriona was running to attack the great man-beast, obviously hoping to protect the others. Kender didn't feel fear for their own safety, but they were concerned for the safety of others, especially those they counted as their friends.

Sindri ran to help Catriona, though he didn't know exactly what he could do. He was reluctant to try a telekinesis spell. The last one he'd attempted hadn't worked. He might well have only once chance at the ogre, and he wanted to make it count.

Catriona ran past the ogre's left side and slashed out with her sword. The blade cut through the ogre's animal-hide tunic but scraped against some sort of armor underneath. From the ogre's lack of reaction and the lack of blood, Sindri figured that Catriona's strike had done little if any damage.

Sindri drew near the ogre, and he knew that if he was going to do anything, now was the time. He hadn't checked his cape pockets in a while. Perhaps he'd conjured something useful since last he'd looked.

Ugo turned away from Nearra and swung his bone club at Catriona's head. But the warrior was too smart and the ogre too slow. Catriona ducked the blow with ease. And as the club swished through the air over her head, she sliced her sword across the bottom of Ugo's forearm. Blackish-green blood gushed from the wound, and this time the ogre bellowed in pain and rage.

Sindri searched his pockets. Let's see, he thought, an ivory carving of a griffin, a necklace made of some sort of animal teeth, a brass doorknob . . .

"That'll do," the kender said to himself. He pulled out the door-knob, took aim, and threw. Sindri wasn't the most powerfully muscled being on Krynn, but he had good aim. The doorknob struck the ogre on the left temple with a meaty thud!

Snarling, Ugo turned to see who his latest assailant was. "A kender!" he roared. "Ugo hates kender! Taste awful!"

Catriona took advantage of the distraction Sindri had provided and again swung her sword at the ogre's wounded hand. This time she sliced the back of Ugo's forearm, releasing another gout of blood. She'd also done enough damage to the muscles and tendons to make it difficult for the man-beast to hold onto his heavy club. It slipped from Ugo's fingers and fell to the ground.

Sindri cheered upon seeing that Catriona had disarmed the ogre, but the kender knew that armed or not, the creature remained extremely dangerous.

"Try to get Nearra away from here!" Catriona shouted. "I'll deal with this—" But her words were cut off as Ugo flicked his bleeding arm toward the warrior. Spatters of blood hit Catriona on the face, getting into her eyes and momentarily blinding her. Sindri knew that a moment was all the time the ogre needed. And the kender didn't think he had any more doorknobs in his cape pockets.

Elidor had raced ahead into the woods, at first trying to lose the others. But he had been unable to shake the minotaur. Jax had spotted Elidor's trail instantly and was now stomping through the underbrush only a few yards behind the elf.

After throwing Jax's steel coins to distract the goblins, Elidor doubted he'd be able to maintain the fiction of being a guide any longer. Though he'd had few dealings with minotaurs in his young life, he knew that they were probably the most stubborn creatures on Krynn, especially when it came to matters of honor. Jax wouldn't stop pursuing Elidor until he'd caught the elf and made him pay—in every sense of the word. The only way out that Elidor could see was to find the others and somehow talk them into convincing Jax to let him go. It was a slim chance, he knew, but he couldn't think of anything else.

While Elidor had by no means mastered all the skills of his father's people, the Kagonesti, he knew his way around a forest well enough and had little trouble finding Catriona and Sindri's trail.

Before long Elidor came to a boulder the color of copper, and for an instant he thought he saw an eye wink on its surface. But when he got closer, all he could see was unbroken stone. He decided his own eyes were playing tricks on him or else some mischievous forest sprite was having fun at his expense. He continued down a short incline and past some damaged trees until he saw the others.

Elidor sighed. This morning it was a dragon, then the goblins, and now an ogre. In the Blind Goose, he'd acted on impulse—as he so often did—when he'd decided to offer his services as a guide. Now he was beginning to wonder if that was one lie he wasn't going to live to regret.

Elidor heard stomping and heavy breathing behind him, and he knew that Jax had caught up to him. The elf didn't turn to look at Jax.

"I understand we have a score to settle," Elidor said. "But I suggest we worry about that after we help the others."

A moment's hesitation, and then Jax rumbled, "Agreed." Without another word, the minotaur ran forward.

Elidor was tempted to take his leave while Jax was occupied with fighting the ogre alongside the others, but both his mother's and his father's people believed most strongly in the principle of honor. And while Elidor had his own way of interpreting the concept—a way neither his father nor mother would have approved of—he too believed in honor, most of the time. And honor wouldn't allow him to abandon the others while they were fighting for their lives.

Elidor drew a pair of his precious throwing knives from their boot sheathes, then dashed forward to foolishly risk his life.

Chaos swirled around Nearra, but she was only distantly aware of it. Davyn lay unconscious on the ground next to her, while Catriona, Jax, and Elidor fought the ogre. Sindri had hold of her left hand and was trying to pull her to safety, but the kender was having no more success than Davyn had earlier. The power inside her was rising, and she was magically rooted to the spot as it happened.

The tingling in her hands had become a raging fire and had spread throughout her body. The sensation wasn't painful, though. It felt almost natural, as if she were *supposed* to feel this way.

She once again became aware of another presence within her. An older, confident, cruel presence.

An ogre, eh? Not much of a threat. At least we've got the others doing our fighting for us; that's a good start. But we could use an ally who's a bit more . . . formidable.

Nearra felt her mouth opening as if it were out of her control, and she whispered a single word.

"Tarkemelhion."

The copper-colored boulder opened its reptilian eyes wide in surprise upon hearing its True Name whispered. The creature was even more surprised to realize there was magic fueling the word—powerful magic that called to him and which he could not disobey.

He spoke his own magic word to dispel the illusion that he was a boulder. The air around him shimmered and the boulder disappeared; in its place now stood a copper dragon.

The dragon, who normally went by the name of Raedon, had been telepathically monitoring the battle. It had been his intention to reveal himself at the exact moment when it looked as if the little ones were doomed. He would then leap to the rescue as Raedon, the Copper-Scaled Savior!

But now it seemed a wizard had tapped into his mind and discovered his secret name. All dragons have a secret name. If anyone else should learn of this name, he or she could gain power over that dragon—which was exactly what had just happened to Raedon.

Raedon coiled his leg muscles, got down low to the ground, and then gave a mighty leap and quite literally sprang into battle.

CHAPTER

17 RESCUE

Nearra felt as if she were waking from a dream. She recalled the voice of the woman speaking to her but she couldn't remember who it had been. She did remember one thing, though. A very long word that she'd never heard before: *Tarkemelhion.*

But none of it seemed important when she saw what was going on in front of her.

The ogre was reaching for Catriona with his massive hands, but she dodged his clumsy swipes with ease. While the ogre was distracted, Jax dashed in and swung his axe at the creature's legs. The ogre howled in pain and turned to strike at Jax. But the minotaur retreated before the man-beast could hit him.

With a graceful flick of his wrist, Elidor threw a knife at the ogre. The blade streaked through the air and lodged in the monster's shoulder. The ogre was now bleeding from a dozen wounds, but he didn't appear to have been significantly hampered by his injuries. It seemed as if they served only to make him angrier. Nearra remembered what had happened. She and Davyn had been running from the goblin raiders when—

Davyn!

She looked down and saw the ranger lying still on the ground. She started to go to him, but something held her back. Still somewhat fuzzyheaded, she turned and saw that Sindri had hold of her left hand and was trying to pull her away.

"Please, let go," she said. "I have to see if Davyn is all right!"

Sindri's face broke into a relieved smile. "Nearra, you can move again! I guess I was able to dispel whatever enchantment had hold of you!"

Nearra didn't know what the kender was talking about, and right now she didn't care. All she wanted to do was check on Davyn. *Please don't let him be dead,* she prayed to no god in particular. She knelt by his side and gently touched his face. His skin was warm, but not feverish. She then moved her hand close to Davyn's nose and felt his breath on her fingertips. Good, he was still breathing.

She took hold of Davyn's shoulders and was about to attempt to shake him awake when a huge copper-colored beast leaped over their heads and landed with an earth-jarring impact in front of Ugo.

It was a dragon! Nearra braced herself for the dragonfear to take hold. But something was different this time. This one's scales were the color of copper and glittered in the sunlight, as if truly made of metal. It was smaller than Slean, perhaps twenty feet from the tip of its snout to the end of its tail. Its wings were folded against its sides, but given the way it could jump, it didn't need those wings at the moment.

Two daggers lodged in the ogre's neck and shoulder. Yet the ogre had still managed to pick up his bone club with his uninjured hand and take a swing at Elidor. But when Ugo suddenly found himself confronted by a copper dragon, he stopped his attack in mid-swing.

He stared at the giant reptile in surprise.

"This some trick!" Ugo said. "Dragons gone. Leave Krynn long time ago!"

"That's true," the dragon said in a pleasant voice that sounded decidedly male. "But now we're back."

Ugo frowned. "What dragon want? To share Ugo's food?" The ogre gestured with his bone club, indicating Nearra and her companions. "Only six, but you welcome to a couple if you want."

The dragon chuckled. "I imagine I am welcome—especially if I help you slay these little ones. They seem to have gotten the better of you so far, while there isn't so much as a scratch on any of them."

"Little ones?" Jax said, sounding offended. Catriona hushed him and motioned to both the minotaur and Elidor to back away from the ogre.

"Bah, these snacks no match for Ugo. Ugo just do as Ugo told. Make good show before killing any."

"Really?" The dragon sounded intrigued. "And who exactly told you to put on a good show?" the dragon asked.

Ugo noticed his three attackers retreating and gave the dragon a sly look. "You no want to help Ugo. You want to help snacks!"

"Well, I am a copper dragon, after all. We prefer not to harm intelligent beings if we can avoid it." The dragon smiled, and though Nearra was certain he was on their side, the sight of his extremely large and extremely sharp teeth was nonetheless intimidating.

"But since ogres hardly qualify as intelligent, harming you won't bother me in the slightest."

Ugo stared blankly at the copper dragon, as if trying to figure out whether or not he had been insulted. He must've decided on insulted, for he raised his bone club and roared.

The dragon didn't seem worried. He took a glance to see if Catriona and the others had made it to safety. Then just as the ogre took a swing, the dragon leaped straight up into the air.

Ugo swung and missed. Growling in frustration, he looked up to see where the dragon had gone. The dragon landed behind him and tapped a claw on his shoulder.

"Tag, you're it!"

Ugo turned around and started to raise his bone club for another blow, but the dragon opened his mouth wide and with a loud hiss, released a stream of copper-colored gas into the ogre's face.

Before Ugo could stop himself, he inhaled the gas. He continued to raise his club for another attack, but he was moving far more slowly than before—so slowly that he almost appeared to be not moving at all.

The dragon laughed. "That didn't turn out so bad after all!" He turned to Nearra and the others. "You may call me Raedon," the dragon said. "Which one of you summoned me?"

"I'm afraid we don't understand," Catriona said. The warrior was sweaty and breathing hard from the battle with Ugo, but otherwise she was unharmed.

"One of you is a wizard," the dragon explained in a tone that indicated he was beginning to wonder if they were any smarter than the near-motionless ogre. "Someone used magic to summon me to your aid."

"Magic?" Sindri said. "Well, I *am* the only wizard in the group."

Raedon eyed the kender skeptically for a moment before walking over on four clawed feet to inspect him. The dragon whispered words in a strange language, then stared at the kender intently.

Finally, he chuckled. "A wizard, eh? Well, why not? I have no objection to playing along." Raedon gave Nearra a quick glance, and for an instant she felt as if the dragon could see inside of her, all the way to the very core of her being.

The dragon nodded at Davyn. "Is your friend seriously hurt?"

"I don't think so," Nearra said. "He has no fever and he's still breathing."

Raedon cocked his head, as if listening to something. "His heartbeat is strong as well. He should recover soon." The dragon returned his gaze to Sindri. "Very well, *wizard*. I have answered your summons and have stopped the ogre with a blast of what in the common tongue would be called slow gas. The ogre will continue to move, but at only a fraction of his normal speed. This will give you all ample time to get away."

"Why didn't you just slay the foul creature?" Jax demanded.

Raedon sighed. "As I told the great smelly oaf of an ogre, I am a copper dragon." He wiggled, making his scales ripple up and down the length of his body.

"Copper?" Nearra said.

Raedon looked at them as if they were complete morons.

"Dragons have only recently returned to Krynn," Elidor said. "Most folk have had little or no experience with your kind."

"I suppose you have a point." Raedon glanced over his shoulder at Ugo, who was still laboring to raise his club. "It might be best if we travel while we talk. That way you'll be far away when Ugo-ly returns to full speed. Where were you headed?"

"To the Temple of the Holy Orders of the Stars," Davyn mumbled.

Nearra looked down and saw that Davyn's eyes were open. She grinned in relief and helped him to his feet. Davyn grimaced and put his hand to his head. His knees buckled, but Nearra steadied him and he managed to remain standing.

"Thank goodness!" Nearra said. "I was so worried about you!"

Davyn gave her a puzzled look. "You were?"

"Of course I was! Are you hurt? Did the ogre hit you with his club?"

"I don't remember. But my head certainly feels as if an ogre bashed it in."

"This is the second time today that you have been rendered unconscious," Jax said. "Perhaps you should consider obtaining a helmet to protect your head."

Nearra had the sense that Davyn wasn't quite telling them the whole truth when he said he couldn't remember. Evidently

Catriona did too, for she was scowling. But Nearra decided not to make an issue of it just now. She was too happy that Davyn was back among the living once more.

Davyn looked at Raedon.

"Where did *he* come from?"

CHAPTER

18 BETRAYED?

Raedon led the companions through the forest on a route he claimed would save them several days of traveling.

"It used to be the main road to the temple," he said. "But when the clerics abandoned the temple, the road fell into disuse. Now, centuries later, you can't even tell where it once was." He grinned. "Unless you're a dragon, of course."

There was another benefit of having Raedon as their escort: with a dragon along, the companions didn't have to worry about anyone or anything else attacking them.

As they made their way through the forest, Raedon told them about dragons. "The chromatic dragons are known by their colors: black, blue, green, red, and white. All are evil to one degree or another. The metallic dragons are known by the type of metal their scales most resemble: brass, bronze, copper, gold, and silver. All of these are good. That's why I didn't slay the ogre. With my breath weapon, there was no need to kill him. It is evil to kill without necessity, and I am not evil."

Catriona frowned. "How can one be fated to be evil or good simply by the type of skin one has?"

Raedon shrugged, the motion making his shoulder scales rustle. "It is the nature of dragonkind. The gods decreed it to 121 be so at the dawn of time, and so it has ever been. Just as they decreed that you little ones could choose between good and evil."

Davyn wished the others would stop talking. Every footstep he took sent vibrations up through his body and into his throbbing head, making it hurt all the more. He was in so much pain that it was an effort to remain conscious. He stumbled, and Nearra took his elbow and steadied him.

"Thanks," he said.

She smiled. "You're welcome."

They continued walking side by side, Nearra still holding onto his arm to steady him. Davyn thought about how concerned she'd been when he'd passed out after trying to use the telekinesis ring. He couldn't remember anyone ever worrying about him like that before. What would she think if she knew what he'd done? He felt suddenly ashamed, and he pulled away from Nearra's touch.

"I'm fine now," he said.

She nodded and smiled once again. "Just let me know if you need any more help."

Jax then spoke to Raedon. "While I admit your slow gas was effective, it is rather passive as weapons go."

Raedon scowled at the minotaur. "I can shoot a stream of acid as well. Would you like me to demonstrate?"

"Perhaps another time," Jax said. He then turned to look at Elidor. "Right now I'm more interested in how the elf came into possession of my money."

"Yes," Catriona said, staring hard at Elidor. "That's a good question."

The elf gave her a wry grin. "I wish I had a good answer."

"You mean a good lie," Jax said.

"That's *precisely* what I mean. But since I don't, I suppose I have no choice but to resort to the truth," Elidor sighed. "As you might've guessed by now, I'm not a guide. Not only do I not know the way to the temple you seek, I'd never heard of it

TIM WAGGONER

122

until yesterday, when Catriona and Davyn mentioned it to the Theiwar at the tavern."

"Theiwar?" Raedon said, sounding surprised.

"Yes," Elidor said, giving the dragon a curious look. "A dark dwarf. Does that mean something to you?"

"Perhaps, perhaps not," the dragon said evasively. "Please, go on."

Elidor gave the dragon another look before continuing. "When we made our rather hasty exit from the tavern yesterday, after Jax came bursting through the door, I paused on my way out and—"

"I *thought* I saw you bend down as you ran by Jax!" Nearra said. "That's when you took his money, wasn't it?"

"Yes," Elidor replied, not sounding the least bit ashamed. "If I'd had any idea that the minotaur would eventually be joining our merry band of travelers, I would have restrained myself."

Catriona snorted. "So you're nothing more than a common thief."

"I'd hardly say 'common,'" Elidor said, sounding offended.

"You don't look like a thief," Sindri said.

Elidor grinned. "You mean because I'm not dressed all in black and don't go around calling myself Elidor Shadowalker or some such nonsense? A good thief needs to blend in and be unnoticed. That's why I wear this." He gestured to his simple gray tunic. "If I had my way, I'd dress like my father's people, the Kagonesti. But an elf tends to draw enough attention in human lands without wearing buckskins adorned with hawk feathers and having a body covered with tribal tattoos."

Despite the pounding in his skull, Davyn managed to ask a question of his own. "Then why did you offer to guide us to the temple if you didn't know the way?"

"He probably wanted to get us alone in the forest and then rob us," Catriona said, her voice dripping with disdain.

"While I understand why you would think that, I assure you that wasn't the case. For one thing, there are too many of you and only one of me. The odds would hardly be in my favor."

"Then why *did* you come?" Catriona asked, clearly exasperated.

"Because I wanted to go to the temple," Elidor said.

"Liar!" Catriona said. "You offered to be our guide before you even knew where we were going."

"Very well. I suppose I did hope to obtain something in exchange for this little misadventure. But I should have known better than to make friends with my targets. Once I got to know all of you, I felt sorry for you." Elidor glanced at Nearra. "I decided I might as well help you to get where you wanted to go. Besides, the temple truly did seem like an interesting place to visit."

"A place full of interesting artifacts, you mean," Davyn said. "And perhaps valuable ones as well."

Elidor smiled. "One can only hope."

"But if you don't know the way to the temple, and we don't know the way, how did you expect we'd make it there at all?" Nearra asked.

"Since I'm half Kagonesti, I know my way around forests. From what you said about the temple, I knew it lay northward. I figured that if we started out in that direction, we were bound to run across it sooner or later."

"Makes sense to me," Sindri said.

"It would," Catriona muttered.

Jax had remained silent during Elidor's confession, but now the minotaur spoke. "Thieves are without honor. They take what they want through trickery and deceit instead of by strength, as would a warrior."

"Speak for yourself," Catriona said.

Jax ignored her and went on. "I should slay you for stealing my purse. But you did use the steel coins as an effective distraction when the goblins attacked. And instead of fleeing once I discovered what you had done, you chose to help battle the ogre." Jax thought for a moment. "Because of the bravery and loyalty

TIM WAGGONER

you demonstrated, I shall spare your life." The minotaur glared at Elidor. "But be warned, elf. If you steal again from me, or any member of this party, then no matter how many brave deeds you may perform, they will not save you from my axe."

Elidor's smile was strained. "I understand."

Jax nodded and then turned away.

"You little ones are amusing," Raedon said. "I'm glad that things worked out the way they did. Listening to you bicker is much more fun than playing a joke on the Theiwar."

"What Theiwar?" Catriona said.

"It couldn't be the same one from the tavern," Sindri said. "Could it?"

"It would be rare to encounter more than one in this area in so short a time," Elidor said.

"It's the same one, all right," Raedon said. "All you little ones look more or less alike to me, but I can tell you apart by the way you smell."

"Excuse me?" Catriona said.

"Nothing personal," Raedon said. "I mean you all have distinctive scents. I can smell traces of the Theiwar's scent on the elf, the male human with the headache, and the disagreeable female with the sword."

"Disagreeable?" Catriona said, her volume rising with each syllable.

"Hush," Nearra said gently. "So it must be the same Theiwar you met in the tavern. When did you see the dark dwarf, Raedon, and why did you wish to play a joke on him?"

"I saw him yesterday," the dragon said. "Normally copper dragons such as myself prefer to live in mountainous regions. My lair is located in the Vingaard Mountains. It's really quite something. I'm young for my kind, so I haven't acquired all that much treasure yet, but I have constructed a fairly elaborate maze to discourage any treasure hunters—" he gave Elidor a look—"or thieves. I dug the tunnels all by myself, though I did use magic to make the process somewhat easier. Speaking of mazes, that reminds me of a joke: what do you call a copper dragon who gets lost in his own maze of tunnels?"

"I hate to interrupt," Nearra said, "but you were going to tell us about the Theiwar."

"But I want to hear how the joke ends!" Sindri protested, but Catriona shushed him.

"Very well," Raedon said, sounding disappointed. "As I was saying, my home is in the mountains, but very few travelers ever come near my lair, so I often come here to the forest to see if I can find any. Copper dragons have a strong sense of fun—one that's much more developed than that of other dragons. But it's not enough to have fun by yourself. We like to have fun with someone."

"By playing pranks on them, I'll wager," Catriona said.

"Sometimes, but only harmless ones." Raedon smiled. "I am a good dragon, remember? But we also like to tell stories, jokes, and riddles. So yesterday evening I was flying over the forest, looking for someone to have fun with, when I spotted the Theiwar traveling through the forest in the company of three goblins."

"Three goblins?" Nearra said. "I was attacked by three goblins yesterday morning when I awoke in the southern forest. Did one of them have large bat ears and the other a small piggy nose?"

Raedon nodded.

"Your situation keeps on getting stranger," Catriona said to Nearra. "The three goblins that attacked you yesterday might well be connected to the Theiwar. And the tavern keeper at the Blind Goose recommended we hire the Theiwar as our guide. Then today we encountered an entire band of goblins."

"What was the Theiwar doing in the forest?" Jax asked Raedon.

"I followed Oddvar and his three goblin friends for a time, making sure that they couldn't see me, of course."

"Oddvar? Is that the Theiwar's name?" asked Catriona. "Can't say I like it, but it suits him."

Raedon nodded again and continued. "Once I was confident I knew the direction they were heading in, I decided to land in the forest ahead of them and disguise myself—"

"As that copper-colored boulder!" Elidor said. "I thought I saw that rock open an eye and look at me!"

Raedon chuckled. "You should've seen your face."

"You were telling us about Oddvar," Nearra prompted.

"Right. So I pretended to be a rock, and Oddvar and the goblins walked past me. I was about to reveal myself when Oddvar called out Ugo's name. Curious, I remained in disguise and listened as the ogre came forth in answer to Oddvar's summons. The dark dwarf then proceeded to give the ogre instructions. He kept them simple, which was wise considering how dumb ogres are. Oddvar told Ugo that there was a good chance a young blond girl accompanied by a ranger, a warrior, a kender, and an elf would be coming his way within the day."

Raedon looked at Jax. "I guess Oddvar forgot to mention you."

"I have only recently joined the group," the minotaur explained.

"Oddvar told the ogre that he could do whatever he liked to the rest of you, but under no circumstances was he to harm the blond girl. If he did, then Oddvar's master, who was a powerful wizard, would punish Ugo most severely.

"Oddvar had to repeat the instructions several times, but eventually he and the goblins departed, but not before giving Ugo a vest made of wyvern scales as payment.

"After that, I remained in disguise. I was curious to see if the stupid ogre would actually remember his instructions. The rest you know."

"Why didn't you warn us before we encountered the ogre?" Catriona asked.

The dragon grinned. "That wouldn't have been much fun now, would it?"

Catriona gave forth an exasperated sigh, but otherwise said no more.

"It's too bad you didn't catch the wizard's name," Sindri said. "Being a mage myself, perhaps I would have heard of him."

"But I did overhear Oddvar speak the wizard's name," Raedon said. "It was Maddoc."

Everyone turned to look at Nearra.

"That's the name of the wizard who rescued you from Slean," Sindri said.

"Slean?" Raedon yelped, but they all ignored the dragon for the moment.

Elidor said, "As I understand the story, Maddoc was the same wizard that suggested Nearra seek a healer in Tresvka. A healer who, in turn, suggested she journey to the Temple of the Holy Orders of the Stars, and who hinted that she might find a guide at the Blind Goose tavern."

"Where the tavern keeper recommended the Theiwar," Jax added.

"You're all overlooking the most important part," Catriona said. "Maddoc wasn't alone when he rescued Nearra. Davyn was with him."

They stopped walking and turned to look at Davyn. The ranger knew he should say something to allay their suspicions, but he couldn't think of anything. So instead he took a deep breath and said, "It's true."

19 BATTLE IN THE SKY

I think he moved!"

"You're crazy!"

"No, Gifre's right! I saw his eye twitch!"

"You only *thought* you saw his eye twitch," Drefan said. "He's been turned to stone or something."

"Then how come he isn't the color of stone?" Fyren asked.

"Yeah, he's still ogre-colored!" Gifre added.

Oddvar did his best to ignore the goblins, though it wasn't easy. They stood in front of Ugo, but not too close. None of them wanted to get bashed by his bone club if the ogre started moving again.

Oddvar and the three goblins had watched Nearra's encounter with Ugo from their hiding place behind a pile of rotted logs. The goblins had picked out the termites that infested the logs and eaten them while the battle took place. And as if that hadn't been disgusting enough, they still had insect parts stuck between their teeth.

There was a flapping of wings as Maddoc's black falcon landed next to Oddvar. The dark dwarf acknowledged his master's presence with a nod. He knew the falcon had been circling high overhead, providing Maddoc with a literal bird's-eye view of the action during the battle with Ugo.

"The girl's luck is unbelievable," Oddvar said. "When you left her in Tresvka, she was alone with Davyn. Since then, she picked up four other companions who are determined to protect her. And now she's befriended a copper dragon, of all things."

The falcon relayed a telepathic message from Maddoc to Oddvar.

The Theiwar turned to look at the falcon. "So it's possible that the spirit of Asvoria has been magically gathering others to help her? But Nearra is not aware that she's doing it?"

Yes.

Oddvar looked back to Ugo. During the entire time they'd been standing there, the ogre's club had moved only an inch or so. At this rate, if the copper dragon's slow gas didn't wear off soon, it might be morning before Ugo's club finally struck the ground.

The goblins, emboldened by Ugo's nearly frozen state, were now taking turns running between his legs and under his club. Even Drefan, the goblins' leader, was participating, laughing along with the other two as they played.

Oddvar sighed. After Maddoc's plan had been fulfilled, he hoped he never had to work with goblins again.

The falcon relayed another message from its master. *Three attempts, three failures.*

Oddvar steeled himself against his master's wrath. He thought Maddoc was surely going to blame him and the three goblins for this latest failure. But as the wizard continued, his telepathic voice sounded thoughtful, not angry.

I never thought Nearra would get this far. But then I didn't anticipate that Asvoria might be able to resist the Emergence, nor that Nearra would acquire so many traveling companions to help her along the way.

"Davyn should have kept anyone else from joining them," Oddvar said.

Yes, he should have. But that isn't important now. What's important is separating Nearra from the others—including Davyn. Without her protectors, she'll be alone and terrified. And her terror should trigger the Emergence.

As near as Oddvar could tell, the girl had been plenty afraid during the earlier attempts to force the Emergence, and it hadn't helped any. But he knew better than to question his master.

"How are we supposed to get her away from her friends?" Oddvar asked.

The falcon cocked its head to one side, and Oddvar could have sworn that there was an evil twinkle in its eye.

I have a plan, naturally.

"What do you wish us to do now?" he asked.

The falcon relayed one last telepathic message from Maddoc before taking wing and rising into the sky.

"Come away from the ogre and let's be off," Oddvar said to the goblins. "Maddoc commands we leave."

"Just a bit longer—please, Oddvar?" Gifre asked, then kicked Ugo in the shin. The ogre, still almost completely motionless, didn't react.

Fyren grabbed hold of the bone club and began to swing on it as if it were a tree branch.

Oddvar looked to Drefan for help, but the goblin leader merely grinned.

"How often is it that goblins can get the best of an ogre?" Drefan said, and then bent down, grabbed a handful of dirt, and threw it into Ugo's face. Again, the ogre didn't react.

"Stop this foolishness at once!" Oddvar shouted. "Maddoc has commanded us to—"

It was at this precise moment that the slow gas wore off. Ugo roared, the goblins shrieked, and the bone club—upon which Fyren was still swinging—came crashing down.

All was silent for a long moment, and then in a small voice, Ugo said, "Oops."

"I lied when I said Maddoc hired me to guide him to Tresvka," Davyn said.

Nearra felt a sudden tightness in her throat, and she thought she might cry. She had only known Davyn for two days, but in that short time she had grown quite fond of him. She couldn't bear to hear that he had lied.

Catriona gave Nearra a smug look, as if to say, *I told you so.*

Davyn spoke. "I was exploring the southern forest when Maddoc first approached me. He said that he was on a mission of vital importance, and that for reasons he couldn't explain, he needed my help. At first I didn't believe him. After all, it was like something out of a child's story—a wizard suddenly appearing and saying he needs your help. But Maddoc wore the white robes, and I knew that meant he was a wizard who practiced his magic in the cause of Good, and so I agreed to help him.

"We traveled together through the southern forest for a day and a half. Maddoc didn't tell me much during that time, only that we were searching for a very special girl who was in great danger. But there's one thing Maddoc made sure I was clear on: the girl would be in a fragile mental state. Because she would be very confused, we needed to keep our explanations simple. He told me to pretend that he had hired me to guide him to Tresvka. Once we reached the village, Maddoc said I should take you to the healer Wynda. Somehow Maddoc knew that if she couldn't help you, she would direct you to the Temple of the Holy Orders of the Stars. And he said we could find a guide named Oddvar at the Blind Goose to take you there."

Davyn looked at Nearra. "I'm sorry that I lied to you, but Maddoc paid me well on the condition that I didn't say a word. I needed the money. Please forgive me."

Nearra wasn't sure what to believe. When Davyn had asked for her forgiveness, he'd sounded sincere. But if he had lied to her once—for whatever reason—then he could lie to her again.

No, she told herself. She shouldn't think such things. Friends were supposed to trust one another, even when they had doubts. Maybe especially then.

Nearra smiled. "Of course I forgive you. You only did what you thought was best at the time."

Catriona hrumpfed but said nothing else. Davyn seemed relieved by Nearra's response, but he didn't look her in the eyes.

"It doesn't make any sense," Sindri said. "If Maddoc is a good wizard, why would he first try to help Nearra by sending her to a healer, then later try to hurt her by arranging for an ogre to attack her?"

"It was Oddvar who set up the attack," Elidor pointed out.

"But he was working for Maddoc," Raedon said. "Unless you mean to imply that I might've heard the dark dwarf incorrectly." Though Raedon was a metallic dragon, and therefore on the side of good, there was still a hint of anger in his voice.

Elidor held up his hands. "Not at all, friend Raedon. Far be it from me to argue with a dragon."

"But how did Maddoc know that Davyn and Nearra would be in the same part of the forest where the ogre attacked?" Sindri continued.

"Wizards delight in complex schemes," Jax said. "Who can say how or why Maddoc has done these things? And in the end, what does it matter? Our goal remains the same: to help Nearra regain her memory. It seems her only hope is to find these clerics at the Temple of the Holy Orders of the Stars."

"Trust a minotaur to see things so simply," Elidor said.

"Of course," Jax replied, as if the elf had paid him a compliment.

So they resumed their journey, Raedon leading them on his shortcut through the forest. Nearra did her best not to worry, but she couldn't help wondering what Maddoc wanted from her.

Slean dozed by the stream, her tail dipped into the cool water. Her wounds still hurt, especially her eye, but they had already done much healing. And they would heal even more, as long as she could continue resting. But then she heard the flapping of a falcon's wings. Her rest was about to be interrupted.

She heard the falcon land on the grass in front of her, and she opened her good eye to look at it.

"Leave me alone, wizard," Slean hissed. "I want to sleep some more."

But Maddoc didn't do as the green dragon requested. Instead, through the falcon, he informed her of how Nearra's encounter with Ugo had turned out—and who had shown up at the last minute to help.

"Raedon," Slean said, snorting twin puffs of chlorine from her nostrils. "He isn't a serious threat. At worst, he's a minor annoyance. I'll take care of him, but later. First I will sleep."

She started to close her eye, but before she could, the wizard sent another telepathic message consisting of a single word.

Vennatherensis: Slean's secret dragon name.

The dragon sighed. "Very well, I shall tend to Raedon now and then fly to the temple and conceal myself in the forest close by. There I shall await further instructions." Slean fixed the falcon with a baleful stare using her one good eye. "But I tell you this, wizard: you had best keep your promise to show me how I can never again be banished from Krynn. If you don't, I'll come visit your keep and bring it crashing down upon your head!"

And with that, Slean spread her wings and launched herself into the air. With slow, powerful strokes of her wings, she flew off in search of Raedon.

The black falcon watched her fly for several moments before taking to the sky itself.

After several hours of traveling through the forest, the companions came to a small creek. On the other side of the creek, the trees appeared to thin.

Raedon stopped. "This is it, little ones. All you have to do now is cross the creek and continue heading northeast. You should have no trouble finding a place that will make a good campsite for the night. Assuming you don't sleep late tomorrow morning, by noon you should reach Heaven's Pass, a trail between two high hills. It's the entrance to the valley that houses the temple. Once you are through the pass, you will have but a short journey to reach the temple itself."

"You're not coming with us?" Nearra said.

Raedon hesitated, as if he wasn't quite sure what he was going to do. But finally he said, "I'm afraid I must go, Nearra." It was the first time he had called any of them something other than *little one*. "I have been away from my lair too long and need to return and check on my treasure. One can't be too careful, you know." He gave Elidor a look. "There are thieves everywhere."

On impulse, Nearra dashed forward and threw her arms around the dragon's scaly neck and hugged him.

"We'll miss you," she said.

Raedon twisted a bit then relaxed into her embrace. Nearra wondered if this was the first time he'd ever been touched by a human.

When she pulled away, Raedon said, "Goodbye, all. I hope the rest of your journey is brief and uneventful." And then he jumped high into the air. Just as he began to drop, he unfurled his wings and flew off to the northwest, toward his lair in the Vingaard Mountains.

"I'm sorry to see him go," Sindri said.

Nearra turned toward the kender, glad that someone besides her was going to miss Raedon.

"Now I'll never get to hear the end of that joke," Sindri said.

"If it's a joke you want," Elidor said, "I have one for you. How many kender does it take to wield a hoopak staff?"

"I've heard that one before," Sindri said, scowling. "And you'd better not finish it!"

"But I thought you didn't like leaving jokes unfinished," Elidor said, smiling innocently.

"I do when the joke is as insulting as that one!"

The elf ignored the kender. "The answer is three: one to hold the staff, one to annoy everyone in the vicinity, and a third to steal everything he can lay his hands on."

"I told you not to finish it!" Sindri ran at the elf, but Elidor jumped gracefully over the creek. Sindri splashed through the water after him, and Elidor fled, laughing all the way, with Sindri in hot pursuit.

"When I catch you, elf, I'll turn you into a toad with pointed ears!" Sindri shouted.

Catriona followed, smiling and shaking her head. Nearra was surprised to hear the normally humorless Jax chuckle.

Davyn gave Nearra a smile. "Come on. We'd better catch up to Sindri and Elidor before they get too far ahead of us."

Davyn and Nearra easily stepped over the small creek and headed after the others, but not before Nearra gave one last glance up at the sky to see if she could still see Raedon. She watched as the dragon became nothing more than a copper-colored speck in the distance, then she turned and followed her companions.

Raedon loved the feeling of wind beneath his wings. Though he was a creature of both land and sky, he felt more at home in the air than anywhere else.

He felt a bit guilty about leaving the little ones—especially Nearra. He sensed a strange sort of bond with her that he couldn't explain. It was almost as if he wouldn't have been able to leave the little ones if she hadn't let him.

Some dragons—both chromatic and metallic—seemed to have a special attraction to humans. Perhaps he was one of those dragons. If so, it was a quality he had been unaware of in himself. But then he was young as dragons went. It only made sense that he would learn new things about himself as he matured.

Raedon had only told the little ones the partial truth about why he was so anxious to check on his lair. Since all dragons used magic to one degree or another, they often collected mystic items for their hoards along with more mundane treasure. Wizards and thieves were known to risk entering a dragon's lair in hope of finding and taking such magic objects.

Raedon was worried that once Ugo had shaken off the effects of the slow gas, the ogre would tell Maddoc how a copper dragon had come to the aid of the little ones. Once Maddoc was aware of Raedon's existence, the dragon feared the mage would seek out his lair in order to steal the few magical items he'd managed to gather so far.

From what the little ones said, it sounded as if Maddoc might not be a white-robed wizard after all. And if this was the case, Raedon couldn't allow his magic items to fall into the wizard's hands.

And so, though he normally took his time when he flew—the better to spot little ones on the ground to play with—he poured on the speed, flying as fast as he could toward his mountain home. But he'd only flown a couple miles when he became aware of another presence in the sky.

Instinct took over and Raedon banked sharply to the right. He saw a flash of green out of the corner of his eye. Then he was buffeted by a blast of wind as something large dove past him, nearly slamming into his wing. He understood at once what was happening.

It was Slean.

All dragons that inhabit a given area are at least acquainted with one another, and he knew that Slean—though roughly the same age as he—was larger and extremely vicious. She was also a highly skilled flyer, and he knew that he couldn't hope to best her in aerial combat. And as a green dragon, she was immune to slow gas, Raedon's most powerful weapon. Since Raedon was smaller and more agile, his best move would be to land and draw her into the forest, where he could—

"Raedon!" Slean's voice rumbled across the sky like thunder. "I do not wish to fight! I only want to talk!"

Raedon turned in the direction of her voice. Slean flew in a circle a dozen yards above him. One of her eyes was squinted closed from a recent wound.

"Is that why you tried to knock me out of the sky?" he said. "Because you want to talk?"

Slean laughed. "I was merely saying hello."

Raedon also began circling, but he didn't fly any closer to the green dragon. He knew better.

"Assuming I believe you—which I don't—what do you want?"

"To deliver a friendly warning. Today you interfered with matters that do not concern you. Do not do so again."

Raedon felt a chill ripple down his spine, but he tried to keep the fear out of his voice. "How do you know, and more to the point, why do you care?"

"Why do *you* care that *I* care?" Slean said in a mocking tone, and then faster than Raedon could react, the green dragon angled downward, flapped her wings, and came streaking toward him.

Raedon thought she intended to crash into him, and as fast as she was moving, there was no way he could avoid a collision. But at the last instant she veered off and Raedon felt a wave of relief.

Just another of her "warnings," Raedon thought.

But as Slean passed him, her claws lashed out. Raedon barely managed to dodge to the side in time to avoid having his right wing shredded.

"I thought you said you just wanted to talk!" Raedon shouted.

Slean turned and soared upward. She flashed him a grin as she passed by.

"I lied."

Raedon could see no advantage in staying to confront Slean, so he did what any other being in his situation would do—he turned and fled.

Slean roared in fury, and Raedon didn't have to look back to know that she pursued him.

He beat his wings furiously and stretched his head out before him as far as it would go in order to make himself as streamlined as possible. He was smaller than Slean, and therefore faster and more maneuverable—provided that he maintained his lead. If Slean managed to catch up to him . . .

He put on a fresh burst of speed.

Raedon had fled without regard to direction, so he risked a downward glance to check his location. If a human could see from this vantage point, the forest below would look like an unbroken canopy of green. But a dragon's vision is far keener than a human's—or an elf's or a kender's, for that matter. Raedon saw an infinite variety of greens, their shades all merging to form a pattern as easy for him to read as a map. He knew at once where he was: not more than fifteen miles from his lair in the Vingaard Mountains. If he could reach his home before Slean could catch him, he would be able to hide from her in the maze of tunnels. All he had to do was keep flying as fast as he could. Faster, faster . . .

He sensed the ripple in the air at the last instant, far too late to do anything more than realize his mistake. When he'd looked down to get his bearings, he'd slowed just a little. But a little was all Slean needed.

A streak of green shot past him and Raedon felt a searing pain in his wing. Slean's claws had found their mark this time. He wobbled, unable to maintain control of his flight with an injured wing, and he tumbled toward the ground, Slean's mocking laughter following him all the way down.

CHAPTER 20 — AMBUSH AT HEAVEN'S PASS

True to Raedon's word, the companions approached Heaven's Pass almost precisely at noon.

After they'd crossed the creek, they'd emerged from the forest and made camp for the night. The next morning, they had set out through the rolling fields of grassland. Within a few hours, they'd found the trail Raedon had called Heaven's Pass, a narrow depression between two high hills.

The companions stopped and considered the trail ahead of them.

"Looks cramped," Elidor said. "Barely room enough for two of us to walk through shoulder to shoulder." He glanced at Sindri. "Or in the case of our kender friend, shoulder to kneecap."

"Very funny," Sindri said. "Well, what are we waiting for? Let's go!"

The kender started running toward the pass, but Jax grabbed him by the arm and lifted him off the ground.

"Hold a moment, small one," the minotaur rumbled. "We might wish to take a different route."

Sindri kicked his legs in the air, looking like an impatient child.

"Why?" he demanded. "Raedon told us to go through the pass.

That means it's safe. Probably boring, too." Sindri muttered this last comment in a tone that indicated boredom was the worst fate imaginable.

But despite his protests, Sindri stopped thrashing his legs. Jax lowered him to the ground, but the minotaur didn't let go of the kender's arm.

"Jax is right," Catriona said. "Considering everything Maddoc has done so far, we can't afford to assume that anything is safe."

Sindri made a face as if he'd just tasted something bitter, but he nodded and Jax released his arm.

Nearra wouldn't have been surprised if the kender had made a dash for the pass anyway, and indeed, Sindri did look longingly at it, but he remained standing where he was.

"Could we climb over the hills?" Sindri asked. "That might be fun!"

Davyn regarded them for a moment. "I suppose. But we have no way of knowing how steep they are on the other side, and we didn't bring any climbing gear with us."

"Besides, there's a reason they call it a pass," Elidor said. "It's usually the only way through."

"Maybe we could go around them," Catriona said.

"Who knows how long that would take?" Davyn said. "It's hard to say if we'd find another way down into the valley no matter which way we went. As Elidor said, there's a reason it's called a pass."

"And Raedon can fly," Nearra said. "He's probably flown over the valley and knows which way is best for us to go."

"I guess we could always . . . " Davyn trailed off and looked up at the sky.

Nearra followed his gaze and saw that he was watching a black falcon circling high above them.

"We have to leave," Davyn said. "Now!"

Nearra and the others looked at him as if he'd suddenly gone crazy.

TIM WAGGONER

"What are you talking about?" Elidor said.

"I don't have time to explain!" Davyn grabbed Nearra's hand and started to pull her away from the pass, but she hesitated. After Davyn had admitted that he'd lied to them, she'd found herself second-guessing everything he said. She knew she should trust him, but she just couldn't—

A chorus of battle cries cut through the air, and a horde of goblins poured over the tops of the two hills.

"Ambush!" Jax shouted. He grabbed hold of his battle-axe and charged forward to meet the onrushing goblins.

"Wait!" Davyn shouted. "There are too many of them! We should run!"

If Jax heard the ranger, the minotaur chose not to reply. He raced toward the northern hill and began running up the slope.

These goblins were dressed and armed similarly to the ones they'd fought in the forest, but here were ten times more of them—at least. Fear surged through Nearra, and now it was she who attempted to pull Davyn away.

"Come on!" she shouted.

"No!" Catriona said as she drew her sword. "Into the pass! It's so narrow that they'll only be able to come at us one or two at a time!"

"We'll be trapped in there!" Elidor said. A pair of throwing knives had appeared in the elf's hands, and he twirled them nervously. "We won't have enough room to maneuver, and the goblins will overrun us by sheer numbers!"

They all looked at Sindri, but the kender just shrugged. "I'd kind of like to stay here and watch the battle."

They didn't have any time left to decide, Nearra thought. The goblins were already three quarters of the way down the hillside. Suddenly, more battle cries erupted behind them, and they turned to see another force of goblins coming at them from the rear.

Now they had no choice. It was the pass or certain death.

As they ran, Catriona shouted, "I'll take the lead! Sindri, you and Nearra come next. Davyn and Elidor can bring up the rear!"

Davyn looked as if he was going to object, but then he nodded and let go of Nearra's hand. As Catriona ran ahead of the others, Sindri reached up to take Nearra's hand, and the companions continued running as fast as they could toward the entrance to the pass.

"What about Jax?" Nearra shouted. She glanced up to see that the minotaur was engaged in battling a group of goblins on the hillside. But a number of the red-skinned creatures had detoured around him and were running down the hill toward her friends. And there was nothing to slow the progress of the goblins racing down the southern hillside, not to mention the goblins coming at them from behind.

"Jax can take care of himself!" Catriona said. "With any luck, he'll join us on the other side of the pass as soon as he can!"

Catriona's words failed to comfort Nearra. Yes, Jax was a skilled warrior, but even the mightiest couldn't defeat an entire army single-handedly, regardless of what occurred in the tall tales bards told. She feared they were abandoning the minotaur to his doom.

But then they plunged into the pass, and Nearra had no more time to worry about Jax. Though it was midday, and the sun shone high overhead, the sunlight failed to penetrate into the pass, and they were instantly shrouded in shadow. The walls were bare earth. The ground was steep and uneven. It was almost impossible to run. The best they could manage was a fast walk.

Rather than feeling safer inside the pass, Nearra felt more vulnerable. The walls were so close. It felt as if they were closing in on her.

"This reminds me of a story I heard once," Sindri said cheerfully. "About a band of heroes who were traveling through a mountain pass much like this one when a demon-mage cast a spell to make the mountains slam together and splat! No more heroes!"

Nearra felt her stomach churn and she thought she might throw up.

"Please, Sindri—not now."

It was difficult to see very far in the gloom, so Nearra more sensed than saw something fall in front of her face. Then she felt a tightening around her midsection, and the next thing she knew, she was yanked off her feet. Her hand tore free from Sindri's as she was wrenched upward.

"Nearra!" Sindri cried. He jumped up to grab hold of her dangling feet. But it was too late. She was already six feet off the ground and moving fast.

The rope around her dug painfully into her armpits. "Help!" she screamed. Someone had lassoed her. She'd been caught like an animal, and whoever had captured her was pulling her up to the top of one of the hills.

"Nearra!"

Davyn heard Sindri shout. He watched as the kender leaped and tried to catch hold of her as she was pulled upward, but he missed.

"Stop running!" Sindri called. "They've captured Nearra!"

The others stopped and they all looked upward. It was hard to see in the shadows, but Davyn could just make out Nearra's rapidly dwindling form.

"Someone lowered a rope and caught her," Elidor said. "I can't see who it is, though."

"Can you cut the rope with one of your knives?" Davyn asked. He knew exactly who had captured Nearra. It was Maddoc, or rather, the wizard's agents.

"I could. The shadows are no problem for my eyes, but if I did, Nearra would have a long fall ahead of her. And none of us are strong enough to catch her."

Davyn knew that Jax might be strong enough, but the minotaur wasn't here. He looked down at the silver ring upon his finger. He could try to use telekinesis to lower her safely, but he wasn't confident that he could catch her using the ring's magic before she struck the ground.

Davyn hesitated a moment, but that was all it took.

"I can't see her anymore," Elidor said. "They've pulled her up and over the edge."

Davyn knew that elves possessed far greater dexterity than humans. "Elidor, can you climb up after her?"

Elidor considered for a moment. "I can try." He jabbed one of his knives into the earthen wall before him. It sank halfway to the hilt and held firm.

"This is going to ruin my knives." Elidor pulled the blade free, reached up as high as he could, and plunged it into the wall again. He hoisted himself up, then reached with his other hand and stabbed the second blade into the earth.

"So what are we supposed to do while Elidor has all the fun?" Sindri asked.

As if in response, a spear thunked into the ground not two feet from where the kender stood.

"Try to keep from making ourselves more of a target than we already are!" Catriona flattened herself against the wall, and Davyn and Sindri did the same as spear after spear rained down upon them.

Ugo grinned as he lifted Nearra up to his face, as if he were a fisherman inspecting his catch.

"Ugo do good!" The ogre licked his lips. He looked as if he were trying to decide whether to eat her now or eat her later.

"Yes, you did. Just remember that she belongs to Maddoc."

Nearra looked down and instantly recognized Oddvar standing next to Ugo, his hood pulled over his head to protect him from the sunlight. She shuddered. Nearra feared the Theiwar as much, if not more, than the ogre because Oddvar worked for Maddoc. Standing behind the dark dwarf and grinning with mouthfuls of sharp teeth were the three goblins that had chased Nearra after she had awakened on the forest path.

Oddvar cupped his hands to his mouth and shouted. "We've got her! Seal off the pass!"

Nearra felt a stab of horror upon hearing Oddvar's command. "You can't do that!"

The Theiwar grinned from within the shadows of his hood. "Of course we can. My large friend here helped us loosen the ground on both hills just above the entrance and exit to the pass. It won't take much to start a pair of avalanches."

Nearra glanced back and forth. Four groups of goblins had jammed spears into the ground on both ends of the hills. As she watched, they pried and pushed and dug until the soil began to tear free and slide down into the pass. Nearra could hear chunks of dirt falling, knocking rocks loose from the walls of the pass as it fell. She prayed that none of her friends were standing underneath either of the goblin-made avalanches.

"Your friends are trapped," Oddvar said. "And don't think that the minotaur will be coming to your rescue any time soon. He has several hundred goblins to deal with at the moment."

Nearra's hopes fell. That's exactly what she had been thinking. She knew she had only one defense; she'd have to try to control the strange power that dwelled within her if she was to have any chance of escaping and aiding her friends. The tingling sensation always seemed to come over her when she was in danger and afraid—and both were certainly the case right now.

"Lower the girl down to me," Oddvar commanded Ugo. The ogre instantly let the rope slack and Nearra fell to the ground. She landed awkwardly on her ankle and the pain shot up through her leg. But she didn't wince.

Nearra willed her hands to start tingling. Come on, she thought.

The Theiwar reached into his tunic and brought out a small bottle and a handkerchief.

"What are you going to do with me?" She felt the first faint sensation of warmth and tingling in her fingers. Just a few moments more . . .

Oddvar uncorked the stopper and poured a small amount of noxious-smelling liquid onto the handkerchief. "This is just a little something to make you sleep so you don't cause us any trouble as we travel."

The warm tingling was growing more intense. "Travel where?"

In answer, the dark dwarf grabbed the back of Nearra's head and pressed the handkerchief against her face. Nearra struggled then tried to hold her breath. She kicked at Oddvar, but it felt as if her foot connected with solid rock.

She could only hold her breath for so long, especially after the exertion of thrashing and kicking, and at last she took in a breath of air, inhaling the foul stench of the chemical that soaked the handkerchief. Her nose and throat burned and her eyes watered. She coughed once, twice, and then she began to feel numb all over, as if she were floating free in space. She grew drowsy, and though she fought her hardest to stay awake, it was a losing battle.

The tingling sensation diminished until it was gone.

"Don't worry about your companions." Oddvar's voice sounded like a faint echo coming from somewhere far off in the distance. "While goblins aren't the most skilled archers on Krynn, they do all right with spears. Once we leave, Drefan, Gifre, and Fyren are going to lead the others in a little target practice—with your friends' help, of course."

Nearra could no longer keep her eyes open. The last thing she heard was the Theiwar's cruel laughter following her down into darkness.

Jax hacked away at one goblin after another. Although he was loath to admit it to himself, he was beginning to tire. Even foes as weak and pathetic as goblins could take their toll on a warrior if there were enough of them.

The minotaur had caught a glimpse of the others running for the pass, but rather than resenting them for abandoning him, Jax approved. Their goal was to help Nearra reach the Temple of the Holy Orders of the Stars, and it was a goal he had made his own. If he had to sacrifice his life to protect her from these goblins, then so be it. His honor would be satisfied with nothing less.

Jax had managed to fight his way almost to the top of the hill when he saw the huge form of Ugo standing over the narrow gap that formed the pass between the two hills. As surprised as the minotaur was to see the ogre here, he was even more surprised to see the man-beast holding Nearra. The girl dangled from a rope that the ogre held, and a small cloaked figure looked to be addressing Nearra. While Jax couldn't see the cloaked being's features, he felt sure that this was the Theiwar of which the others had spoken. It seemed the wizard Maddoc had struck again.

Jax bellowed a war cry and fought with increased ferocity. He needed to reach Nearra before anything happened to her. But although goblins fell before his axe like blades of grass, he made slow progress. As he fought, he could only watch as goblins thrust spears into the earth at both ends of the pass and forced loose a shower of soil and rock, sealing off the pass. His friends were trapped.

Jax looked back toward Nearra just in time to see her lying slack in the dwarf's arms. The dwarf gestured toward the ogre and the great brute slung the unconscious girl over his shoulder. Then he followed the Theiwar north along the top of the ridge.

"Stop, cowards!" Jax shouted. "Stay and fight!" But if the dark dwarf or the ogre heard him, they didn't look back.

As if obeying an unspoken order, half the goblin force broke off the attack and began streaming after the Theiwar and the ogre, no doubt to help escort their prisoner to wherever it was they were taking her. A trio of goblins garbed in black tunics appeared over the ridge, one of them covered with bandages around his arm and leg. The largest one shouted out a command to the remaining half of the goblin army and a number of them began hurling spears down at Jax's trapped companions.

Jax was no longer concerned for his own safety. He ran for the top of the ridge ignoring the goblins who swiped at him with short swords, hand-axes, and flails. He took a dozen different wounds as he ran, but he ignored the pain and kept going.

As he gained the top of the northern hill, he ran along the gap, cutting down spear-wielding goblins as he went. Bellowing in fury, bleeding from numerous wounds, he did not slow as he wielded his axe like some sort of bull-headed demon. So fearsome was the minotaur that the rest of the goblins shrieked in terror, dropped their spears, and begin fleeing after the Theiwar and the ogre. The trio of goblins in black tunics looked around at their retreating brethren, considered for a moment, and then turned and ran after them, the wounded one hobbling as fast as he was able.

Jax wanted to give chase, but exhaustion was catching up with him. Besides, his friends were still trapped in the pass, perhaps wounded themselves. He couldn't leave them.

The minotaur was about to peer over the edge of the gap to see if he could spot his companions when Elidor's head appeared. The elf looked around, saw the retreating goblins heading north along the ridge, then grinned up at Jax.

"Looks like you've been busy."

Using broken lengths of goblin spears, the trapped companions were able to fashion climbing pegs that they fit into the holes made by Elidor's knives. Before long, Davyn, Catriona, and Sindri stood on the ridge along with Jax, Elidor, and quite a few dead goblins. Luckily, the three that had been trapped in the pass had suffered no major wounds, though Davyn had a cut on the back of his left hand and Sindri's right leg had been grazed by a spear tip.

Jax told them how Oddvar and Ugo had stolen away with Nearra, accompanied by a force of goblins.

"More of Maddoc's doing," Catriona said, glaring at Davyn. The ranger didn't acknowledge the accusation implied in her glare, though. Instead, he gazed to the west.

Catriona then walked over to Jax. "Let me take a look at your wounds."

"There is no need," the minotaur said stiffly.

"Shut up and stand still," Catriona replied.

Jax scowled, but he did as the warrior said. She looked him over, then pronounced, "You're lucky your hide's so tough. These wounds are mostly superficial, but we should clean and dress them as soon as possible. And don't tell me it's 'not necessary.'"

"Bah," Jax muttered, but he didn't dispute her further.

"Where do you suppose they're taking Nearra?" Sindri asked, his voice full of concern.

Davyn looked at the kender and smiled. Though Sindri's people might not fear for their own safety, it appeared they did fear for the safety of their friends.

"I don't know," Davyn said. "But the goblins didn't bother to conceal their trail. Tracking them will be easy enough." The only question is, thought Davyn, can we find her in time?

21 IN THE DARK, BUT NOT ALONE

The first thing Nearra was aware of in the darkness was a throbbing pain in her head. She tried to open her eyes, but it hurt too much to perform even that small action.

I was . . . drugged, she remembered. *My body must . . . not be working right yet.*

She decided to lie still for a bit and give her body more time to recover.

Seems like I'm always waking up in interesting places. If her head hadn't hurt so much, she might have laughed at the thought.

Nearra brushed her fingers lightly over the ground beneath her and found it cold, hard, and uneven. She was lying on rock. She inhaled slowly and found the air cool, damp, and stale. She finally managed to open her eyes and saw only darkness. She blinked several times, but the darkness that surrounded her remained unbroken.

Paladine above, I've been blinded, she thought. Fear gripped her and she tried to sit up, but the action caused fresh waves of agony to erupt in her skull and she had to lie back down. Her hands began to tingle.

Calm yourself, a voice whispered through the pain in her mind. **153**

A wave of soothing energy washed over Nearra. She felt her fear subside as she relaxed against the cool stone.

The time is not right. Control your anger. Control your fear. If you do not, you will die.

"Who are you? What do you want from me?" Nearra screamed silently. But as quickly as it had come, the voice was gone.

The throbbing in her head began to subside a bit, and Nearra decided to risk sitting up again. She moved slowly and gently, and this time she managed to sit up and remain that way. She realized she must be in some sort of cavern.

Was the dark dwarf going to leave her here to rot? Maybe someone would find her. Her friends would surely be looking for her.

Then she remembered the goblins. Her heart sank. Had her friends made it through the pass alive? They had done so much to help her and now—

She pictured Davyn stabbed with dozens of goblin spears. Tears welled in the corners of her eyes.

No! She swiped the tears away with her thumb. Whoever or whatever that voice was, she knew it was right. She was through being a victim. There was no one here to protect her. She would just have to protect herself. Whatever Maddoc wanted from her, she wasn't going to let him have it. She had to find a way out. Now.

She sat for a time, trying to decide what to do. It was obvious she was shut into some kind of cave. Waiting here for someone to get her was out of the question. She could stand and try to walk, assuming her head had cleared enough to allow it. But in this kind of darkness, she couldn't walk about safely without a light of some sort to guide her. What if she came to a drop-off and fell?

She felt a flash of fear at the thought, but she immediately suppressed it. All right then. If she couldn't stay here and she couldn't walk, then she'd just have to crawl. That way, she could move slowly and feel her way as she went. That decided, she had only to choose a direction. She had no way of telling which direction she could go in this darkness, though, and the idea of choosing a direction at random didn't appeal to her. She had no idea how much time she had before Maddoc or one of his agents decided to take a more direct—and potentially deadly—approach. But how could she determine which direction to try when she couldn't use her eyes?

Then it came to her: sight was only one of the senses she possessed. She had four others. Maybe if she made a noise, she could learn something about the shape and size of the cavern from the way the sound echoed. At least it was worth a try.

She opened her mouth and in a normal tone of voice said, "Hello."

The word immediately began echoing all around her.

Instead of growing softer and dying out the way echoes usually did, the sound increased in volume and continued to do so as it bounced around the cavern.

HELLO-HELLO-HELLO-HELLO-HELLO-HELLO-HELLO!

Nearra covered her ears and tried to shut the sound out, but it was no use. She could feel the simple word she'd spoken vibrating through the flesh and bone in her hands and penetrating deep in her skull. The sensation soon became painful, far worse than the throbbing in her head. It felt as if two red-hot pokers were being thrust into her ears.

Finally, Nearra couldn't take it anymore and she screamed.

And as the cavern's acoustics picked up and magnified her scream a thousandfold, her pain truly began in earnest.

In a nearby tunnel, Oddvar and the three goblins stood listening to the echo of Nearra's screams.

"How long are we supposed to leave her in there?" Fyren asked, covering his ears. It was clear from his voice that the sound was causing the goblin pain.

Truth to tell, the sound disturbed Oddvar as well, though he'd never admit it to these three morons. "As long as it takes." The Theiwar didn't add that he hoped it wouldn't take very long.

"We've been following the goblins' trail for nearly two days, and this is where it ends?" Elidor said. "A small hillock surrounded by a growth of thorns?"

"You should have spent more time among the Kagonesti," Davyn said. "Maybe then you'd notice that, unlike the others, the ones in front of us aren't alive. They're brown and dry."

Elidor stepped forward to examine the thorn bushes, then turned to Davyn. "So they're dead thorns. What's your point?"

Though the sun was still up, dusk wasn't far off. Davyn had never been to this part of Solamnia, but from what he'd heard about the creatures that lived here, he knew they didn't want to be out in the open when the sun set.

Jax took a turn examining the thorns. "They are camouflage."

Davyn nodded. "That would be my guess. Unless the goblins have somehow learned to disappear into thin air."

Sindri's eyes widened in wonder. "Do you think they have? I wonder if I can get one of them to teach me how. I've already mastered conjuring and levitating. I'd so love to add disappearing to my magical repertoire."

Elidor looked at Sindri for a moment before finally shaking his head. "I won't say it—it's too easy."

Davyn choked back a laugh as Sindri shot Elidor a dirty look. But the ranger's amusement soon died away. They were here for one reason: to rescue Nearra. It had been two days since Oddvar, Ugo, and the goblins had taken her. Who knew what they might have done to her in that time? Or whether she was even still—

No, Davyn told himself. Don't even think that.

Catriona drew her sword. "Let's get to work. Once we cut away the thorns, we'll be able to see what they're hiding."

But before the warrior could take a swing at the thorns,

Davyn said, "Wait a moment." He stepped forward, unslung his bow, and used it to prod the thorns. His suspicions confirmed, he hooked the bow around a branch of thorns and began tugging backward. The bush moved easily; in fact, it wasn't a bush at all, but rather a collection of branches woven together to resemble one.

Catriona used her sword to help Davyn drag the camouflage. When they'd pulled it far enough away, Elidor walked up and peered closely at the section of hillock the thorns had been concealing. He cautiously touched his fingers to the surface of the mound—mostly bare earth covered with patches of scrub grass. The elf moved his hands so lightly over the mound that it seemed he didn't so much as disturb a single blade of grass.

He turned to the others and grinned. "There's a door here."

Davyn let out a sigh of relief.

"It's locked, I suppose," Sindri said.

"Of course," Elidor replied.

"And trapped as well," Catriona added.

Elidor grinned even wider. "I certainly hope so. Otherwise, breaking in won't be nearly as much fun."

"Can you open it?" Davyn asked.

Elidor gave the ranger a look as if the question was the gravest of insults. "Of course. But that's not our major concern. If the goblins have guards posted on the other side of the door, no matter how quietly I open it, they'll be alerted to our presence."

"You worry about the door," Catriona said, flourishing her sword. "We'll take care of any goblins."

Elidor nodded and eagerly returned his attention to the hidden door. The elf's fingers danced over the surface, touching here, poking there, pushing, prodding, and tapping in what appeared to be a random pattern. Davyn was beginning to wonder if Elidor had lied to them about being able to open the door—after all, weren't thieves supposed to use lock picks and similar tools?

Finally there was a soft *snik!* and a round section of the hillock swung inward.

They waited several moments, weapons drawn and ready, but no guards came running out of the open doorway.

"I guess the goblins didn't post any guards." Sindri sounded almost disappointed.

"With this kind of locking mechanism on the entrance, they probably don't see any need for guards," Elidor said. "It's a pressure lock. Different switches on the door must be pressed in a specific order. Quite sophisticated, really. I'm surprised to find such a complex device being used for a goblin lair."

Catriona peered at the open doorway. "It doesn't seem large enough for Ugo to go through."

"The ogre could pass through if he crawled," Jax said. "Though even then it would be a tight fit."

"Maybe the ogre left after he delivered Nearra," Sindri said.

"Let's hope," Catriona said. "It'll be difficult enough fighting an army of goblins within their own stronghold without having to face Ugo again."

"I hope it won't come to that," Davyn said. "Not if we're quiet and careful."

Jax snorted. "It is not the way of my people to slink around in the dark like vermin."

"What do you suggest?" Elidor asked. "That we shout for the goblins to emerge and return Nearra to us?"

"Yes." The minotaur sounded as if this were the only logical course of action.

"Our goal is to rescue Nearra," Davyn said. "Not slay goblins. If we can find where they're holding her and escape without attracting the goblins' attention, so much the better."

Jax scowled, but he said nothing more.

Davyn turned to Elidor. "Any traps to worry about?"

In response, Elidor turned to Sindri. "Have you happened to conjure anything small lately, such as a stone or perhaps a piece of fruit?"

Sindri rummaged through his cape pockets for several moments before finally bringing forth a handful of walnuts. "Will these do?"

"Perfectly." Elidor took three and Sindri put the rest back. The elf thief then walked back to the entrance of the goblin stronghold and tossed the walnuts onto the ground. Sharp wooden stakes shot forth from the floor, walls, and ceiling of the entrance. The tips of the stakes were coated with a greasy, foul-smelling substance. Undoubtedly, it was poison.

Elidor turned and grinned at Davyn. "To answer your question: not anymore."

"How are we supposed to get through now?" Catriona asked. The stakes filled the entranceway, save for a small round space barely large enough for a kender to fit through.

"Very carefully," Elidor said. He then backed up and ran toward the ring of poisoned stakes. Before anyone could stop him, he dove through the space in the middle, hit the ground, and rolled gracefully into a standing position. He turned around to face his companions and executed a graceful bow.

"Ta-dah!" he said.

Sindri clapped. "That was great! Now it's my turn!"

But before the kender could take a step, Catriona moved in front of him and blocked the way.

"Oh no you don't! I haven't kept you alive as long as I have just to watch you die from attempting a somersault."

"I don't think somersault is the right word," Sindri said. "I mean, you have to dive through the ring before—"

"There's no need for the rest of you to resort to acrobatics." Elidor walked farther into the tunnel, his hands moving as quickly as spiders over the walls. "Ah! Here it is." He pressed his palm against a certain section of the wall, and the ring of stakes began to slowly retract. A moment later, they disappeared into the earth.

"The trap's been reset," Elidor said. "It's safe to enter—provided you don't step where the stakes emerged."

The remaining companions entered the tunnel. Jax went last, turning behind him to carefully drag the thorn camouflage back into place, using only his bare hands. His hide was so tough that not a single thorn pierced his skin.

"What about the door?" Davyn asked as they joined Elidor.

"It's simple to open and close from this side. All you have to do is push."

Jax started to push the door closed, but Davyn said, "Hold a moment." He removed a lantern from his pack, then used his flint and striker to light the wick. "Should I unhood the lantern?"

"No," Elidor said. "I should have no trouble leading you all in the dark. A light would simply announce our presence to our enemies."

Davyn nodded and pulled shut the thin metal door that cut off the lantern's light, leaving it lit, just in case.

Jax then pushed the door shut easily, sealing it tight and plunging them into total darkness.

"I suggest we keep our weapons drawn and ready," Catriona said, her voice sounding both louder and muffled at the same time. "We are in an enemy stronghold, after all."

It was a sensible precaution, but Davyn thought he detected a slight quaver in Catriona's voice. Was the warrior afraid of the dark?

"Let me carry the lantern," Sindri said. "That way, you can keep your bow strung with an arrow ready to fire."

Another sensible suggestion, but Davyn wasn't sure whether he could trust Sindri with the lantern. He imagined the kender opening the hood out of curiosity and releasing a beam of light just as a squadron of goblins came tromping around a corner.

Sindri sighed. "I promise not to play with it, all right?"

Davyn hesitated a moment more before finally holding out the lantern for Sindri to take. He couldn't see the kender, nor could he hear his footfalls. But the lantern left his hand so gently that Davyn began to wonder if Sindri really did possess levitation magic.

Then the kender's voice came from directly in front of him. "I have it, Davyn."

"Good." Davyn then strung his bow, removed an arrow from his quiver, and nocked it. He didn't need light to perform this maneuver. The action was as natural to him as breathing.

"Stay close to each other," Elidor advised. "And try to keep a free hand on the wall to guide you. If you need to stop for any reason, tell the rest of us. It's too easy to get lost in the dark, and I'll be too busy watching the way ahead of us to keep tabs on the rest of you. And from now on, don't speak unless it's absolutely necessary—"

"That means you, Sindri!" Catriona said.

"Even the smallest of sounds can travel far underground," Elidor finished.

For a moment, Davyn reconsidered allowing the elf to lead. He'd lied to them about knowing the way to the temple, and he was a thief. How could they trust him?

But you've lied to them, too, Davyn thought. And far worse than Elidor ever did. If there's anyone in this group who doesn't deserve to be trusted, it's you.

He was surprised at how painful this thought was to him.

"Everyone ready?" Elidor whispered.

There came a chorus of whispered agreement.

"Then let's go."

CHAPTER

22 UNDERFELL

Darkness surrounded them like a shadowy cocoon. Davyn felt as if he were lost, cut off from the real world and stranded in some strange dimension. He felt the uneven stone floor of the tunnel beneath his boots, and he breathed stale air that had been trapped too long underground.

The tunnel wound and curved as it continued to angle downward, deeper and deeper into the earth. After a time, it became wider, and from the feel of it, hard bare rock gave way to smooth carved stone.

We must be getting closer, Davyn thought. He then became aware of a rank odor, one that he'd smelled before, back in the forest. It was goblin-stink.

They continued downward for a bit longer, and then Davyn realized he could see again. He couldn't make out much, just the shadowy outlines of the others, but it was enough to tell him that they were approaching a light source of some kind. And down here, where there was light, there would be goblins.

"This is a lucky break," Elidor whispered. "You can extinguish the lantern now, Sindri. I don't think we're going to need it."

"Why?" Davyn asked. But before Elidor could respond, Sindri closed the tiny shutter on top of the lantern to cut off its air 163 supply. The fire inside soon would die out.

"It appears the goblins have their own manner of light source," Elidor said. "Let's see if I can . . . got one!"

Elidor turned to the others and held out his hand. Caught between his thumb and forefinger was a small beetle. It looked ordinary enough, except that its shell emitted a faint glowing light.

"There are only a few of these insects in this portion of the tunnel," Elidor said. "I imagine they will become more numerous as we continue." He placed the beetle back on the wall and it scuttled off.

"How marvelous!" Sindri said. "I wonder if these glitter-beetles are natural or the result of some sort of spell?"

The latter, Davyn guessed. These insects looked like some magical combination of cave beetle and firefly.

"We shall need to be even more cautious now," Jax said. "If we can see the goblins, then they in turn will be able to see us."

They continued downward, more slowly than before, weapons held at the ready. The number of glitter-beetles increased, as did the light, until all the companions could see without any trouble, though the tunnel remained shadowy and the insects' light painted everything in eerie hues of bluish-white. They could now see that the tunnel opened into a larger chamber. They crept quietly up to the edge of the doorway and peered in.

The chamber was in actuality a gigantic cavern, so high and wide that the ceiling and walls weren't visible. On the cavern floor was a haphazard conglomeration of stone structures: towers tilting at all angles, if not broken off altogether; buildings that leaned on their sides, as if they'd been frozen in the process of sliding into the earth; fragmented arches; scattered blocks of stone. Swarming over it all were uncountable numbers of glitter-beetles.

"What is this place?" Jax whispered. "Have we descended to some realm of demons?"

"Not unless goblins count as demons," Catriona said. She

pointed toward a partially collapsed building, in front of which a group of goblins were playing some sort of game. They were laughing as they kicked a ball back and—

No, Davyn realized with sudden nausea. It wasn't a ball they were kicking; it was a head. A hand of ice gripped his heart. Please, don't let it be hers, he prayed.

Davyn turned to Elidor. The elf's eyesight was far better than his. "Is it . . ."

"It's one of their own kind," Elidor said.

To make matters worse, Ugo sat close by, watching the grisly game, laughing and clapping for the players. Davyn had hoped the ogre would prove too large to travel through the tunnels, but he obviously wasn't.

"I imagine that this was once a surface city," Elidor said. "And after the Cataclysm, it ended up down here, still partially intact."

"It must have been a mighty city indeed to withstand the Cataclysm as well as it did," Jax said.

"I wonder what it was called?" Sindri said.

Elidor shrugged. "None of us are scholars, but even if we were, it's quite possible that there are no longer any records that exist of this place. Perhaps only the gods know its name now."

They fell silent for a moment, as if feeling the weight of antiquity suddenly settle upon them.

"Let's go," Davyn said. "The longer we stay here, the longer we risk getting caught."

"Go where?" Catriona asked. "Can you read tracks on solid rock?"

"No," Davyn admitted. "But we don't need a trail to follow. Not when we have a city full of goblins to question."

Elidor gave Davyn an incredulous look. "You aren't seriously suggesting that we walk up to one of those loathsome creatures and say, 'Pardon me, but would you mind telling us where you're keeping the blond human girl who was abducted two days ago?'"

Davyn laughed. "Not we. Jax."

The minotaur tightened his grip on the haft of his axe and slowly smiled.

The entrance to the chamber was flanked by two large stone columns that rose so high, Davyn couldn't see where they ended. Both columns tilted inward slightly and cracks covered the stones. Large pits, where whole chunks of column had fallen out, met Davyn's gaze at eye level. Davyn had the impression that it wouldn't take much to bring the columns down.

The companions passed between the columns and began to make their way through the underground city. They kept to the shadows and hid behind piles of rubble to avoid being spotted by goblins—and especially by Ugo. Though Davyn knew it was a sensible precaution, he thought they needn't have bothered. The goblins were so preoccupied with drinking, eating, bickering, and fighting that the companions could have walked around in full view and likely gone unnoticed.

"There!" Catriona pointed to a broken statue of an armored warrior missing its head, arms, and legs. The statue rested on its back, and sitting on its chest, guzzling drink from a wineskin, was a lone goblin.

"He'll do," Davyn said. "We need a way to lure him—"

But before Davyn could finish, Jax stalked over to the statue, grabbed the goblin by the neck, and threw him onto the ground. The goblin screeched in outrage, but when he saw who had pulled him off the statue, he began whimpering.

"Please don't hurt me!" The goblin's lips and chin were smeared with wine and his tunic was dotted with stains. He held up the almost empty wineskin. "There's still a bit left, and I'm willing to share. After all, we're one big, happy, mercenary family here in Underfell, eh?"

Elidor frowned. He turned to Davyn and whispered. "Why isn't he raising an alarm?"

TIM WAGGONER

"Probably had too much to drink," Davyn said.

"We have a question to ask you," Jax said. "If you answer truthfully, you can go back to drinking. If not . . ." He gave his axe a shake.

The goblin's eyes widened in terror and he held up his hands in a placating gesture. "Of course, of course! You have only to ask!"

"A Theiwar and an ogre brought a human girl to this place not long ago," Jax said. "Where is she being held?"

The fear didn't leave the goblin's eyes, but now it was joined by suspicion. "Are you new here? I don't remember seeing you five in Underfell before."

"Whether you've seen us or not doesn't matter," Jax growled. "If you don't tell us what we need to know, you won't be seeing anyone ever again!"

The goblin's gaze darted back and forth as he sized up each of the companions. Davyn knew the goblin was trying to decide if they were allies or enemies. If he decided they were the latter, the goblin might get out a warning cry before Jax could silence him. And from the nervous way the goblin kept looking at them, Davyn doubted the creature was going to decide they were allies. But the creature clearly wasn't very bright. Maybe if they just played along.

"Maddoc hired us," Davyn said, trying to put a rough edge into his voice.

"Oh. You must be the mercenaries from the west I heard about." The goblin's eyes narrowed as he glanced at Sindri. "I never would have thought the wizard would hire a kender . . ."

"This kender is a wizard as well," Davyn said. Sindri struck a mystic pose.

The goblin shrank away from Sindri's outstretched arms. "Stay away from me, wizard. What business do you have with the human girl?"

Davyn felt a surge of hope. It wasn't exactly a confirmation that Nearra was being held captive here, but it was a good sign.

Before Davyn could think up another lie, though, Catriona jumped in.

"Maddoc sent word that he wants us to check on the girl. He's thinking of moving her to a different location and wants us to determine if she's fit to travel."

The goblin's eyes narrowed even more. "Why would newcomers such as yourselves be given a task by Maddoc?"

Davyn cursed inwardly. It seemed that the wine hadn't completely dulled the goblin's wits after all.

Sindri walked up, grabbed a fistful of the goblin's tunic, and pulled him forward until their noses were almost touching. "Because he knows better than to trust your kind with any job that actually requires a brain to perform."

The goblin looked at Sindri for a moment, shaking as if the cavern's temperature had suddenly dropped a few dozen degrees. "All right, wizard! I'll tell you!"

Sindri glared at the goblin one last time before letting go of his tunic and stepping back.

Jax snorted, and Davyn guessed the minotaur was unhappy at using subterfuge to gain the goblin's cooperation. To a minotaur, such lying wouldn't be honorable. It was, however, most effective.

"The girl you speak of is being held captive in a place so terrible that we rarely speak of it." The goblin's voice dropped to a fearful whisper. "The Crypt of a Thousand Voices."

23 GETAWAY

S he's been quiet too long."

"Maybe she fell asleep."

"Maybe she's dead."

"You three had better pray that she's still alive. Because if she dies, Maddoc will see to it that you do, too."

"You mean, he'll see to it that we *all* die."

Davyn recognized the voices. The first three belonged to Drefan, Gifre, and Fyren. The fourth was Oddvar's. Though Davyn knew sound could echo in strange ways underground, he thought the Theiwar and the goblins stood just around the next bend in the tunnel. Davyn motioned for the others to stop.

"They must be talking about Nearra," Catriona whispered.

"Then the Crypt of a Thousand Voices must be nearby," Elidor added.

"We have to draw them away from the entrance somehow," Davyn said.

"Well, that's easy enough." Sindri suddenly raised his voice. "Hey, you red-faced cave-rats! We're over here!"

Davyn groaned. That wasn't exactly what he'd had in mind.

"Quick, against the wall!" Davyn ordered, and the companions flattened their bodies against cold stone—all except Sindri. **169**

The kender stood in the middle of the tunnel, oblivious to the sound of goblins charging toward him.

Or maybe he's looking forward to it, Davyn thought. He reached out, grabbed Sindri's arm, and hauled the kender over to the wall with the rest of them.

As the sound of pounding footfalls drew closer, Davyn motioned to Jax. The minotaur nodded and crouched down in a fighting stance, though he did not draw his axe. As Drefan, Gifre, and Fyren came running around the bend, poison-tipped daggers clutched in their hands, Jax swept his arm forward and struck all three goblins in the throat. The goblins crashed to the ground, wheezing as they struggled to breathe.

Oddvar came racing around the bend. But when he saw his three goblin henchmen writhing and gasping on the tunnel floor, he slid to a stop, turned, and tried to run back the way he'd come. Unfortunately for the Theiwar, Jax was faster. The minotaur made a fist and slammed it down on top of the dwarf's head. Oddvar's eyes rolled white and he collapsed to the floor.

Sindri grinned. "See? I told you it would be easy!"

Davyn ignored him. "Let's go find Nearra."

Nearra crouched on her hands and knees, unmoving and silent. She concentrated on taking slow, shallow breaths, and even then the sound echoed back to her as loud as a howling wind. She could hear her own heartbeat pounding loud as a drum. Though it might have been her imagination, she thought she could even hear the blood flowing through her veins like a rushing river.

Stay calm, she told herself. Calm.

Her pulse began to slow and her breathing became ever shallower.

Good . . . that's good.

When she'd first started screaming, the pain of the reflected sound was so intense that she thought she might lose her mind.

But then her common sense had taken over. She was the one making the sound; therefore, she could stop it. And though it had taken some effort, she'd managed to stop screaming long enough for the echoes to fade away. Now she was ready to try and find a way out of this awful place.

She moved her right hand forward the merest inch. The sound of her flesh sliding across the stone floor was amplified to the point where it seemed some large beast slid across the ground on its great leathery belly. She then moved her left hand the same distance, and again the noise was magnified. Still, it wasn't nearly as loud or painful as her screaming had been. She could handle it.

Next she moved her right knee, then her left, and soon she was crawling forward, but slowly, inch by torturous inch. But at least she was moving.

She knew that there was almost no chance that she'd discover a way out going at this speed. She'd most likely succumb to thirst and hunger before she managed to explore more than a fraction of this cave—and that was assuming she didn't crawl around in circles in the dark. But there was nothing else that she *could* do, and almost no chance was better than absolutely none, so she continued to crawl along the cavern floor like Krynn's largest snail. If she were lucky—*very* lucky—she might stumble across a way out. If not, well, at least she would have tried.

She didn't know how long she crawled after that, or for that matter, how far she crawled. Time didn't seem to pass in this place of no sight and far too much sound. After a while, though, she became aware that her mouth and throat were parched, and her stomach was aching to be filled. She felt weak and dizzy, and she wondered how much longer she could keep going on like this. She hadn't even come to a wall yet!

Fear started rising within her and this time, she didn't struggle to hold it back. There was no hope. Her head began to fill with pressure and her skin felt as though it were on fire. That strange power she'd felt so many times was coming back. She knew she should fight against it but she was so very tired.

But then the darkness was broken by a gentle blue glow. As Nearra watched, the glow came closer and closer until she could see the outline of a human form. No, not a human—an elf. It was Elidor, and the blue-white glow came from a number of small insects he held in the palm of his hand.

Nearra was so happy to see Elidor that, without thinking, she opened her mouth to call out his name. But Elidor quickly put a finger to his lips to indicate that she should remain silent, and she nodded.

Elidor then knelt and lowered his hand to the floor. He let the glowing insects crawl off his hand. Nearra heard the sound of their tiny legs on the stone as if it were the pounding of horses' hooves. And then Elidor reached over and gently picked Nearra up and cradled her in his arms.

Elidor stood and began walking, his footfalls making only gentle whssk-whssk-whssk sounds, no louder than the noise a human might make walking through a field of tall grass.

Nearra relaxed in Elidor's arms as he carried her silently through the darkness.

"The goblin we questioned told us how the crypt worked," Davyn whispered. "So Elidor decided to go in to get you. He can move more quietly than the rest of us, and with the way these walls echo, we knew you'd need a quiet escape."

The group crouched in a shadowy alcove, not far from the place where Nearra had been imprisoned. Nearra chewed a mouthful of biscuit given to her by Catriona. She took a drink of water from the warrior's water skin to wash it down, then smiled gratefully at the elf. "And I'm so very glad he did. It was awful in there." She shuddered. "I don't think I'll ever be able to explain just how bad it was, but if you hadn't come to my rescue, I believe I would have eventually gone mad."

Elidor executed a gallant bow. "Think nothing of it, milady. It's all in a day's work for a daring rogue-adventurer such as myself."

Nearra laughed, but as she did, she noticed Davyn scowl and look away. Was Davyn jealous?

Nonsense, she told herself. It was only her imagination.

They'd gagged Oddvar and the three goblins and bound their hands and feet. Catriona had wanted to throw them all into the Crypt of a Thousand Voices, but Nearra wouldn't allow it. The place was so horrible that she wouldn't put the Dark Queen Takhisis herself in there. So they'd left the goblins and Oddvar farther back in the tunnel, where, with luck, they wouldn't be discovered until after the group had departed Underfell.

"We're not out of here yet," Catriona said. "We still need to get past the rest of the goblins—as well as Ugo—and then return to the surface."

"It shouldn't be that hard," Sindri said. "We were able to sneak in, weren't we? We should be able to sneak out the same way."

"There's one difference this time," Davyn said. "Now we have Nearra with us."

"So?" Jax said. "She can pretend to be another mercenary if necessary. Not that I condone such deception," he hastened to add. "But in this situation, it seems to be less distasteful than it might be."

Elidor shook his head. "You refuse to kill Oddvar and the goblins because of your honor—although doing so would have made our escape more certain. But you find the idea of telling a little lie 'distasteful'?"

Jax frowned and his thick bovine lips curled away from his broad, flat teeth. "There is no honor in slaying such pitiful opponents, especially once they are no longer a threat."

"We'd never get away with Nearra posing as a mercenary," Catriona said. "The goblins would recognize her as Oddvar's captive."

"Oh, for Paladine's sake!" Nearra snapped. "We don't have time to stand around and argue. Every moment we stay here increases our risk of capture. I don't know where my pack is—Oddvar must've taken it when I was unconscious—but if one of you would lend me a rain cloak, I'll wear it and keep the hood up to hide my face. That should be enough of a disguise to get me out of here."

The rest of the companions looked at each other.

"Sure," Davyn said. "You can wear mine."

Nearra wondered why they were suddenly looking at her so strangely. Then she understood. Despite the fact that they were her friends, they viewed her as someone who needed help, not someone who could help herself.

Davyn removed the rain cloak from his pack and handed it to Nearra. As she put it on, she thought, just because I lost my memories doesn't mean I've lost the ability to think.

She pulled up the hood of the rain cloak and said, "All right. I'm ready."

Davyn nodded and the six companions continued down the tunnel toward Underfell's main cavern.

Nearra had been unconscious when she'd been brought to Underfell, so she'd never seen the vast cavern and the ruins it held. Despite the danger they were in, it was hard to resist gazing in awe upon the remnants of the ancient city and the millions of glowing insects that illuminated it. But Nearra knew that if she did, she risked drawing the attention of the goblins milling about. So she kept her hood up and continued walking as if she were unimpressed with her surroundings.

They were halfway across the cavern city when their path was suddenly blocked by the hulking figure of Ugo the ogre. The great man-beast sniffed the air several times before looking down at them and grinning.

"Ugo thought he smelled something familiar, but Ugo not

remember what it was. But now Ugo know—it you!" The ogre scowled then and his grin fell away. "Hey, you those brats that hurt Ugo." He looked at Nearra, who was doing her best to try to disappear into the folds of her rain cloak. "You girl Ugo caught for dwarf. What you doing out running around with these others?" A sly look came into his eyes. "Say, you trying to escape, aren't you?"

Jax and Catriona started to reach for their weapons, but Davyn said, "We can't fight—there are hundreds of goblins in Underfell. All we can do is—" Ugo roared and lunged toward Davyn, "—run!"

The companions detoured around the slow-moving ogre. Behind them, Ugo howled in frustration and turned around to give pursuit. Alerted by the ogre's cries, goblins turned away from their drinking and fighting to join in the chase, and soon it seemed that every inhabitant of Underfell was coming after them.

Nearra was breathing hard and sweat poured off her, making her skin feel clammy in the cool cave air. She'd been starved for the last two days, and her body was still suffering from the effects of the chemical Oddvar had used to render her unconscious. Her head began to throb and she felt suddenly weak and dizzy. She stumbled and started to fall, but then Davyn was at her side. He put an arm around her waist to steady her, and together they continued running.

"Stop!" Ugo bellowed. "You not supposed to run away! Wizard be very mad if you don't come back!"

The goblins were shouting now too, though they spoke in their own guttural tongue and Nearra didn't know what they were saying. But she didn't need to speak goblin to know it was probably all variations of "Get the human girl!"

Nearra saw the tunnel entrance ahead of them. It was flanked by two towering stone columns that leaned inward. And then they were past the columns and inside the tunnel. Unable to run any longer, even with Davyn's help, Nearra's legs folded beneath her and she slumped to the ground.

"Get up!" Davyn said as he tried to pull her to a standing position. "We're not in the clear yet!"

"I don't think I can run anymore." Her vision began to go gray, and she feared she was going to faint.

"Let me carry her," Jax said. The minotaur scooped her up in his powerful arms as if she weighed less than a feather. But before they could start running again, there was a loud *whumpf!* The tunnel shook and a shower of rock-dust fell from the ceiling.

Nearra turned her head and saw that Ugo was wedged in the tunnel opening between the two columns. The ogre grunted in frustration as he struggled to free himself.

"Ugo forgot to get down and crawl like dwarf showed him. Now Ugo stuck!"

"Come on!" Catriona shouted. "We have to reach the surface before the ogre gets free!"

"If he does free himself, then we'll have both him and several hundred goblins pursuing us!" Elidor said.

"What's wrong with you, Ugo?" Sindri called out. There was a harsh, mocking edge to the voice of the normally sweet-natured kender. "I can't believe an ogre as strong as you would let something as insignificant as a pair of stone columns stop him. I've heard it said that ogres are as stupid as they are strong, but now I know that ogres are way stupider than that!"

The ogre growled and pushed harder. The columns trembled slightly, but that was all.

"Oh, come on!" Sindri said. "Is that the best you can do? Those columns are so old that my arthritic grandmother could shove them aside without breaking a sweat!"

Ugo shrieked in frustration and rammed his body into the columns. They trembled once again, and this time the cracks on the ancient stone widened and began to spread. Bits of rock fell from the tunnel ceiling.

"Let's move!" Davyn shouted.

Catriona grabbed Sindri's hand and the six of them started

running once more. As they ran, Sindri fired off a last parting shot.

"An imp could do more damage to those columns than you!"

Ugo screamed in rage and threw himself against the columns with all his might. The tunnel filled with a loud cracking noise.

"Uh-oh," Ugo said.

And then the columns—and all the rock and soil they had held up for so many centuries—came falling down upon Ugo's head, burying the ogre and sealing off the entrance to Underfell.

Nearra sighed in relief. They were safe, thanks to Sindri's taunting. She started to thank the kender, but weariness finally caught up with her and she fell asleep in Jax's arms as the minotaur, along with the others, continued running.

CHAPTER 24 ALMOST THERE

She stood upon the battlements of a high stone tower. The wind was coming from the north and she faced into it, her long raven-black hair streaming behind her. A wind this strong normally meant a storm was coming, but the night sky was free of clouds and the stars shone clear and bright like chips of ice.

Two of the moons—Solinari the silver moon and Lunitari the red moon—were in low sanction this night. They hung near the horizon, their power weakened. A third moon, one that few on Krynn knew about and even fewer could see, was moments away from being at high sanction, the point of its greatest power. And when the moon Nuitari reached that point, it would be directly over her tower. It had been for this reason alone that she'd had the tower constructed on this very spot in the first place.

She had worked for many years to prepare for this night. She had studied ancient and forbidden mystic texts. She had built this tower and had fought to protect it from those who either wanted to stop her or to steal her prized magical possessions.

But soon all her efforts would bear sweet, dark fruit. For in mere moments, when Nuitari had reached the proper position in the sky, she would begin the spell she had created. And then, using her tower as a focusing and channeling device, she would tap the vast mystic power of the moon and draw its dark energies into herself. When she was finished, she would be like a god. No, she would be a god, and then no living being on Krynn could stand against her.

She lifted her hands high and turned her face toward Nuitari. Cold horror washed over her soul as she saw not a dark moon, but rather a huge ebon eye glaring down upon her with fury and hatred.

She tried to begin the spell, but instead of words of magic, all that came out of her mouth was a terrified scream.

"Nearra, wake up!"

The voice seemed to come from a great distance away, but she latched onto it as a drowning person would to a rope and used the sound to pull her out of the darkness.

She opened her eyes and saw Davyn's concerned face looking down at her.

She grew quiet and gave Davyn a sheepish smile. "Let me guess. I was having a nightmare." Slowly, her confusion began to give way to memory. She lay in a bedroll upon the soft grass of the field where they had made camp for the night. The silver light of the two-thirds full Solinari painted the clearing with gentle illumination, more than enough to see Davyn's face—as well as those of the others, who were all awake and looking at her with concern.

"I'm sorry I woke you all," Nearra said.

Catriona was on her feet, sword in hand, and Nearra knew that the warrior had armed herself the instant she'd heard her friend scream. Jax had grabbed his battle-axe, and Elidor was balancing a throwing knife on the tip of his index finger.

Catriona lowered her sword, but she didn't sheathe it. "That must have been quite a dream," she said.

"I suppose," Nearra said. "I don't remember much of it." She wasn't sure why she said this, for she remembered the dream in vivid detail. But some instinct told her not to say anything more about it. Besides, it was just a bad dream. And it wasn't as if it was about her. The woman in the dream was older and had long black hair.

Davyn was kneeling next to Nearra, holding her hand. The contact felt nice, especially after that awful dream.

Nearra shivered, as much from the cool night air as from the memory of her dream. "I wish we could build a fire," she said.

"Me, too!" Sindri agreed. "Then we could all sit around it and tell ghost stories."

"I've heard it said that speaking of ghosts summons them from their shadowy realm," Elidor said. He tossed a throwing knife into the air, caught it, and slid it back into its boot sheath.

"Really?" Sindri said, excited. "Let's try it!"

The idea of being visited by spirits disturbed Nearra. "I'd really rather not, Sindri," she said.

The kender looked disappointed, but he nodded.

"We didn't build a fire because we didn't wish to alert anyone or anything to our presence," Catriona said. "Especially Oddvar and the goblin raiders—assuming that they were able to dig their way out of Underfell."

"Nearra screamed so loudly, I doubt there's anyone in Solamnia who isn't aware of us now," Elidor said.

"The elf speaks true," Jax rumbled. "If you wish to build a fire, I shall keep watch." The minotaur glanced up at the night sky. "Dawn is not far off, and my people can go without sleep when we need to."

"Thank you," Nearra said, "but I'll be fine in a bit. One bad dream isn't enough reason to risk a fire when we have enemies about."

Jax nodded. "Then I shall return to sleep. Wake me if I am needed." The minotaur lay down on his bedroll, put his axe on the ground next to him, and rolled over on his side.

Nearra envied the minotaur. She wished she could go back to sleep so easily.

"Since I'm awake, I think I'll go off and explore a bit," Sindri said. "I imagine there must be all sorts of strange and interesting things about." Before anyone could stop him, the kender scampered off into the trees and disappeared.

Catriona let out a sigh of frustration. "I hate it when he does that."

"Should we go after him?" Nearra asked, worried about Sindri's safety in the night.

"There's no need," Elidor said. "He's a kender. They're harder to kill than cockroaches. I'm sure he'll return by morning, safe and sound." And with that, the elf lay down on his bedroll and closed his eyes.

"Elidor is right," Catriona said. "You'd think the way kender eagerly throw themselves into dangerous situations, they wouldn't live long, but somehow they always manage to survive." She smiled. "Sometimes I think the gods gave their kind extra luck just to keep them alive. I shall stand watch, though, just in case. I suggest you try to go back to sleep." She gave Davyn a distrustful look. "Both of you. Dawn will come soon, and you'll need your rest for tomorrow's trek to the temple. You are still certain that you want to go?"

"I know it may be dangerous," Nearra said. "There's no way of knowing whether or not it's another trap. But it's the only hope I have to regain my memory. We have to try."

Catriona nodded in silent agreement, then moved off a dozen yards. She squatted on her haunches and held her sword in front of her. Both of her hands rested on the hilt, with the sword's point touching the ground. She stared in the direction Sindri had run off. Nearra knew Catriona wouldn't move before sunrise.

Nearra and Davyn were now alone, more or less. Davyn didn't let go of her hand, and she didn't try to take it away.

"It's funny," he said in a low voice.

"What?"

"How devoted Catriona is to Sindri. They don't seem to have anything in common, and the kender drives her crazy. Yet I believe she would give her life for him without a moment's thought."

"It's not so strange," Nearra said. "Catriona made a vow to take care of Sindri, and she'll do everything she can to fulfill that promise. Isn't that what friends do? Take care of each other?"

Davyn looked away. "I . . . I never really had friends before. I'm not sure what they do."

Nearra smiled. "It's never too late to learn, you know. Look at me. When you and Maddoc found me, I was alone. Now I have five good friends."

Davyn looked back at her and smiled. "That's because you're a kind, caring person, Nearra."

"I don't know what sort of person I am. Or was. Who knows what I was like before I lost my memory? I might have been perfectly horrid."

"You weren't," Davyn said.

Nearra laughed. "How could you know?"

Davyn looked uncomfortable. "I, *uh*, believe that a person is more than the sum of his or her memories. A person has an inner spirit that doesn't change. And you have a very beautiful spirit."

Nearra looked into Davyn's eyes for a long moment, but eventually the ranger looked away, clearly embarrassed. She decided to change the subject. "I wish I could understand why Maddoc is doing all this. You told me that he was looking for me in the forest. Was he there to help me or hurt me? Does he know who I really am? Could he be my father . . . or a friend of my family? What does he *want* from me?"

Davyn jerked his hand away from Nearra and jumped to his feet. "I wish I had answers for you, but I've told you all I know. I should let you get back to sleep." He walked over to his bedroll and lay down.

Nearra lay back herself and drew the cover of her bedroll up to her chin. She looked over at Davyn. She knew he was deeply troubled by something, but she had no idea what it might be. She wished that he would confide in her. If he did, perhaps she could help him.

She decided she would just have to wait until he was ready to tell her what was wrong. She just hoped that if and when he did, it wouldn't be too late.

"Stop scratching, Sindri," Catriona said.

"I can't help it! It itches like mad!"

As Elidor had predicted, Sindri had returned to the camp by sunrise. Unfortunately, he had brought with him a bad case of poison ivy.

"Why not use your magic to stop the itch?" Jax asked.

"Magic doesn't work like that," Sindri said as he vigorously scratched the strawberry-colored rash on the side of his neck. "I don't know any anti-itch spells." He frowned. "At least, I don't think I do."

"I know a number of plants that can be used to make a medicine for such a rash," Davyn said.

"Really?" Sindri asked hopefully.

"However, they are rare this far north," Davyn answered. "I've been keeping an eye out for them since we broke camp this morning, but I haven't seen any."

Sindri groaned in disappointment and scratched all the harder.

"We should arrive at the temple by afternoon. Perhaps the clerics will have a supply of such plants," Elidor said. "After all, they are supposed to be skilled in healing."

"These clerics are supposed to use their holy powers to heal people," Sindri said. "They don't need medicine."

Elidor shrugged. "So? What does it matter how your discomfort is relieved, as long as it is? Besides, though I have heard

TIM WAGGONER

stories that healing magic returned to Krynn after the War of the Lance, I have not observed such magic at work, and I doubt the stories are true."

"Let's hope they are," Catriona said. "For Nearra's sake."

They continued walking in silence after that. Nearra was puzzled. Though Davyn was a ranger and thus well-versed in plant lore, he had said on several occasions that he was unfamiliar with the north. But if he truly didn't know anything about this area, how did he know that the plants he needed to help Sindri were rare here?

Perhaps it was merely a detail he'd noticed while they'd traveled, she told herself. Or maybe he really did know these parts and for some reason had lied about it.

She sighed. Once you began doubting someone, it was hard to trust again.

They were forced to climb over one of the hills since Heaven's Pass was still blocked. As they mounted the hill's peak, the temple came into view. It was nestled within a small valley, surrounded by green fields and white birch trees. The valley possessed an atmosphere of quiet calm, and Nearra knew this was a place of safety and tranquility. She couldn't imagine a more appropriate setting for a temple of healing.

The temple was dome-shaped and constructed from large blocks of white stone. A circular wall thirty feet high ran around the outside of the main building. The only way to enter, at least that they could see, was an iron gate set into one section of the wall.

They started to descend the hill but after a few steps, Catriona put up her hand. "Hold a moment," she said. "Jax and I should go first to check for any danger."

Nearra shivered in spite of the warm sun.

Jax nodded and heaved his battle-axe over his shoulder. Without another word, he and Catriona padded their way down the hillside, weaving back and forth among the birch trees. The others crouched low, watching from the hilltop. When the warriors came to the temple, they circled the wall. Then Catriona waved her arm above her head, motioning for the group to join them.

"All clear!" she shouted.

Nearra jumped up and bounded down the hill, her friends close behind. It won't be long now! she thought.

As they drew closer, they could see that the temple's outer wall was riddled with cracks. Large chunks of stone had fallen to the ground. Nevertheless, the wall appeared intact, if only just. While the noonday sun shining on the stone's surface had made it appear white from a distance, up close the stone looked a shade closer to dingy yellow-gray. The iron gate was shedding flakes of rust, and the courtyard visible between its bars, was nothing but dry, cracked earth.

Nearra tried to keep the disappointment she felt out of her voice. "Somehow I thought it would be—"

"Less of a ruin?" Elidor suggested.

"It's an *ancient* temple," Catriona pointed out. "Of course it's going to look old."

"Actually," Sindri added, "it's something of a miracle that the temple survived the Cataclysm in such good shape."

"Perhaps it was indeed a miracle," Jax said in a soft, reverent voice.

Elidor peered through the gate. "It appears no one is home."

"Well, the healer Wynda did say it was *rumored* that clerics had returned to the temple," Catriona said. "Maybe those rumors were false."

"If that's so, then we've come all this way for nothing," Nearra said. And if that were the case, then perhaps she would never solve the mystery of her lost memories or learn the truth behind whatever game Maddoc was playing.

Jax gripped the gate and tried to open it, but it wouldn't budge. "Locked," he said.

"I'll go see if I can find someone to let us in," Sindri said. He

TIM WAGGONER

started to slip his small body between the bars. It would be a tight fit, but it looked as if the kender was going to make it. But before he was halfway through, there was a bright flash of light. Sindri was thrown backwards.

Jax, moving with surprising dexterity for a being of his size, caught the kender before he could strike the ground.

"Are you harmed, small one?" the minotaur asked as he gently set Sindri on the ground.

"I don't think so. What an interesting experience. It felt as if I were shoved back by a giant hand. I wonder what kind of magic it is?"

He darted forward, obviously intending to attempt to step through the bars again, like a child eager to go on a festival ride one more time. But before he could reach the gate, a voice came from the other side.

"I wouldn't do that if I were you. Your minotaur friend might not be able to catch you next time."

A tall man in a dark blue robe approached the gate. A white rope tied about his waist served as a belt, and he wore sandals on his feet. Embroidered on the chest of his robe was a pattern of white dots. As Nearra looked more closely, it seemed the dots formed a shape. Then it came to her—the robe's dark blue color was supposed to represent the night sky, and the dots made from white thread were stars. The image was a constellation . . . a dragon.

The man's hair was black, with a touch of gray at the temples. His smile was friendly and his eyes were kind. He gave off an aura of quiet power that made Nearra feel safe and secure, despite the image of the star dragon that adorned his robe.

"I am Feandan, priest of the god Paladine, and this is the Temple of the Holy Orders of the Stars. What brings such an interestingly diverse band of travelers such as yourselves to our gate?"

"Well, I have this rash—" Sindri began, but Catriona shushed him.

"My name is Nearra. A healer in the village of Tresvka suggested I come here. My friends came along to make certain I reached your temple safely."

The priest smiled. "Then they are indeed true friends. So now I know what brought them here: you did. But why have you come, young lady?"

"I have lost my memory and seek to have it restored," Nearra said. "I just want to know who I am and where I come from."

The priest gave her a sympathetic look. "You poor child. Come inside. We shall do all that we can to help you." He unlocked the gate and opened it. The ancient hinges groaned and creaked in protest.

Remembering what had happened to Sindri, they all hesitated.

Feandan chuckled. "No need for concern. The temple's protective barrier is deactivated when the gate is unlocked. You may all enter without any trouble now."

The six companions walked into the courtyard, and Feandan closed and locked the gate behind them. None of them noticed the black falcon perched on a branch of a nearby white birch tree—a falcon which had seen, and more importantly heard, everything that had just taken place.

25 THE TEMPLE

Nearra blew on her vegetable soup before taking a sip. The companions sat at a polished wooden table, eating a meal of hard bread and goat's milk along with the soup.

"I'm sorry we do not have a more elaborate meal to offer you," Feandan said. "But we weren't expecting guests."

Feandan and his three associates—the only clerics that currently inhabited the temple—sat at a nearby table. They had already eaten, Feandan had explained, and so they merely sat while their young guests filled their bellies.

"There is no need to apologize, Master Cleric," Catriona said. "Humble food is often the most filling."

Jax snorted, and Nearra thought the minotaur would have preferred more substantial fare, but he continued eating without further complaint.

While the temple looked like a ruin on the outside, the inside was well kept and clean. Nearra looked around. The dining hall was smaller than she would have expected, but it possessed a simple elegance that she found pleasing. She glanced down and saw that the floor was covered with aquamarine tile, while the walls had been constructed from smooth marbled stone. The tables and chairs were made from polished oak, and **189** brass wall sconces, with glowing white candles, illuminated the hall. As near as she could tell, no matter how long the candles burned, they never seemed to grow shorter.

Sindri was eating happily, his poison ivy rash gone. The first thing Feandan had done after letting them in was to lay a hand on the kender's shoulder, close his eyes, and whisper a prayer to Paladine. A moment later, Sindri's rash was gone and his skin was once more smooth, pink, and free of itching. Nearra knew that curing a case of poison ivy was far different from restoring lost memories, but seeing Feandan demonstrate true healing magic had filled her with hope that maybe—just maybe—she could be healed, too.

Elidor nodded at the elaborate mosaic that adorned the walls opposite the tables. The mosaic stretched from floor to ceiling—a full fifteen feet—and was made from thousands of miniature colored stones. "It's very beautiful. What sort of stones are they?"

Elidor's tone was innocent enough, but Nearra knew what the elf thief was really asking: Were the stones valuable?

One of Feandan's fellow clerics, a pretty young woman named Nysse, answered. "Though each stone was smoothed and painted by hand, they have little worth individually. It's only when they work together as one that they acquire true value."

Elidor gave Nysse a skeptical look, as if he thought she might be lying to conceal the stones' actual worth, but then he returned to eating his soup.

Together the stones created an image of a black-haired woman garbed in a dark blue robe. In her arm, she held a bow, string pulled back and ready to release. The arrow was made from white wood, with an ivory point and white feathers for fletching. Before the woman stood a fierce red dragon easily ten times her size, wings outspread, eyes gleaming with hate, mouth opened wide to release a blast of flame.

"Is the picture accurate?" Sindri asked, his voice muffled by the mouthful of bread he was still chewing. "Is that really what Elethia looked like when she fought the dragon?"

A third priest, a plump bald man named Pedar, answered. "None of us were there to bear witness, my dear kender." Pedar appeared to be in late middle age, though there was something about his face and manner that reminded Nearra of a chubby child. "Some of us may be old, be we are a bit younger than that!" The priest chuckled. "But according to all written accounts—including those penned by Elethia's own hand—the scene is correct in every detail."

"She looks so fierce," Nearra said. "She's not at all what I imagined a priestess would look like." The longer Nearra looked at the mosaic, the more real it seemed to her. She could almost feel the heat from the dragon's flame, and the arrow appeared to glow with a bright light. She had the impression that if she reached out and touched the arrow, she would feel not polished stones set into the wall, but rather the smooth wood of the arrow's shaft, the softness of the feathers in its fletching, the sharp point at its tip. She marveled at the artistry it had taken to create such a beautiful and realistic piece of work.

"Appearances should never be trusted." The fourth cleric was an old woman named Gunna. "According to the temple histories, Elethia was gentle and soft-spoken—until there was a need to be otherwise."

"And then watch out!" Pedar said. Gunna gave the jesting cleric a disapproving look, but Feandan and Nysse laughed.

"It's true, though," Feandan said. "Elethia could fight most strongly for what she believed in. She needed to have an iron will to attempt what she did."

"You mean slaying the dragon?" Davyn asked.

"Yes, but more than that," Feandan said. "Do any of you know about the Holy Orders of the Stars?"

"We've heard one story about it." Nearra smiled at Sindri. "But please tell us more."

"The Holy Orders of the Stars is the collective term for the priests and priestesses of all the gods," Gunna said. "Good, Neutral, and Evil."

Feandan continued. "It was Elethia's belief that despite their differences, all the gods are necessary for Creation to function. She was a cleric of Zivilyn, who is also called the Tree of Life. Zivilyn is a Neutral god who represents balance and wisdom. Elethia dreamed of creating a single temple where clerics of all gods could come to worship, share their knowledge and faith, and work to fulfill the roles the gods had chosen for them."

"As you might imagine, it was far easier said than done," Pedar said. "The priests who worshiped gods of Good and gods of Neutrality came, but those who were devoted to gods of Evil were somewhat less than enthusiastic." He grinned. "Evil clerics aren't exactly known for working and playing well with others."

"And those few evil clerics that did come caused more than their fair share of trouble," Feandan said.

"Still, it was a lovely dream," Nysse said as she glanced at the mosaic of Elethia fighting Kiernan the Crimson. "And she accomplished so much of it."

Feandan continued. "After Elethia grew old and died, the temple continued to function, but without her leadership to hold them together, the other clerics eventually began to drift away one by one. And then the Cataclysm came. The blessings the priests had placed on the temple and the wall surrounding it prevented their complete destruction, though they were left somewhat the worse for wear. After that, the gods appeared to abandon Krynn. But during the War of the Lance, it was revealed that it was we mortals who had abandoned the gods, not the other way around. And once this was known, people returned to their faith and healing magic returned to the land."

"All of us are scholars in our various orders," Gunna said. "I belong to the order of the god Majere and Feandan to the order of Paladine. Pedar is a worshiper of Gilean, and Nysse is devoted to Mishakal, the goddess known as the Healing Hand. During our studies, we had read about Elethia and the temple she founded, and we all—separately and at the same time—had the idea of seeking out and restoring her temple to its former glory so that Elethia's dream might live once more."

"It is our belief that the gods themselves guided us here," Feandan said, "for it is their wish that the physical temple not only be restored, but that it once again become a center of knowledge and healing in Ansalon."

"The mystic shield that protects the temple did not keep us out when we first arrived," Gunna said. "We took this as further proof that the gods wish us to be here."

"And now," Pedar said, his eyes twinkling, "you fine young folks are our first customers, so to speak."

The companions had remained silent while the clerics told their tale, listening with rapt attention. But none of them seemed as caught up in the story as Jax.

"I wonder," the minotaur said. "If healing magic has returned to Krynn, can minotaur clerics now perform miracles in the name of our gods?"

"Quite possibly," Feandan said, and Jax nodded, looking thoughtful.

Feandan stood. "I believe we've kept our 'customers' waiting long enough. If it's agreeable, Nysse and I shall take Nearra to the Chamber of the Sky to determine what is wrong with her and what can be done about it."

"I have sworn to protect Nearra," Catriona said. "I would like to accompany her to this chamber if permitted."

"I understand, my child," Nysse said, "but the fewer people who are present when Feandan and I attempt the healing, the better. You have my word that we shall safeguard your friend at the cost of our lives if need be."

Catriona didn't look happy about it, but she agreed.

"Then it's settled," Nysse said. She and Feandan stood and the two clerics walked over to the table where Nearra sat with her friends. Nysse held out her hand and gave Nearra a reassuring smile.

"Come with us, my child," she said.

Nearra wanted to reach out and take the cleric's hand, but she hesitated. This was the moment she had worked for, ever since waking on the forest trail. If all went well, she would soon have her memories restored. But as bad as it was not to remember her past, what if knowing it was even worse?

She looked to her friends for guidance. They were all smiling, even Jax.

"Go on," Catriona said. "It will be all right."

Sindri, Elidor, and Jax all wore similar expressions of encouragement. Then she looked to Davyn. At first it seemed as if he were unsure what to say, but finally he smiled along with the others.

"This is something you need to do," he said.

Deciding that she felt as brave as she was going to get, Nearra took Nysse's hand and allowed the cleric to help her to her feet.

Nearra turned to give her friends one last look. "When we next see one another, I might be a completely different person."

"Then we shall have the pleasure of getting to know you all over again, won't we?" Elidor said.

Nearra hoped it would be so, but there was no way to foretell what the future might hold. All she could do—all anyone could—was keep moving forward and hope for the best.

She turned to Nysse. "I'm ready."

26 STARS AND RELICS

T his is the Chamber of the Sky," Feandan said in a reverent voice that was also tinged with pride.

Nearra couldn't respond; she couldn't breathe. It was so beautiful.

Inside the chamber it appeared to be night, and above them stretched what seemed to be a star-filled sky. But these stars were larger and brighter than true stars, and the white light they gave off was cool and soothing. The illusion was perfect, save for the smooth stone floor beneath her feet and the marble dais in the center of the room.

"How—?" Nearra began, but she wasn't sure how to frame the question.

Nysse laughed softly. "To be honest, we're not certain. We believe it is some manner of enchantment placed here by one or more of the clerics from Elethia's time. Perhaps even Elethia herself." Before entering the chamber, Nysse had gone to her room and retrieved a staff carved from white wood. She now carried the staff in her right hand, its white wood seeming to glow in the light of the chamber's stars.

"We do know that the temple clerics came here for prayer and meditation," Feandan said. "They also used the chamber as a 195 place of both physical and spiritual renewal."

"It was here that the greatest healings were performed," Nysse said. "Since your situation is unique, this seemed an appropriate place to bring you."

The atmosphere in the Chamber of the Sky was so peaceful that Nearra no longer felt any fear about what might happen next.

"What should I do?" she asked.

"Climb onto the dais and lie down," Nysse said.

Nearra did so without hesitation. Nysse walked over to stand on Nearra's right side.

Feandan stood on Nearra's left. "Look up, child." He pointed to a particular configuration of stars that formed the image of a dragon. "That is the constellation of Paladine."

The dragon of Paladine's constellation seemed nothing like Slean. To Nearra, it looked like a proud and noble creature, good in every sense of the word. The longer Nearra looked, the more it seemed to her as if she stared not at a mere pattern of stars, but at an actual Stardragon. And it seemed to be looking back at her with eyes filled with love.

Nysse pointed with her staff. "That is Mishakal's constellation. It's in the shape of a figure eight lying on its side."

Nearra found it easily. It was very close to the dragon.

"Mishakal is Paladine's daughter and a true goddess of healing. I will now call to her and beseech her to restore that which has been lost to you."

Nysse spoke a soft prayer, and one of the stars in Mishakal's constellation broke free of the others. It drifted down toward Nysse and settled onto the tip of her staff. The star glowed with a gentle blue-white light, and Nysse lowered her staff until the star touched Nearra's forehead.

Nearra felt drowsy all of a sudden and she closed her eyes. She felt light as a feather, as if the slightest breeze could send her into flight, floating up through the air to join the rest of the stars in the heavens.

Images tumbled through her mind then: the faces of a man

and a woman, both with blond hair; a small cottage on the edge of some woods. The man was driving a wagon full of firewood down the lane while the woman stood in the cottage's doorway waving goodbye. This scene was quickly replaced by a series of narrow stone corridors, dark and gloomy. Nearra felt herself walking down one of the hallways, carrying buckets full of water. She felt weary, on the verge of collapse, as if she had worked for days without rest. There was also a sensation of uneasiness, as if she were afraid of something, but she didn't—

Another face—this one belonging to Maddoc. The wizard was looking down at her, chanting words that she didn't understand. The robe he wore was as black as midnight. She looked up and saw a tapestry hanging above a cold, empty fireplace—a tapestry that depicted a woman with raven-black hair and cruel violet eyes.

Those eyes began to glow with magenta fire and Nearra screamed . . .

Nearra sat up abruptly. All she saw now were the concerned faces of the two clerics. The star on the tip of Nysse's staff had gone out.

"I'm sorry. It was starting to hurt." Her head pounded and her stomach was queasy. She felt so weak that she was afraid to try to get off the dais, let alone walk.

"Rest a moment, child," Feandan said. "The discomfort should pass soon." But the cleric sounded uncertain.

"Tell us, Nearra, what did you experience?" Nysse asked.

"I'm not sure I can describe it. I saw things . . . people, places, but I don't know who and what they were." A tear slid down her cheek.

Feandan patted her hand. "Whatever enchantment has befallen you is very strong—too strong for us to easily remove." His tone was apologetic, but also confused. Clearly, he couldn't fully comprehend what had just taken place.

"We are all new to the practice of healing magic," Nysse said, "and we still have much to learn. But do not give up hope. We shall continue to search for a way to help you. And we *shall* succeed." But Nysse didn't sound very confident.

Nearra's head and stomach were already beginning to feel better, but doubted if any amount of time would alleviate the despair she felt in her soul.

From somewhere deep inside her—so deep that Nearra was only barely aware of it—came the sound of cruel, mocking laughter.

"And this room houses the archive, where our various books, scrolls, and parchments are kept," Gunna said.

Davyn and the others, along with their two guides, stood outside a room that was literally overflowing with papers of all sorts. They were jammed onto shelves, stacked on tables, and spread all over the floor in lopsided piles.

"Obviously we haven't gotten around to cataloguing the collection yet," Pedar said wryly.

Davyn was only partially paying attention. He was worried about how Nearra was doing in the Chamber of the Sky. Whatever happened, he hoped Nearra wouldn't be harmed.

"Given how long the temple was abandoned, I'm surprised the pages are still intact," Elidor said. "I'd have thought they would have crumbled to dust long ago."

"It's magic, of course," Sindri said.

"Of course it is," Gunna said gruffly. "Some manner of preservation spell was cast on the archives by the clerics who used to live here. The books and scrolls are as fresh as the day they were made."

"Really?" Elidor said, eyeing the cluttered collection with obvious interest.

"As long as they remain in that room," Pedar said. "The magic only works inside it. If you take one of the writings out, *poof!* It

TIM WAGGONER

turns to dust in mere moments. That's why there are so many works crammed in there. They cannot be moved anywhere else."

"I see," Elidor said, sounding disappointed.

Davyn had to fight to keep from smirking. Those books were truly thief-proof!

Pedar closed the door to the archives, and then he and Gunna led the companions farther down the hallway. They stopped in front of a polished mahogany door with a golden handle that had been shaped to resemble a graceful swan.

"And this—" Pedar said in the tone of a proud owner about to show off his most prized possession—"is the repository."

He opened the door, then stood back and gestured for the companions to enter. They did so, Catriona leading the way while Davyn brought up the rear. When they were all inside, the two clerics followed.

This room was no larger than the archive, but since it contained far fewer items, there was much more space to move around. Recessed display areas had been carved into the stone walls, sixteen of them in all. In addition, five small marble columns were placed around the room: one in each of the corners, while the fifth stood in the middle. In the wall recesses and on top of each of the columns rested a different object, each more intriguing than the last—a small bell with a handle carved to resemble an armored warrior, a silver needle and a spool of golden thread, an eagle's claw encased in amber, a skull with runes carved into the bone, and many more. In the middle of the room, resting atop one of the columns, lay a white arrow.

"Is that Elethia's arrow?" Catriona asked. "The one she used to slay Kiernan the Crimson?"

"We believe so," Gunna said. "The temple had been abandoned for centuries before we came here, and what records we have managed to discover are incomplete. But we know that the repository is where holy objects were kept, so we can only assume this is Elethia's arrow."

"Amazing," Sindri reached out to touch the white arrow, but Catriona—who had been keeping a close eye on the kender the entire time—swatted his hand before he could touch it.

Sindri jerked his hand back and gave Catriona a resentful look, but he didn't try to touch the arrow again.

"It is curious, though," Pedar said. "The objects can be taken from the repository without any difficulty."

"How interesting," Elidor said.

"Aren't you worried they might be stolen?" Catriona said, giving Elidor a look that said he'd better keep his hands to himself.

"No," Pedar said. "These objects don't have any real value aside from their mystic powers. And I'm afraid that the blessings placed upon them might have somehow worn off. We've attempted on several occasions to use the objects—under carefully controlled conditions, of course. But we've never been able to make any of the items actually *do* anything."

"Maybe it's because the objects knew it was only a test," Sindri said. "Maybe if there really was a need for them, their magic would activate."

Pedar and Gunna looked thoughtful then.

"That's a very good point," Gunna said. "You may be correct."

Pedar then clapped his hands and rubbed them together. "Well, then. Shall we go see how your friend is doing?"

They gathered in the dining hall once more, and Feandan and Nysse gave the others the bad news.

"The malady that has afflicted Nearra appears to be sorcerous in nature," Feandan said. "And at the moment, there is little we can do to help."

"Why?" Catriona asked. "Are you telling us that wizardry is more powerful than the gods?"

"Not at all," Feandan said. "But wizardry comes from the gods as well as healing power. The moons grant magic to wizards on behalf of the gods whose names they bear: Solinari, Lunitari, and Nuitari. Because of this, the healing magic given to me by Paladine and to Nysse by Mishakal was ineffective. Not because their power is weaker than that of the gods of magic, but because the gods are reluctant to interfere with each other's spheres of influence unless absolutely necessary."

"And evidently Paladine and Mishakal do not believe it's desirable to intervene in Nearra's case," Nysse said.

Nearra felt the crushing weight of hopelessness settle on her soul. If the gods wouldn't help her, who would?

As if she'd read Nearra's mind, Nysse added, "Do not fear that the gods have abandoned you, my child. You were in a great deal of pain. Perhaps the gods recognized you would be injured if the healing continued."

"And it's possible they believe that a sorcerous problem requires a sorcerous solution," Feandan added. "All four of us will need to meditate upon the matter so that we might determine our next course of action."

The other clerics nodded their agreement with Feandan's words.

"So what are the rest of us to do in the meantime?" Jax asked.

Feandan smiled. "Your journey, while not that long in terms of distance, was nevertheless most eventful. I imagine you could all use a bit of a rest."

"And a bath, too," Sindri said, wrinkling his nose. "Jax's fur is really starting to smell."

"WHAT?" the minotaur roared, and Sindri scampered behind the clerics for protection.

The others laughed, but the best Nearra could manage was a thin smile. She didn't know how she could possibly hope to rest after their failure in the Chamber of the Sky. Not only did she still not know who she was or where she came from, it was beginning to look like she'd never find out.

27 NIGHT WALK

"Can't sleep?" Catriona asked.

Nearra sat up. The clerics had provided simple mattresses stuffed with leaves and grass for their guests—not the most comfortable of beds, but they were all they had to offer.

"No. I just can't stop thinking, I guess."

Catriona nodded and returned to looking out the window.

Catriona's mattress was next to Nearra's, but the warrior wasn't lying on it. Instead she sat cross-legged on the stone floor, still wearing her armor, of course. Both moons were visible. Solinari and Lunitari, silver and red, one close to full and the other little over halfway there. If what Feandan had said was accurate, the moons' light radiating down upon Krynn was in truth magic power wizards drew upon to fuel their spells. Nearra would never look at moonlight the same way again.

A sudden rumbling-snorting sound came from the room next door, and Nearra chuckled. "How can you meditate with Jax snoring like that?"

Catriona took a deep breath, held it for several long moments, and then let it out slowly. When she was finished, she turned and crawled over to her bed. She lay on her side facing Nearra, and propped herself up with an elbow.

The warrior smiled. "It isn't easy. So what have you been thinking about?"

"Everything." Nearra wanted to share her concerns about Davyn with someone, but Catriona was already suspicious of him. She didn't want to make things worse by expressing her worries about the ranger. "What if the clerics can't find a way to restore my memories? What will I do then?"

Catriona thought for a moment before answering. "The only thing you can do—make new memories."

The thought made Nearra feel better. She still intended to try to recover her memories, but if she couldn't, it wouldn't be the end of the world. One way or another, she would be able to go on with her life.

"Would you like to join me in meditation?" Catriona offered. "It will clear your mind so that you can sleep."

Jax's snoring suddenly became louder. It sounded as if he had a hive full of angry bees stuck in his throat.

Nearra laughed. "I don't think I'm up to the challenge tonight, but thanks for the offer."

Catriona nodded, then returned to her position in front of the window. Nearra lay back down, closed her eyes, and tried to ignore the minotaur's snoring. Despite the noise, she was soon fast asleep.

Next door, Davyn lay awake while Jax, Sindri, and Elidor slept. Jax's snoring kept Davyn from dozing off. The minotaur was making more noise than an avalanche! Davyn had no idea how Sindri and Elidor could ignore the sound and sleep, but they did. Davyn envied them.

Like the girls next door, Davyn had left the window open to let in the cool night air. But Davyn had another reason for wanting the window open—he was expecting a summons.

Davyn's heartbeat thundered in his ears and the vegetable soup they'd eaten for supper roiled in his stomach. He didn't know if he could bear to keep up this act much longer.

Everything had begun to go wrong almost from the moment Nearra had awakened in the forest, Davyn thought. Maddoc had said he'd planned for every eventuality, but even a wizard as powerful and intelligent as Maddoc wasn't perfect. How could Maddoc have possibly foreseen that Davyn and Nearra would encounter Sindri, Catriona, Elidor, Jax, and Raedon, let alone the impact they would have on his plans?

Of all of them, the one who had most interfered with Maddoc's plans was Davyn himself. At first, he had done as the wizard had asked of him. He'd helped hire Nearra to serve in Maddoc's keep, and had stood by while the wizard had conducted the mystic rite that transferred the spirit of the ancient sorceress Asvoria into Nearra's body. And when Asvoria's personality failed to take control of Nearra, Maddoc had come up with a plan to force the sorceress to, as he called it, emerge. Maddoc cast a spell to rob Nearra of her memories, so as to make more room for Asvoria's personality. Then he cast a sleep spell on Nearra and Davyn had carried her into the forest. It had been Davyn who had laid her on the path. Then he had run back to join Maddoc in the clearing, where they watched as the goblins chased Nearra directly into Slean's path. Maddoc believed that when Asvoria's new life was in danger—or at least, when she *believed* it was—the sorceress would take control of Nearra's body in order to protect herself. But when that didn't happen immediately, they had been forced to attempt an alternate plan, with Davyn leading Nearra on a quest to restore her memories.

Maddoc never expected they would actually reach the Temple of the Holy Orders of the Stars. Davyn was supposed to use the journey as a ruse to lead Nearra into danger and force the Emergence. As instructed, he had guided Nearra into another encounter with Slean and a confrontation with the goblin band in the forest, and finally he had led her to the ogre. And when Nearra and the others had begun to suspect him, he'd lied to them . . . lied to people who had become his friends.

205

He had done as Maddoc had instructed in every way but one. Several times now, Nearra had shown signs of the Emergence, but instead of letting it happen, Davyn had stepped in to prevent it, and Nearra had returned to normal each time. Maddoc wanted the Emergence to take place—it was what he had worked so long and so hard for. Davyn should have helped the Emergence occur, not stop it. But he hadn't, and he wasn't sure why.

Davyn thought of Nearra and the way she looked the night before as they'd talked. Her eyes had sparkled in the moonlight, blue as the evening sky. He thought of how she had insisted they continue the journey to the temple. She was strong and brave, in spite of everything that had happened to her.

But most of all, the concern she had shown for him after he had passed out during the battle with Ugo tugged at his conscience. While it was difficult for Davyn to believe—especially after all he had done—it was clear that Nearra genuinely cared for him.

Davyn had to face facts. Though he knew he shouldn't have allowed himself to become emotionally attached to Nearra, he had. After Davyn had helped rescue Nearra from Underfell, in spite of his knowledge of Maddoc's plan, he could no longer deny the truth about his feelings for Nearra. He had to admit, he'd grown fond of the others, as well. They were the closest things to friends that he'd ever known. How could he betray them?

It was quite late, and Davyn didn't think he could resist sleep any longer. He was just about to drift off when he finally heard what he'd been listening for: the cry of a falcon.

He rose slowly from his bedroll and stood. He'd lain down fully dressed—he'd even kept his boots on—so he'd be prepared. He briefly considered bringing his bow and quiver of arrows in case he needed them, but he decided against it. He was afraid of making too much noise and waking his roommates. Even with the sound of Jax's snoring to drown out any noise he might make, Davyn wasn't certain he could keep from waking his companions. None of the three were human, and while they possessed heightened senses, Davyn wasn't sure just *how* heightened they were. He decided it would be best to be cautious, so he left his bow and arrows on the floor.

He stepped carefully to the window and peered out. Thankfully, their room was on the ground floor. Davyn climbed over the windowsill and dropped lightly to the ground, making no sound as he landed.

He crouched there for a moment, listening. But all he heard was the minotaur's snoring. Satisfied that he hadn't woken anyone, Davyn clenched his fists and stalked toward the temple gate.

Davyn had made up his mind. He was going to find a way to convince Maddoc to abandon his plan. It wasn't worth hurting so many people.

He knew it wouldn't be easy to change Maddoc's mind. Maddoc did not take kindly to dissension. The last time a servant had questioned Maddoc's wisdom, the wizard had thrown him off the top of the keep. Thereafter, any servant who could no longer stand working for the wizard would simply sneak out in the night. But Davyn didn't have the luxury of quitting the wizard's service and finding work elsewhere. For there was one more thing Davyn had lied about.

Davyn wasn't Maddoc's servant.

Davyn was Maddoc's son.

Elidor was normally a light sleeper. In his line of work, one had to be. Plus, his hearing was able to block out the truly thunderous noise of Jax's snoring while still being able to hear the *scuff-scuff-scuff* of Davyn's boots as he walked across the stone floor.

Elidor came instantly awake, but he didn't open his eyes, not yet. He might have been young for an elf, but he knew enough not to give himself away.

When he heard Davyn jump to the ground, Elidor rose, slipped on his boots, and then glided over to the window with liquid grace.

His kind were gifted with the ability to see almost as well at night as they could in the day—provided there was at least a little light for their eyes to use. And the illumination from the two moons was more than enough for Elidor to see Davyn sneak across the temple's courtyard and head for the gate.

What an interesting turn of events, he thought. He then jumped out the window, landing cat-silent, and jogged after Davyn, determined to learn what the ranger was up to.

So far, the temple had proven to be a disappointment for Elidor: books that couldn't be removed from their library, and a repository full of worthless holy relics, not one made of anything valuable, like diamond or steel. But sometimes information could be the most valuable thing of all—depending on what it was, and more importantly, how it could be used.

He continued moving through the night, just one more shadow among all the others.

Who knows? he thought. I might actually be able to make a profit from this little adventure after all.

28 TALKING IN THE DARK

Davyn unlocked the gate as he had watched Feandan do and opened it enough so he could step through. He knew that he had deactivated the temple's defensive barrier, but he wasn't concerned about the possibility of an attack. Maddoc just wanted to talk.

Davyn didn't have far to walk. The falcon was waiting for him on a birch branch, just a few feet from the temple's exterior wall.

Davyn's throat felt dry as dirt, his stomach like a solid block of ice. Now that he was actually about to confront his father and try to talk him out of his plan to attack the temple, he wasn't certain he could go through with it. But he knew he had to—for Nearra's sake.

Beneath the tree stood Oddvar and two of the goblin bandits, Drefan and Fyren. Fyren looked worse than he had the last time Davyn had seen him, and he guessed the goblin had been severely wounded when Ugo knocked down the columns in Underfell. Both of Fyren's arms and one of his legs were bound in splints, and he was wrapped in so many cloth bandages that he could barely move. Now that it was night, Oddvar wore the hood of his cloak down, and the Theiwar's eyes seemed as large as an owl's.

"I see you managed to survive the cave-in," Davyn said, making sure to keep his voice low. He looked at Fyren. "Though some fared better than others, it appears. Ugo?"

"Dead," Oddvar said without emotion.

"Several tons of rock falling on your head will do that," Davyn said. "Gifre, too?"

"That's none of your concern, boy."

"All right, be secretive," Davyn said. "See if I care." He looked up at the falcon, knowing that by doing so, he was also looking at his father. "What do you wish of me?"

The falcon relayed a telepathic message from Maddoc.

Davyn was astonished. "Do you mean it? You're really not going to go through with your plan to attack the temple?" In the event that Nearra reached the temple, Maddoc had planned to have Slean lay siege to it. But now it seemed that wasn't going to happen.

"Maddoc believes the situation has become too complicated," Oddvar said. "In addition to the companions Nearra has acquired on her journey, she is now protected by four clerics. To make matters worse, a mystic barrier guards the temple. Given all these factors, the odds are slim that an attack would succeed in causing the Emergence to take place."

Davyn felt a wave of relief. His father was a reasonable man after all. He decided to press the matter further.

"I . . . I don't think we should keep trying to make the Emergence happen anymore. Nearra . . . she's so kind. She doesn't deserve this. I want her to stay the way she is."

The falcon gazed at Davyn intensely then, and the young ranger heard his father's voice whisper in his mind.

You're a love-addled fool, boy! Haven't I taught you that sacrifices are unavoidable along the path to ultimate power? Such sentimentality, such weakness disgusts me.

Davyn's face burned with shame and anger, but he didn't reply.

Oddvar reached into his tunic pocket and brought forth

a scroll bound by a black ribbon. "Maddoc believes that the clerics, having failed to heal Nearra on their own, will search for a wizardly solution. This document tells of an enclave of wizards in the Vingaard Mountains who are especially skilled at removing curses. Maddoc wants you to place this scroll in the archive for the clerics to find. With any luck, they will believe the scroll to be one of the temple's documents, and they will advise Nearra to seek out the mages in the mountains. Once you have reached this new destination, we shall again attempt to force the Emergence."

Davyn took the scroll and placed it in one of his own pockets. He looked at the falcon's eyes, and he thought he could sense his father, miles away, sitting in his favorite chair before the fireplace, gauging the level of his son's sincerity. Finally, the ebon falcon nodded once, then took to the sky, quickly melting into the night.

"Maddoc wants to give you one last chance to redeem yourself, boy," Oddvar sneered. "But I disagree with him. I think you've come to care too much about that girl and can no longer be trusted. For his sake, I hope you prove me wrong."

With that, the dark dwarf turned and began walking away. The two goblins followed, Fyren leaning on Drefan for support.

Davyn turned and headed back for the temple. He didn't see Elidor—who had been listening from behind the wall—hurry back to get to the temple door before Davyn came through the gate.

Elidor had learned a great deal about the ranger this night. Now he had to figure out a way to use this knowledge to his best advantage.

Oddvar and the goblins continued walking through the valley away from the temple until they came to a birch tree that had one branch broken off. They found it without any trouble. After all, Drefan had been the one who'd broken it. They stopped there and waited.

"Do you think he fell for it?" Fyren asked. His voice was garbled due to his swollen lips and a number of missing teeth.

"Of course," Oddvar replied. "Davyn believed it because it was what he wanted to hear. Humans are like that."

Drefan chuckled. "Humans are such fools."

Oddvar looked at the goblin leader. He was about to tell him that goblins were ten times the fools that human were. But before he could speak, the black falcon landed on the protruding stub of the broken branch, just as they'd planned.

The falcon relayed a message from its master.

"I'll try," the Theiwar said. "But once the attack begins, it will be difficult if not impossible to ensure Davyn's safety. If it comes down to a choice between the Emergence taking place or Davyn getting hurt, what do you want us to do?"

The bird passed on another message.

The Emergence is more important than anything.

"Even more important than your son?" Oddvar asked.

Anything.

There weren't any good places to hide in the courtyard—no trees, no large rocks—and the temple's dome shape didn't offer any convenient nooks and crannies to conceal one's self in. Gifre was glad that Oddvar had insisted he wear one of the Theiwar's dark cloaks. It now provided his only camouflage. But he had taken other precautions against being seen. He lay on the ground as flat as he could, covered by the black cloak. He'd also chosen a spot close to the temple, but far away from the main gate and any windows. He was confident that no one would detect his presence before sunrise, and by then it would be far too late.

He had sneaked into the courtyard when Davyn had left the gate unlocked and the mystic barrier deactivated. He knew the barrier would start functioning again the instant Davyn

TIM WAGGONER

returned, closed the gate, and locked it. But that didn't matter now that Gifre had managed to make it inside the wall. Gifre would spend the rest of the night on this side of the barrier. When the sun began to rise tomorrow morning, he would go to the gate, throw open the lock, and the magic barrier would fall. And once that happened, there would be nothing to prevent the rest of the plan from falling into place.

Gifre almost giggled at the thought, but he clamped his hand over his mouth to stop himself. Oddvar was always telling him and the other two goblins how stupid they were. Well, tonight he'd show that slug-skinned tunnel dweller that goblins weren't so dumb after all. He'd lie here still and silent until morning and then he'd do his job.

And after that, the fun would truly begin.

CHAPTER

29 DRAGONSTRIKE

Nearra awoke to the sound of a loud crash.
"What was that?" she said as she sat up.

Catriona was already dressed and putting on her boots. "I believe we are under attack."

Nearra felt a stab of fear. She threw her blanket aside and reached for her own boots.

Catriona stood and buckled on her sword belt. "Stay here, Nearra, and shut and bar the window. Whatever is happening, you'll be safer inside." Without waiting for Nearra to reply, Catriona opened the door of their room and dashed into the hallway.

Nearra could hear the sounds of yelling and of feet pounding down the corridors as people ran. She could make out various voices: Davyn's, Sindri's, Jax's, and Elidor's, as well as those of the clerics. Everyone was rushing to see what the trouble was and to do something about it. Everyone except her.

Whatever was happening, she felt sure it had something to do with her. And she couldn't just sit here while the others might well be putting themselves in danger's way on her account, no matter how afraid she might be.

She finished putting on her boots and then rummaged through Catriona's pack until she found a dagger. Nearra had 215 lost her own weapon along with everything else back at Underfell. She knew Catriona wouldn't mind if she used her dagger. It might not have been much of a weapon, but it was all she had.

As she dashed into the hallway and ran after her friends, she couldn't help thinking it was a shame that Raedon had left them to go check on his lair. She had a feeling they could use the copper dragon's help right now.

Raedon dwelled in a darkness that was at once both like and unlike sleep. He had no idea how long he had been in this nonplace, but he thought it had probably been a while; hours certainly, perhaps even days. It wasn't such a bad place, really. For one thing, it was quiet. For another, he didn't feel anything except for a pleasant numbness.

No, all in all, he could have spent a great deal more time here—perhaps even the rest of his life. But then he heard a woman's voice calling him by his true dragon name.

Tarkemelhion.

He tried to ignore the voice, but he heard it again, and with it came a powerful feeling; the little one called Nearra needed him.

He said a reluctant goodbye to the soothing darkness and opened his eyes. He regretted it at once. Pain flooded through his body as awareness returned—more pain than he'd ever known in his life, so much that he was surprised he wasn't dead.

He wanted to close his eyes and return to the darkness, but he knew he couldn't. He forced himself to wake up even more and tried to determine where he was.

Leaves surrounded him and thick branches supported his body. He was in a tree. He ached all over, but his worst pains were in his head and his right wing. His wing felt as if the membrane had been torn somehow, but he didn't . . .

And then it came back to him. Flying to check on his lair, encountering Slean, talking with her, Slean diving, clawing at

Tim Waggoner

his wing as she passed, and then he had fallen, spinning and tumbling out of control.

He understood then what had happened. He'd landed in this tree, struck his head, and had passed out into the deep, dark sleep of the seriously wounded. He might never have woken if it hadn't been for Nearra's summons.

He needed to get down from this tree—now. Moving as quickly as his sore, battered body would allow, Raedon gingerly lifted himself off the branches and began to crawl downward, gripping the bark with his claws so he wouldn't slip.

His head pounded so hard he thought he might pass out before he made it to the ground. Once on the forest floor, he lay still for several moments, breathing deeply and trying not to think about how much he hurt all over.

He was in a heavily wooded section of the forest, one that he didn't recognize. It couldn't be far from where Slean had attacked him. He then moved his head, neck, legs, tail, and wings. Although his limbs were stiff and sore, none felt as if they were broken.

He turned in the direction he felt Nearra calling from—the direction in which the Temple of the Holy Orders of the Stars lay. Spreading his wings and coiling his powerful but aching leg muscles, he launched himself into the sky.

Immediately he crashed back to the ground. His wing was too badly damaged to keep him aloft. But if he couldn't fly, how could he reach Nearra in time?

He lied to me! Davyn thought. My own father lied to me!

He ran out of the temple's main entrance and joined Jax and Catriona, who were already standing in the courtyard. The sun had just started to come up, and while the rest of the sky was still purple and a scattering of stars remained visible, the eastern horizon was tinted pink and orange.

Slean crouched by the main gate—or rather, where the gate

had been. That section of the wall was now empty, and the gate, twisted and mangled, lay on the ground below a newly-made hole in the temple. Slean had torn the gate from the wall and hurled it at the temple building. It had been the sound of the gate's impact that had wakened everyone.

Davyn had no idea how Slean had gotten past the temple's mystic barrier. He had triple-checked last night to make sure he'd locked the gate when he'd returned. He started to wonder if Maddoc had managed to find a way to neutralize the protective spell.

Then he thought of Gifre. Last night, Oddvar wouldn't say where the goblin was. When Davyn had left the gate unlocked to go outside and meet Maddoc, Gifre must have sneaked in.

How could I have been so blind, thought Davyn. His father hadn't really wanted to speak to him last night, he'd merely wanted to lure him into leaving the gate open so that Gifre could enter the temple. Maddoc had not only lied to him about the attack, he'd used Davyn as if he were merely another pawn in the wizard's grand scheme.

As angry as Davyn felt, he was also strangely relieved. Now he knew for certain what to do. He pulled the scroll out of his pocket, struck a spark off his flint, and dropped the parchment as it burned. Stamping out the ashes, he resolved that whatever happened, he wasn't going to be a pawn any longer. He had to do everything he could to protect Nearra.

Slean reared up on her hind legs, spread her wings wide, and roared.

"Bring me the girl!"

Elidor and Sindri came running outside then, followed by the four clerics. The kender grinned upon seeing the dragon again, but the clerics paled. Davyn understood why an instant later.

Dragonfear crashed into him. He began to tremble and he thought he would drop his bow and run back inside the temple and hide. But then Feandan, Nysse, Pedar, and Gunna began chanting prayers. Davyn felt the dragonfear diminish slowly.

It didn't go away entirely, but it decreased to the point where he could handle it.

He looked to his companions and saw expressions of relief and surprise on their faces—all save for Sindri, since the kender had felt no fear in the first place.

"We have just asked the gods to grant us all strength to resist the dragonfear," Feandan explained.

Davyn was impressed. He'd had no idea that clerics could do more than heal the sick and injured.

"I wonder how Slean got through the barrier," Sindri said. "Shall we go ask her?"

But before the kender could take a step toward the green dragon, Slean shot a blast of chlorine gas straight up into the air.

"Bring me the girl now, or I shall destroy this temple and kill you all!"

Even though Slean hadn't released her gas toward them, the acrid smell stung the back of Davyn's throat and made his eyes water.

Elidor put his hand over his nose and mouth as he turned to the clerics. "I don't suppose you can use your holy powers to turn chlorine into something more pleasant, like the scent of horse manure?"

"I'm sorry," Nysse said. "We don't know a prayer for that."

Gunna stepped forward. "Stay back now, children, and let the four of us handle this."

"Children!" Catriona and Jax said at the same time, but the clerics ignored them as they stepped forward to confront the dragon that had invaded the temple's courtyard.

"What are they doing?"

Davyn turned to see that Nearra had joined them. He was mildly surprised to see that she was armed with her dagger. "They're going to try to stop Slean, I think," he said.

"Can they?"

Davyn shrugged. "Elethia stopped Kiernan the Crimson, didn't she?"

The clerics, standing side by side and wearing looks of grim determination on their faces, approached Slean until they were within twenty feet of the green dragon.

"What do you want here, foul beast?" Feandan demanded.

Slean eyed the clerics with amusement. "Are you deaf? I said it twice already. Bring me the girl!"

"I assume you speak of either Catriona or Nearra," Nysse said. "Regardless, we will not grant your request. All within these walls are under the protection of the gods we serve."

Slean snorted. "I care not for your gods. But I do care for that one." She nodded toward Nearra. "The blond human in the dress. Give her to me and I shall depart in peace."

"Why do you want her?" Pedar asked.

"That is my concern, not yours," Slean said. "I'm starting to lose my patience. Quit stalling and give her to me."

Gunna stepped forward. "Never!" Around her neck the cleric wore a pendant in the shape of a rose—the holy symbol of the god Majere. She clasped the rose in her hand and whispered a prayer.

The barren ground around Slean suddenly burst into life as grass and weeds sprouted from the earth. They grew with lightning speed and wrapped themselves around Slean's limbs, twisting and entwining until the dragon was tightly bound.

"What are you doing?" Slean roared. "I cannot move!"

But then Gifre, garbed in a black cloak, came rushing up from the other side of the temple, holding a good-sized rock in his hand. When he was close enough to the clerics, he drew back his arm and prepared to throw the stone.

"Gunna, beware!" Catriona shouted, but it was too late. Gifre hurled the rock and struck Gunna on the side of the head. The cleric groaned and slumped to the ground.

Gifre giggled and clapped his hands.

Slean had managed to keep her mouth free of the entangling plants and she now used her teeth to tear at the greenery that bound her. The plant tendrils shredded in her jaws until Slean was able to break loose.

"I'm free!" the dragon shouted, flapping her wings and whipping her tail about as if to emphasize her point.

"Foul goblin!" Jax roared and took off running toward Gifre, battle-axe held high.

The goblin screamed in terror at the sight of a furious minotaur coming at him in full battle-rage. Gifre turned and ran toward the open gateway. Unfortunately, that was where Slean stood. The dragon's thrashing tail clipped the goblin on the side of the head and sent him crashing into the stone wall. Gifre hit the wall with a nasty thud, then lay still.

Seeing there was no longer any need to attack the goblin, Jax changed his course and ran toward Slean. Nysse was kneeling next to Gunna, her hands on the older cleric's head, no doubt attempting to heal the wound she had sustained.

"The rest of you stay here!" Catriona said. "I'm going to help get Gunna to safety!" The redheaded warrior took a deep breath, then dashed across the courtyard toward the clerics.

"Stay? She's got to be joking!" Sindri started to run forward, but Davyn grabbed the kender's arm and stopped him.

"Hold back a moment, Sindri," Davyn said. "We need to keep your magic in reserve, just in case the clerics fail."

"I'd listen to him, Sindri, if I were you," Elidor said, glancing at Davyn. "I've a feeling our ranger knows more about magic than you'd expect."

There was something almost accusatory in the elf's tone, but Davyn didn't have time to worry about what he meant.

"I suppose you're right." Sindri didn't sound happy about this, but when Davyn let go of his cape, the kender stayed put.

Slean turned to meet Jax's approach, inhaling deeply in preparation for releasing another deadly blast of chlorine, this one aimed straight at the charging minotaur.

But before she could breathe out, Jax—still running—hurled his axe at the green dragon. The weapon tumbled end over end to lodge in Slean's open mouth. The dragon roared in pain as blood gushed from her wounds, then she coughed and choked as she swallowed her own chlorine.

Though he no longer had a weapon, Jax continued running toward the dragon.

"Sindri!" Nearra said. "Use your magic to send my dagger to Jax!" She pressed the blade into the kender's hand. "He needs it far more than I do."

"I'm not really sure . . ." Sindri began, but then Davyn concentrated and activated his magic ring. The dagger flew out of Sindri's hand and streaked across the courtyard toward the minotaur.

"Jax!" Nearra yelled.

The minotaur flicked a glance toward Nearra, saw the dagger flying toward him, caught it, and launched himself into the air. He landed on Slean's back and began stabbing at her with the dagger. But her scales were too hard and the blade caused no damage.

Meanwhile, Catriona and Nysse had pulled Gunna back to the temple entrance. Nysse continued to tend to her wounded friend, while Catriona ran back toward Slean.

Feandan and Pedar were in the process of performing another miracle. Beams of light were shooting out of their hands to strike Slean in the face. The dragon roared, sounding more angry than hurt, and spun around, sweeping her tail at the two clerics. The dragon's tail slammed into them with all the force of a green-scaled battering ram. Feandan and Pedar flew through the air and landed in a heap, unconscious or worse.

"We can't just stand here!" Nearra said. "We have to do something!"

Davyn looked at her with concern. She hadn't been present when the clerics had cast their blessing of calmness on the companions. If she continued to be worried and afraid, there was an excellent chance the Emergence would be triggered—which of course was exactly what Maddoc wanted. Davyn had to think of some way to get Nearra away from here.

Jax was now attempting to climb up Slean's neck, obviously hoping to get at her vulnerable eyes. But Slean thrashed her head back and forth, and it was all the minotaur could do to hold on.

Catriona had reached the dragon and was hacking away at the beast's underbelly with her sword, but like Jax before her, she was having no success.

"Slean's hide is too tough," Davyn said.

"Too bad we don't have a blessed arrow like Elethia did," Sindri said.

Davyn, Nearra, and Elidor turned to look at the kender.

"What, did I say something wrong?"

"No, my small friend," Elidor said. "You said something very right."

"I have a bow," Davyn said.

"We can get the key to the repository door from the clerics," Nearra said.

"No time for that. I can pick, I mean, open the lock," Elidor said. "Give me a moment." With that, the elf dashed back inside the temple.

"Do you really think it will work?" Nearra asked.

"I don't know," Davyn admitted. "It's been in the repository for centuries. The blessing may have faded by now. But it's our only chance."

It was at that moment that Slean finally managed to dislodge the battle-axe from her mouth. She spit the weapon onto the ground—along with a good amount of blood. And then, eyes gleaming with hate, she sucked in a breath, curled her long neck around toward Jax, and released a yellow-green cloud of chlorine directly into the minotaur's face.

Elidor raced down the temple hallways, moving with a speed and grace of which only elves are capable. Though he ran as fast as he could, his feet barely made any sound as they touched the stone floor.

He soon reached the repository. He crouched down before the door and removed a leather pouch from his tunic. He paused a moment to examine the lock. It was a sturdy thing, made of iron, and despite its age, it looked as if it had been installed only yesterday. More of the temple's magic? he wondered. He opened the pouch and selected a long pick from among his assortment, then he stretched forth his hand to insert it into the lock—and stopped.

His hand was trembling.

Elidor was so shocked that he nearly dropped the pick. He had picked hundreds of locks, and his hand had never shook before. He was an elf; he was able to keep his hands as steady as if they were carved of stone. But not this time. What was wrong?

And then it came to him: This time, he wasn't picking a lock for his own amusement and enrichment. This time, he was doing it for others, for his friends. They were outside in the courtyard, confronting Slean, perhaps even dying—while he dithered here before the door, his hand shaking like a leaf caught in a storm wind. He frowned in concentration and willed his hand to be steady, and though the trembling subsided, it didn't go away entirely. Still, it was enough. It had to be.

He inserted the pick and began probing the lock, testing it, teasing it, coaxing it to open for him. Moisture beaded on his brow. He was surprised to discover he was sweating. He kept imagining his friends engulfed by chlorine gas, coughing as they desperately struggled to draw breath. He saw their bodies rent by dragon claws, savaged by dragon teeth, crushed by powerful blows of Slean's whip-like tail . . .

His fingers slipped and the pick tumbled from his hand. With inhuman speed, he snatched the pick out of the air before it could hit the floor. He forced himself to take a deep, calming breath before inserting it into the lock once more.

Stop it! he told himself. If you don't do your job, those imaginings may well come to pass. And if they do, it'll be your fault for failing to pick a lock so simple that a blindfolded infant could—

The lock clicked open.

Elidor was so surprised that for an instant, he couldn't quite believe he'd done it. But then he quickly stood and opened the repository door. He hurried inside and stepped up to the pedestal where Elethia's arrow rested. He started to reach for it, but then he hesitated. What if some sort of enchantment protected it from theft? He could be burned to a crisp or turned to stone the instant he touched the arrow.

But he knew his friends couldn't afford to wait any longer. Gritting his teeth and muttering a quick prayer to whatever god looked after elf thieves, he tensed his muscles, squinted his eyes, and snatched up the arrow.

Nothing happened.

Relieved, he turned and ran out of the repository, carrying with him the key to Slean's doom and his friends' salvation.

30 THE ARROW OF ELETHIA

Nearra was horrified as she watched Jax fall off the dragon's neck and strike the ground. The minotaur was coughing violently, as if his lungs were being eaten away by the deadly gas.

Nysse stood. "I can heal him, but only if I can get to him quickly enough!"

"What about Gunna?" Nearra said.

"She'll be fine. She just needs to rest. But Jax will surely die if we don't do something quickly!"

"What of Feandan and Pedar?" Davyn asked. "They've been wounded, too."

"They would both want me to tend to Jax first," Nysse said, "and that's precisely what I intend to do—if I can reach him."

Elidor chose that moment to reappear. Despite the speed at which he'd run, the elf wasn't out of breath. He held out Elethia's arrow.

Nearra turned to Sindri. "Can you use your magic to pull Jax toward us while Davyn fires the arrow?"

Sindri frowned. "Jax is awfully big and heavy, but I can try."

Nearra looked at Davyn and was surprised to see the ranger biting his lower lip, as if he were struggling to make a decision of some sort. Then a look of determination came over his face.

He reached for the arrow. As he took it from Elidor's hand, Davyn's fingers jerked, and he dropped it.

"Nervous, I guess," Davyn said. He bent down to retrieve the arrow—which had fallen close to Sindri's left foot. As he did, he slipped the silver ring off his finger and left it on the ground. Then he picked up the arrow and stood.

As he began to nock the arrow, Davyn said, "Hey, Sindri—what's that by your foot?"

"Look at that!" Sindri reached down and snatched up the ring. "It's quite lovely! I must've conjured it without knowing, and it fell out of one of my cape pockets when I wasn't looking." He slipped it on. "It seems a little loose . . . no, there we go. It fits fine now."

Davyn smiled. "All right, let's go help Catriona and Jax. I'll need to be closer to Slean to get a good shot at her. I figure that her wounded eye is her most vulnerable spot right now. Elidor, can you distract Slean while I get into position?"

"I have only a couple throwing knives left." Elidor didn't seem to move as a blade appeared in each of his hands. "But they're at your service."

Davyn grinned. Then he turned to Sindri. "Concentrate when you try to bring Jax over here. Picture him moving in your mind and then will it to happen with all your strength."

Sindri looked offended. "Of course I will! Who's the wizard around here, anyway?"

"My apologies, friend," Davyn said. Then he turned to Nearra. "Try to stay calm."

It seemed an odd request, but she nodded. Davyn then looked at Elidor.

"Let's go."

The elf nodded and the two of them ran toward Slean.

While the others had talked, Catriona had continued to battle the dragon alone. Slean, moving more slowly now due to the amount of blood she'd lost from her mouth wound, had tried several times to gas Catriona. But each time, the nimble warrior had managed to dodge the deadly clouds of chlorine.

Nearra remembered then that dragons were also able to cast spells. She wondered why the dragon didn't try to cast a spell on Catriona. Perhaps Slean was in too much pain from her mouth wound to concentrate effectively.

Sindri furrowed his brow and set his jaw in a determined line. But Jax—who had stopped coughing and now lay as still as death—wasn't moving toward them.

"Strange," the kender said. "It was never this hard before." He frowned more deeply and pointed both hands toward the minotaur. Sweat began to bead on Sindri's forehead, and then Jax began to slide across the ground toward them. Within moments, he lay next to Nysse. She put her hand on his black-furred chest and began to pray.

Sindri wiped the sweat from his brow with the back of his hand. "I feel as if I'd just carried him over here myself!"

"But it worked!" Nearra gave the kender a quick hug, then turned to watch Davyn and Elidor.

Davyn stood to Slean's left, arrow nocked and ready to fire. Catriona continued to hack away at the dragon's belly. Elidor, off to Slean's right, juggled his two knives in an elaborate pattern, hoping to catch the great beast's attention.

They're wasting their time, a woman's voice whispered in Nearra's mind. *That's not the arrow—it's only a replica.*

Nearra recognized the voice as the one she'd heard before. Somehow, she knew it spoke the truth.

Just as she was about to shout a warning to Davyn, Elidor flipped one of his knives toward Slean. The dragon jerked her head to avoid being struck in her good eye, exposing her wounded one to Davyn.

The ranger fired.

Davyn's aim was perfect. The arrow hit Slean's wounded eye and lodged in the socket. Fresh blood welled forth from the wound, and Slean shrieked in agony. But the dragon did not die.

Instead, Slean went berserk, lashing out with her claws, tail, and teeth. Elidor tried to jump out of the way of her talons, but as swift as he was, the elf was still too slow. He staggered backward and fell to the ground. Catriona was struck by Slean's tail, and she too hit the ground. Only Davyn remained standing. He continued nocking and releasing arrows, one after the other, but they merely bounced off Slean's armor-tough scales. Then the dragon butted Davyn with her head and the ranger went down to join the ranks of the fallen.

Only Nearra, Sindri, and Nysse remained conscious, and the cleric was too busy praying to be of any help. So it was down to the two of them: a kender wizard of dubious power, and a young girl with no idea who she really was.

Slean, breathing hard, blood still dripping from her mouth, and an arrow protruding from one eye socket, looked around. Seeing no other opponents, she turned to Nearra and grinned. The sight of the dragon baring her blood-slicked teeth sent a surge of terror through Nearra's being.

"I have to admit, your friends put up a good fight," Slean said. "But there's no one left to protect you now, girl."

The dragon started toward Nearra.

"It's over, girl," Slean said.

"What do you want with me?" Nearra cried, overcome with frustration and grief for her fallen friends.

At that moment, three figures entered through the temple's gateway, walking slowly toward Nearra. It was Oddvar and two of the bandit goblins.

"We don't want anything with *you*," Slean said. "It's what's *inside* you that matters." The dragon continued in a sing-song voice, "Come out, come out, wherever you are."

Nearra grew furious at the dragon's mockery. She felt the familiar tingling sensation begin. Only now, instead of being confined to her hands, she felt it throughout her entire body.

Sindri stepped in front of Nearra. "You cannot have her, fell beast. I, the great wizard Sindri Suncatcher, shall stop you!"

Slean stretched her neck toward them as far as it would go, until her head was only a few feet away.

"I hate kender," the dragon said, and chuffed a tiny amount of chlorine gas into Sindri's face. Sindri began coughing violently. He fell to his knees and clawed at his throat, trying to breathe.

"Well, girl, it appears as though you're all out of protectors," Slean said.

"I don't know about that," came a voice, and then Raedon leaped through the air and crashed down upon Slean's back.

There was the sound of cracking bone and Slean howled in agony. She whirled around to meet this new attack. But before she could do anything, Raedon opened his mouth and shot a jet of black acid into her face. Slean screamed as her flesh sizzled.

The green dragon bucked and threw Raedon off of her. The copper dragon flapped his wings to try to keep himself from falling, but Nearra saw that one of his wings was torn, and he couldn't keep himself from hitting the ground.

Hissing, Slean struck out like a serpent and fastened her teeth around Raedon's neck. Raedon clawed at Slean's belly with all four of his feet, but the evil green dragon stubbornly held onto his neck. She continued to exert pressure until her teeth began to penetrate Raedon's metallic scales and small rivulets of blood trickled forth.

Oddvar and the goblins laughed, and Nearra felt her head swim. She feared she was going to pass out.

Nearra struggled to think. If only we had Elethia's arrow. The arrow from the Repository was a copy, so the real arrow must be hidden somewhere else in the temple—somewhere no one would ever think to look for it.

And then Nearra remembered the feeling she'd had in the temple's dining hall . . . how the image of Elethia in the mosaic had seemed almost real, as if she could reach out and—

Nearra turned and ran back inside the temple. She flew down the corridors until she reached the dining hall. There, in the mosaic, was the image of Elethia, aiming the white arrow at the great red dragon called Kiernan the Crimson.

Nearra hurried over to the mosaic and reached out with trembling fingers. But when she touched the mosaic, all she felt were smooth stones.

"Please," she said.

This time her fingers closed around a shaft of wood, and when she withdrew her hand, she was holding the true arrow of Elethia.

She didn't have time to feel wonder and awe at the miracle that had just taken place. Her friends needed her.

She ran out of the dining hall, through the corridors and out to the courtyard, stopping only when she reached the tail of the green dragon.

"Slean!" Nearra shouted.

The green dragon didn't release her grip on Raedon's throat, but she turned her good eye to look at Nearra.

"Elethia sends her blessings!" And then Nearra raised the arrow and plunged it down point-first into Slean's tail. There was a burst of white light as the holy weapon released its power.

Slean's death scream was so loud it seemed to shatter the world.

CHAPTER 31 ONWARD

Sindri hurried through the temple courtyard. He was following a very interesting butterfly. It was twice as large as an ordinary one, and the colors on its wings seemed to change with every flap. He wanted to get close enough to the insect to see if the colors really were changing, or if it was just a trick of the sunlight.

The kender was grateful for the distraction. It had been several weeks since they'd defeated Slean, and all they'd done was remain here while the injured finished healing and the clerics researched a way to help Nearra regain her memories. The healing had been completed a while ago, but despite all their efforts, the clerics still didn't know what was wrong with Nearra or how to fix it.

The iridescent butterfly fluttered up to a tree seedling and landed on a thin, delicate branch. The courtyard had been transformed since the battle with Slean. Once nothing but barren earth, the yard was now covered with lush green grass, blooming daisies, and white birch seedlings.

The new growth had begun precisely at the spot where Gunna had cast her spell of entanglement. The remnants of the tendrils had taken root and sprouted, spreading throughout the courtyard at a fantastic rate. A true miracle, indeed, Sindri thought.

This butterfly was something of a miracle as well. Sindri approached it slowly, not wishing to startle it into flying away. Kender can move with almost supernatural stealth when they wish. Sindri was able to walk up to the seedling and sit down on the grass next to it without making a sound. The colorful butterfly remained on the branch where it had landed, undisturbed.

Grinning with delight, Sindri leaned as closely as he dared and watched as the butterfly's wings transformed. Red turned to orange; green changed to purple, swirling and merging like the colors of a kaleidoscope. The effect was so beautiful it was almost hypnotic.

As Sindri sat mesmerized by the butterfly's light show, his hands moved of their own accord through the grass. His nimble fingers grabbed whatever they might find: an odd-colored stone, a prickly weed. Then Sindri's fingers brushed against something dry and crinkly. He snatched up the object and lifted it to his face.

"What's this?"

He sniffed the rolled yellow parchment. Not only did it look old, it smelled old, too. It took Sindri mere seconds to untie the black ribbon binding the parchment and unroll it. The document was covered in writing, though Sindri didn't recognize the language. Still, he knew it had to be important, or else why would he have conjured it? He jumped to his feet and ran toward the temple. He had to show this to the clerics!

Had he thought to look back at the butterfly, he would have witnessed an even more amazing sight.

The butterfly shimmered once more and then vanished without a trace.

"This is intriguing," Feandan said. "The scroll tells of a village called Arngrim on the eastern slope of the Vingaard Mountains. According to this, the village is home to a group of powerful wizards."

The companions and the four clerics stood in the dining hall, the scroll spread out upon a tabletop before them, the image of Elethia looking on from the mosaic on the wall.

Feandan continued. "The scroll goes on to say that these wizards specialize in countering the effects of magic, especially evil magic." The cleric looked up at Nearra. "This could be exactly what you're looking for."

Davyn tried not to frown. It seemed there was no escaping Maddoc's manipulations.

He had tried several times over the last few weeks to tell the others the truth about who he was and his relationship to Maddoc. But each time, his courage had failed him. He was afraid his friends—the only ones he'd truly ever had—would come to hate him if they knew the truth.

Now, somehow, Sindri had managed to "conjure" a scroll identical to the one Davyn had burned—no doubt left somewhere by Maddoc for the kender to stumble across. But there was no way Davyn could tell this to his friends.

"That scroll looks ancient," Davyn said. "Even if Arngrim was ever more than a legend, I doubt it's still there. It was probably destroyed in the Cataclysm."

"The temple survived the Cataclysm," Catriona said. "Perhaps Arngrim did, too."

"If there's even a chance that there are wizards in Arngrim who can help me, it's worth traveling there," Nearra said. "At least, it's worth it to me."

"There's no way of knowing how dangerous the journey may be, but so far we've managed to hold our own. I think it's a risk worth taking," Catriona said.

"Me, too," said Sindri. Elidor nodded.

They all looked at Davyn, and he knew there was no way he would be able to dissuade the others without revealing the truth to them.

He forced a smile. "Arngrim it is, then."

"Are you certain you won't come with us?" Catriona asked.

"It won't be the same without you," Nearra said.

The companions and the four clerics stood in the temple courtyard. It was a bright, sunny morning with few clouds in the sky. Though it was late summer, there was a crisp scent in the air that hinted at autumn's approach.

"I am certain," Jax said. His voice wasn't quite as deep as it had been before he'd inhaled Slean's chlorine gas. Jax had nearly died, and though Nysse had managed to heal him, he had been left with a higher-pitched, raspy voice. But otherwise, he was as strong and healthy as ever.

"Without the protection of the mystic barrier, the temple needs a guardian," Jax said. "I used to make my living guarding trading caravans. It will be satisfying to guard something more important than a merchant's wares for a change."

Despite the minotaur's gruff manner, Davyn had grown fond of the man-bull, and he would miss him. Davyn knew there was more to Jax's decision than he'd said. The minotaur's people lived by a strict code of honor. Jax believed he owed a debt to Nysse for saving his life, and he was determined to repay it. Davyn also thought that remaining to guard the temple was a way Jax could honor the memory of his cleric ancestors. Perhaps the minotaur would even become a cleric himself one day.

"No matter how long it will be until we meet again, remember that you will always be my friends." Jax's eyes twinkled and he almost smiled. "Even the kender."

Sindri grinned, but his own eyes were moist with tears.

Catriona turned to the clerics. "Will you continue to try to restore the mystic barrier?"

"We have given the matter much thought," Feandan said, "and we have decided not to attempt to recreate it. It is possible the barrier was meant to come down. It protected the temple during the centuries it was abandoned. Now the four of us have arrived here, and we want to make it a center of healing and wisdom once more. Such a place should not be separated from the rest of the world by a barrier of any sort."

"You do not have to leave just yet, you know," Gunna said. The elderly cleric had softened toward the companions during their stay, almost becoming a surrogate grandmother to them. "The passage into the Vingaard Mountains will be long and difficult. You shall need to be in full health to make such a hard journey."

"We're fine," Nearra said. "Thanks to the care we received from the four of you, we couldn't be more healthy."

"And we need to enter the mountains while it's still summer," Catriona said. "Or else we risk the way to Arngrim being blocked by an early snowfall."

Davyn had no idea if Arngrim was real or just another of his father's lies.

Still, he was determined to keep a close eye out for Maddoc's trickery. His father had failed to cause the Emergence this time, but Davyn now knew he would never give up.

Davyn glanced at Nearra. She had a streak of black in her blond hair, a sign of how close she'd come to undergoing the Emergence. The clerics had theorized that the change had somehow been caused by Nearra wielding the blessed arrow. After all, Elethia had possessed black hair. But Davyn knew better.

A shadow passed over the courtyard, and they all looked up in time to see Raedon come gliding in for a landing. The copper dragon's flying skills were still a bit wobbly from the wound he'd sustained to his wing, but otherwise he was fully healed.

"I had a feeling you little ones were going to be leaving today. Where are you off to now?"

"A place called Arngrim, on the other side of the Vingaard Mountains," Nearra said. She went on to tell Raedon about the wizards who were supposed to live there.

The dragon frowned. "Arngrim. It sounds familiar. But I can't remember anything specific about it. That's a long trip for folk who can't fly. I could give you a ride there one at a time. It would save you all a great deal of time and effort."

"No offense," Elidor said, "but I don't quite trust that wing of yours yet."

"It's strong enough that I don't have to hop everywhere I go anymore." Raedon flexed the wing in question and winced. "Still, perhaps you're right."

The clerics had tried to heal Raedon's wing after the battle. But they were injured themselves and they'd spent so much of their strength fighting Slean and healing the companions that they'd had only minimal success.

"If I can't perform as your steed, then I'll be a watchdog instead," Raedon said. "I'll try to fly by from time to time to see how you're progressing on your journey. How does that sound?"

Nearra patted Raedon on the snout. "That sounds wonderful—thank you."

"Whatever happens to us along the way," Elidor said, "it cannot possibly be as bad as burying Slean. My lower back still aches when I think about it."

It had taken all of them working together, along with help from Raedon, to dig a pit large enough to hold the body of the green dragon. They'd chosen to bury her in the temple courtyard out of sheer practicality; she was too big to move elsewhere. Her burial mound was the only place in the courtyard that wasn't covered with new growth. The ground there remained barren and cracked.

Pedar chuckled. "The pain is all in your mind, my boy. Your back is fully healed by now."

Elidor looked skeptical, but he didn't say anything.

Davyn wasn't sure why the elf thief was going with them. In fact, Elidor had never openly declared his intention to do so. It was just understood that he was coming along. Perhaps, Davyn thought, since he was half Kagonesti and half Silvanesti—half wild, half civilized—he too had found a group of friends to which he belonged. And, like Davyn, perhaps for the first time.

"Tell me, Elidor, why have you decided to accompany us?" Davyn asked. "Tired of a life of crime?"

He'd meant it as a joke, but the elf looked at him with a raised eyebrow.

"Oh, the usual. Adventure, friendship, loyalty—you know all about loyalty, don't you?" Elidor's smile was almost, but not quite, a sneer.

Davyn's heart skipped a bit. What did he know? He briefly considered confronting Elidor and demanding an explanation, but it wasn't the time or place. He'd have to let the matter drop—for now.

"It's too bad we can't take the arrow with us," Sindri said. "We might need it if we ever run into another dragon." He gave Raedon a look. "An evil dragon, I mean."

After Nearra had killed Slean, the arrow had vanished, only to reappear once again as a part of the mosaic. The clerics had tried several times to extract the arrow, but without success.

Nearra had her own theory about that. "Even if the gods allowed us to borrow it once," she said, "the arrow will remain part of the mosaic until it is truly needed again."

"Well, then," Feandan said. "I suppose there's nothing more to do than wish you all farewell."

"Good journey," Nysse added.

"Be careful," Gunna warned.

"And may the gods watch over you and guide you along your way," Pedar said.

The companions then turned and headed for the gateway, Raedon walking alongside them. As the dragon began telling a joke about a barbarian, a griffin, and a centaur, Davyn had the feeling that they were being watched. He looked up and wasn't at all surprised to see a black falcon circling overhead.

The story continues in

THE
DYING KINGDOM

by Stephen D. Sullivan

Acknowledgments

Thanks to Mark Sehestedt and Nina Hess. This is a much better book because of their editorial guidance. Extra-special thanks to my most important editor: my daughter Devon, who read the first draft of the manuscript and gave me excellent suggestions from a kid's point of view. Thanks to my agent, Jonathan Matson, for believing in me all these years. And, of course, deep gratitude to Margaret Weis and Tracy Hickman for creating a wonderful world and granting me the privilege of living there for a little while.

Enter a World of Adventure

Do you want to learn more about the world of Krynn?
Look for these and other **Dragonlance®** books in the fantasy section
of your local bookstore or library.

Titles by Margaret Weis and Tracy Hickman

Legends Trilogy

Time of the Twins, War of the Twins,
and Test of the Twins
A wizard weaves a plan to conquer darkness—
and bring it under his control.

The Second Generation

The sword passes to a new generation of heroes—
the children of the Heroes of the Lance.

Dragons of Summer Flame

A young mage seeks to enter the Abyss in search of his lost uncle,
the infamous Raistlin.

The War of Souls Trilogy

Dragons of a Fallen Star, Dragons of a Lost Star,
Dragons of a Vanished Moon
A new war begins, one more terrible than any in Krynn have ever known.

Dragonlance and its logo are trademarks of Wizards of the Coast, Inc.
in the U.S.A. and other countries. ©2004 Wizards.

WANT TO KNOW HOW IT ALL BEGAN?

WANT TO KNOW MORE ABOUT THE DRAGONLANCE° WORLD?

FIND OUT IN THIS NEW BOXED SET OF THE FIRST DRAGONLANCE TITLES!

A RUMOR OF DRAGONS
Volume 1

NIGHT OF THE DRAGONS
Volume 2

THE NIGHTMARE LANDS
Volume 3

TO THE GATES OF PALANTHAS
Volume 4

HOPE'S FLAME
Volume 5

A DAWN OF DRAGONS
Volume 6

Gift Set available September 2004
By Margaret Weis & Tracy Hickman
For ages 10 and up

Dragonlance and its logo are trademarks of Wizards of the Coast, Inc.
in the U.S.A. and other countries. ©2004 Wizards.